Sydney Shaw, 34
Accountant

 Marital status: Single

Kids: Want kids

How do you spend your leisure time?
I like to try to see if I can take a fitted sheet and fold it carefully so that it looks indistinguishable from a folded flat sheet. Oh, and long walks in Central Park.

What are you most passionate about?
I am really passionate about having my coffee order ready when I get to the front of the line. I mean, the menu doesn't change from day to day! There's no reason for it to take five minutes to order a small Americano half-caff no cream, especially since you probably ordered the exact same thing yesterday! That should take literally like five seconds, seriously! Sorry, I'm just really passionate about this.

What is your best life skill?
I can get bloodstains out of anything.

What are you looking for in another person?
I am looking for a guy who dresses nicely, uses proper punctuation in text messages, doesn't talk about his mother or his exes too much, and also, won't murder me at the end of the date and throw my body in the Hudson River. Especially the punctuation part.

What are four adjectives your friends would use to describe you?
Quirky. Quixotic. Quick-witted. Quacky.
Wait, why did I read that question as adjectives that had to start with Q? And why won't this let me delete and rewrite my answer?? Argh!!!

Hi there, Walmart readers!

I'm so thrilled you've purchased this special edition of The Boyfriend!

This book was a bit traumatic to write, because it brought back memories of all the many bad dates I have been on over the years. It's definitely been a while, but some of them still haunt me. For example, this guy I went to brunch with, who put peanut butter on his waffles. Syrup or butter or even a sunny-side-up egg would have been acceptable choices but peanut butter? Clearly, he was a psychopath.

But I dug deep for the sake of giving you, my readers, a wild ride. Whether you're reading in bed with a flashlight or under your desk at work, I hope you'll enjoy reading my little tale of dating gone horribly wrong. And just remember, if a potential date starts bragging about his large kitchen knife collection, you might want to swipe left!

Happy wishes and happy reading…and may your shopping trips be filled with unexpected surprises (of the non-murderous variety)!

Freida

ALSO BY FREIDA MCFADDEN

THE
BOYFRIEND

FREIDA McFADDEN

Poisoned Pen
PRESS

Published by Poisoned Pen Press, an imprint of Sourcebooks
P.O. Box 4410, Naperville, Illinois 60567-4410
(630) 961-3900
sourcebooks.com

Cataloging-in-Publication Data is on file with the Library of Congress.

Printed and bound in the United States of America.
LB 10 9 8 7 6 5 4 3 2 1

PROLOGUE

BEFORE

TOM

I am desperately, painfully, completely, and stupidly in love.

Her name is Daisy. We met when we were four years old. I've been in love with the girl since age four—that's how pathetic I am. I saw her at the playground feeding bits of her sandwich to the hungry squirrels, and all I could think was that I had never met any living creature as beautiful or as kind as Daisy Driscoll. And I was gone.

For a long time, I didn't tell her how I felt. I couldn't. It seemed impossible that this angel with golden hair and pale blue eyes and skin like the porcelain of our bathroom sink could ever feel a tenth of what I felt for her, so there was no point in trying.

But lately, that's changed.

Lately, Daisy has been letting me walk her home from school. If I'm lucky, she lets me hold her hand, and she gives me that secret little smile on her cherry-red lips that makes my knees weak. I'm starting to think she might want me to kiss her.

But I'm scared. I'm scared that if I tried to kiss her, she would slap me across the face. I'm scared that if I told her how I really feel, she would look at me in sympathy and tell me she doesn't feel the same way. I'm scared she might never let me walk her home again.

But that's not what I'm most scared of.

What I am most scared of is that if I lean in to kiss Daisy, she will let me do it. I'm scared that she will agree to be my girlfriend. I'm scared that she will allow me into her bedroom when her parents aren't home so that we can finally be alone together.

And I'm terrified that the moment I get her alone, I will wrap my fingers around her pretty, white neck and squeeze the life out of her.

CHAPTER 1

SYDNEY

Who is this man, and what has he done with my date?

I'm supposed to be meeting a man named Kevin for dinner tonight at eight o'clock. Well, it was supposed to be drinks at six o'clock—drinks are easier to escape from—but Kevin messaged me through the Cynch dating app that he was running late at work and could we push it to dinner at eight?

Against my better judgment, I said yes.

But Kevin seemed really nice when we were texting. And in his photos, he was cute. *Really* cute. He had this boyish smile with a twinkle in his eye, and his light-brown hair was adorably messy as it fell over his forehead. He looked like a young Matt Damon. I've been on a lot of bad dates through Cynch, but I was cautiously optimistic about this one. I even arrived early at the restaurant, and I have spent the last ten minutes eagerly waiting at the bar for him to arrive.

"Sydney?" the man standing before me asks.

"Yes?"

I stare at the man, waiting for him to tell me that Kevin was killed in a tragic taxi accident on the way to our date, because this guy is definitely *not* Kevin. But instead, he sticks out his hand.

"I'm Kevin," he says.

I don't budge from my barstool. "You are?"

Okay, let's be real here—nobody looks as good in real life as their dating-app photos. I mean, if you're looking to score a date, you're not going to snap a photo of yourself when you're rolling out of bed with a hangover. You're going to doll yourself up, take about fifty different shots from every conceivable angle and with a dozen lighting options, and you're going to pick the very best one. That's just good sense.

And hey, maybe that one perfect photo was taken ten years ago. I don't agree with this logic, but I understand why people do it.

But this guy…

There's no way he is the same man as in his Cynch profile. Not ten years ago—not *ever*. I just don't believe it.

Even though it's an obnoxious move, I grab my phone from my purse and bring up the app right in front of him. I compare the boyishly handsome man in the photo to the man standing in front of me. Yeah—nope.

My date for the evening is at least ten years older than the guy in the photo and bone thin, bordering on gaunt. I think his eye color is different too. His blond hair is badly receding, but what's left of it is long and pulled back into an unkempt ponytail.

This is not the same man as in the photo. I'm even more sure of that than I am of the fact that I enjoy long walks through Central Park and bingeing Netflix.

"Yes, that's me," Fake Kevin assures me. (Although really, the guy in the photo is Fake Kevin. Maybe the photo really *is* of Matt Damon. I'm starting to think it might be.)

I begin to protest that he doesn't look anything like the photo, but the words sound so superficial in my head. Okay, yes, Kevin looks vastly different from his profile photo. But does that really matter? We have been texting through Cynch, and he seems like a nice enough guy. I should give him a chance.

And if it's not going well, my friend Gretchen will be calling me in twenty minutes with a manufactured excuse to get me the hell out of here. I never, *ever* go on a date without a planned rescue call.

"It's really great to meet you in real life," the real Kevin says. "You look exactly like your photo."

Does he expect me to say it back? Is this some kind of test? "Um," I say.

"Come on," he says. "Let's get a seat."

We snag a booth in the corner of the bar. As we're walking over there, I can't help but notice the way Kevin towers over me. I tend to like tall men, but he badly needs a little meat on his bones. It feels like I'm walking next to a broomstick.

"I'm so glad we are finally doing this," Kevin tells me as he slides into the seat across from me. Why is his ponytail so messy? Couldn't he have at least combed it before our date?

"Me too," I say, which is only slightly a lie.

He rakes his gaze over me, an approving expression on his gaunt face. "I have to tell you, Sydney, now that we're actually meeting in person, I genuinely feel like you are the perfect woman."

"Oh?"

"Absolutely." He beams at me. "If I closed my eyes and imagined the perfect girl, it would be you."

Wow. That's…sweet. Possibly one of the nicest compliments I have received on a date. Thank you, Real Kevin. I'm starting to feel glad that I stayed. And like I said, I do like tall men, so even though he looks vastly different from his profile, I get a tiny tug of attraction. "Thank you."

"Well," he adds, "except for your arms."

"My *arms*?"

"They're kind of flabby." He wrinkles his nose. "But other than that, wow. Like I said, you're the perfect woman."

Wait. My arms are *too flabby*? Did he really just say that to me?

Worse, now I am straining to surreptitiously examine my bare arms. And why did I wear a sleeveless dress tonight? I have only two sleeveless dresses in my closet. I could have worn something with sleeves that would have concealed my apparently hideous arms, but no, I chose *this*.

"Can I get you two something to drink?"

A waitress is standing over us, her eyebrows raised. I pry my gaze away from my monstrous arms and look up at her. "I…I'll have a Diet Coke."

"A Diet Coke?" Kevin seems affronted. "That's boring. Get a real drink."

I never drink alcohol when I'm on a first date with a man I've met on Cynch. I don't want to impair my judgment in any way. "Diet Coke *is* a real drink."

"No, it's not."

"Well, it's a *liquid*." I glare at him across the sticky wooden table. "So I would call it a drink."

Kevin rolls his eyes at the waitress. "Fine, I will have a Corona, and she will have a *Diet Coke*." Then he winks at the waitress and mouths the word *Sorry*.

I glance over at my purse next to me. When is Gretchen going to call? I need an escape route.

But maybe I'm not being fair. I've only known Real Kevin for five minutes. I should give him more of a chance. That's why I told Gretchen to call twenty minutes into the date after all. Five minutes is a snap judgment. If I can't give a guy more than five minutes, I'm going to be having first dates for the next twenty years. And now that I'm thirty-four years old, I don't have that luxury.

"Hot damn," Kevin remarks, following the path of the waitress with his eyes as she goes to get our drinks. "She has *really* nice arms."

Gretchen, where are you?

CHAPTER 2

"So you have to pay two thousand dollars if you're a new member joining the group," Kevin explains to me, "but for every vacation package you sell, you earn a five-thousand-dollar commission. Pretty amazing, right?"

I drag one of my french fries through a little trail of ketchup on my plate. We are nearly forty minutes into this date, and I am inexplicably still here. Stupid Gretchen. She's making out with her boyfriend or something and has forgotten all about poor little me. I even texted her "SOS" and she still didn't call me.

"I could definitely get you into the group." Kevin chomps on one of his spicy barbecue chicken wings—he's got an incredibly healthy appetite for such a skinny guy. I pointed out to him once that the barbecue sauce was getting on his cheek, and he wiped it off that time, but every single time he takes a bite, more of it gets all over his face. At some point, I got sick of telling him his face was dirty. "Do you want me to call Lois at the corporate headquarters? This is an amazing opportunity, Sydney. You're lucky I came along."

"No, thank you," I say.

Kevin reaches over and grabs my Diet Coke. When his wings arrived, he complained they were too spicy, and then, over the course of fifteen minutes, he proceeded to drain his beer, then a second beer, and now he has commandeered my Diet Coke. "Why not? Why would you turn down an opportunity to make, like, six figures a year?"

"Because it's a pyramid scheme?"

"A pyramid scheme!" Kevin chuckles. "Why would you think that?"

"Because I am an accountant and I know what a pyramid scheme is?"

"No, you just don't understand," he insists. "Look, I'm trying to do you a favor, Sydney. You've got this super boring job crunching numbers all day. Wouldn't you rather make a few sales a year and relax the rest of the time on your own luxury vacation property?"

I don't know what to say to that, so instead, I grab my purse. "I'm going to the bathroom."

I hope the bathroom has a window I can climb out of.

When I get to the ladies' room, I find that there is sadly no window. So I actually use the toilet, then I spend another two minutes looking at myself in the mirror, carefully examining my "flabby" arms. They don't look that bad, do they?

Do they?

I am googling "arm slimming exercises" on my phone when it starts to ring. Gretchen's name pops up on the screen, and my jaw tightens. *Finally*, she's calling. Forty-five freaking minutes into the meal. I swipe to take the call.

"Seriously, Gretchen?" I bark into the phone without even saying hello. "I have been on the worst date ever, and it's pretty much all your fault."

That's not entirely fair. The real Kevin deserves at least 50 percent of the credit for this awful evening. But I'm pissed off, and I need to take it out on *somebody*.

"I'm so sorry!" Gretchen cries. "Randy and I were watching a movie and we just lost track of time…"

"Uh-huh."

"I didn't even want to watch the movie," she insists. "Randy promised me he wouldn't let me forget about the call, but then, well, you know."

I can hear Randy in the background, saying, "Hey! Don't tell her it's *my* fault!" And then Gretchen giggles like he's tickling her or something. I bite my lip, resentful of how cute Gretchen and Randy are together. When she and I became friends, she was single, like me. Then one day, we were riding up in the elevator together, and she started gushing about how adorable the super in my building is. And now they've been dating for, like, six months!

Don't get me wrong. I'm happy my friend has found the guy of her dreams. I'm just still trying to find mine.

"Where are you now?" she asks.

"Hiding in the bathroom, obviously."

"Oh God. I'm so sorry."

"It's fine," I grumble. "You were probably making passionate love to your boyfriend, while I'm stuck here with a guy who is trying to talk me into a pyramid scheme."

"Oh no, Syd! Seriously?"

"That's not even the worst of it," I say. "His mother tried to FaceTime him in the middle of our meal, and he actually took the call. I had to say hello to her! His *mother*, Gretchen! On our first date!"

"I'm truly sorry," she says, even though I can tell she's trying not to laugh.

"I'm sure."

"Really, Syd. I'm the worst. Tomorrow after yoga, lattes and muffins are on me."

I suppose I can accept that apology. Anyway, the date is almost over. I am about five minutes away from never seeing Real Kevin or Fake Kevin ever again. Well, I might see Fake Kevin again if I go to a Matt Damon movie.

I tell Gretchen goodbye, take one last critical look at my arms (which are *fine* the way they are, Kevin!), then I head back out to the table. And lo and behold, a miracle has occurred and our check is on the table, waiting for me. I might get out of here sooner than expected.

"You were in there forever," Kevin comments. He wipes his lips with the back of his sleeve. It gets the sauce off his lips but smears it all over his white-and-red-checkered shirt. I don't even care anymore. "Did you fall in?"

I manage a thin smile. "Thanks for dinner."

"Sure thing." Kevin slides the check across the table to me. "Your share comes to thirty-eight dollars."

I wouldn't have wanted Kevin to treat me to this meal, because I don't want to owe him, but I'm having trouble figuring out how my small salad and Diet Coke plus tip somehow cost thirty-eight dollars. The accountant in me wants to pick up the check and calculate my actual share of the meal, but the woman in me doesn't want to prolong this another second. So instead, I toss two twenties on the table.

While Kevin is climbing out of the booth, the song "Eye of the Tiger" comes on the radio. He grins at me and winks. "This is my favorite song. Isn't *Rocky* the greatest movie of all time?"

"I haven't seen it."

Kevin clutches his chest in astonishment, like I just told him I kill puppies for fun. "You haven't *seen* it?"

"Nope."

"Well, now we know what we're doing on our second date."

I decide not to dispel him of the notion that there will be another date. But as soon as I get out of here, I am blocking him on Cynch. He doesn't have my real phone number, so he has no way of contacting me again.

"And then," he adds, "we can watch *Rocky II* on our third date. And *Rocky III* on our fourth date!"

He is in the midst of planning our seventh date (*Rocky VI*) when we get out of the bar. It's smack in the middle of August, which is a great time to wear a sleeveless dress that shows off my grotesque arms but also peak humidity time in New York City. Despite my leave-in conditioner and my careful efforts with the curling iron, my hair has started to frizz. Thankfully, I couldn't care less what my date thinks of my hair right now.

"I'll walk you home," Kevin tells me.

I nearly choke. "No, that's okay."

He sticks out his chin. "I absolutely insist. It's dark out. What sort of gentleman would I be if I let you walk home yourself in the dark?"

"It's okay. Really."

"You could be *killed*, Sydney."

That seems unlikely. Anyway, I'm willing to risk death just to get away from this guy. But he has a determined look on his face, and I'm starting to suspect that the easiest option would be to just let him walk me home. Not that I am *actually* going to let him walk me home. I live about ten blocks away, and I figure after three or four blocks, I'll just point out a random building and tell him it's mine. Then I'll be free of Real Kevin forever.

"Fine," I grumble. "Let's go."

He grins at me. "Lead the way."

Given that it's a Tuesday night rather than a weekend, the streets are emptier than they usually are when I'm out after dark by myself. Especially since I usually travel in a busier area, and now I am cutting through a more residential area just to get this over with as quickly as possible. The residential areas are always quieter, and they also smell less strongly of urine than the more populated path back to my apartment building. It's deserted enough here that it's not terrible to have Kevin's company.

That said, there's no way I'm going to let him see where I live. I'll never get rid of the guy.

I stop short at a brownstone a few blocks away from my actual apartment building. I gesture at the banister. "Well, this is me!"

Hopefully he won't insist on walking me into the building, because I have no way to get inside. But he seems very reluctant to leave.

"I had a great time, Sydney," Kevin tells me.

I can't quite bring myself to return the sentiment, even just to be nice. "Uh-huh."

A corner of his lip quirks up. "How about a hug?"

"Um…" I eye his outstretched arms and the pit stains that have gathered since we've been walking in the humid August air. "I don't hug on first dates."

"Oh." At first, I think he's going to protest, but then he says, "Well, how about a kiss then?"

Is he out of his ever-loving *mind*? I didn't even want to hug him, but I definitely don't want this guy's slimy lips touching mine.

"Come on," he says. "I bought you dinner. You're really not going to kiss me?"

He bought me dinner? On what planet does my paying forty dollars for a salad mean that *he* bought *me* dinner? "I don't kiss or hug on first dates," I explain. And then, in case he asks to bump hips or God knows what, I add, "I have a strict no-touching policy."

"Seriously?"

He takes a step closer to me. He towers over me, but I can still smell the sour stench of beer on his breath. I take a step back, bumping into the short set of stairs up to the entrance of the building I claimed I live in. I scan the street, dismayed there isn't another pedestrian in eyeshot. I thought Kevin was a dud, but I had labeled him as harmless.

Big mistake.

"Come on, Sydney." He takes another step closer to me—this time uncomfortably close. Kevin may be skinny, but he looks strong. Stronger than me, that's for sure. "You can't tease me like that. All I'm asking for is a kiss, for God's sake."

"I think this date is over," I say firmly.

"Don't be a tease." He frowns, his features contorting in the dim glow of the streetlight above us. "All you women are the same. You're never going to land a husband if you won't even kiss a guy on a date, you know."

My mind races, thinking through the contents of my

purse and what I could use as a weapon. Gretchen gave me a can of Mace, but I took it out at some point because it kept leaking all over my purse and I had never been in a situation where I was close to needing it. I do have a spritz bottle of hand sanitizer. If I sprayed him in the eyes with hand sanitizer, would that do the trick? Of course, that would mean I would have to locate it in my gigantic purse, which is probably 80 percent crumpled tissues at this point.

I decide the best bet is to push past him and make a run for it. In another block or two, I'm certain to run into another person.

"Sydney," he says.

I avoid eye contact as I try to dart around him. But Kevin is quicker than he looks. His fingers close around my wrist, pinning it against the jagged brick wall of the building. His spindly fingers bite into my flesh.

"Come on, Sydney," he says. "Don't cut our night short. The fun is just getting started."

CHAPTER 3

Kevin has his body pressed against me. The stench of sour beer is almost overwhelming, and I have to turn my head away as I attempt to wriggle free.

He doesn't just want to kiss. He wants something more than that. And he's not going to leave until he gets it. I should never have let him walk me home.

God, why is he so *strong*?

"Let me go!" I hiss at him.

"I told you," he says through his teeth, "to stop being a tease."

His body is pressed against me now, hot and uncomfortable. I open my mouth, ready to let out an ear-shattering scream. There are buildings on this block. Someone is sure to hear it, even though all the windows are closed and the air conditioners are blasting inside. But before any sound passes through my lips, a voice booms from behind me:

"Hey! *Hey*! What are you doing over there?"

Kevin eases his grip on my wrist. He backs away from me an inch or two, and I decide to take advantage of the fact that I can now move again. Bracing myself on a metal trash can next to me, I lift my right leg and knee him in the groin as hard as I can.

It's gratifying how quickly Kevin goes down. I've never nailed a guy in the balls before, and wow, that works *really* well. He crouches down, clutching his family jewels, his face bright red. It's quite a rush—well, until I lose my balance in the process and tumble to the ground, clocking my head on the metal garbage can.

"You bitch!" Kevin gasps. "What the hell is wrong with you?"

As I gingerly get back to my feet, I squint into the shadows at the figure who came to my rescue. It's too dark to see clearly, but it's obviously a man, about average build and height. He's looking down at Kevin, who is still doubled over, but then he glances up at me.

"Are you okay, Miss?"

"This is none of your business!" Kevin spits out at him. "We were on a date, you asshole. We were having a great time."

The mystery man continues to look at me, waiting for my answer, his eyes dark shadows.

"I'm fine." I brush sidewalk dirt off my sleeveless blue dress, which I will probably never wear again for a multitude of reasons, including self-consciousness about my unacceptably flabby arms. I should just throw it out after this. "I mean, *now* I'm fine."

"*You're* fine?" Kevin bursts out. "I should sue you for assault!"

Mystery Man lets out an astonished snort. "I *saw* what

17

you were trying to do. I'd be happy to call the police and let them know all about it."

With those words, he pulls his phone out of his pocket, as if about to call 911. He looks at me again, as if for permission, and I shake my head. That is not how I want this evening to end. I just want to go back home and soak in my bathtub. And block Kevin on Cynch. I can report him to the admins, since they have all his personal information.

For the first time, Kevin looks properly worried. He manages to straighten up with some effort. "Hey," he says. "Hey, look, maybe you got the wrong idea. I wasn't going to—"

"Get out of here," the mystery man cuts him off. "*Now*. Before your date changes her mind about calling the cops." His voice lowers a few notches, almost to a growl. "And if you *ever* bother her again, I'm happy to testify to what I saw you do. Do you know what jail is like for a sex offender?"

Kevin's eyes widen. He finally gets the idea.

I watch my date limp down the street, in the opposite direction of my apartment building. It's only when he disappears from sight that I finally feel my shoulders relax.

"Are you sure you're okay?" Mystery Man asks me.

I swivel my head in the direction of his voice. He has stepped into the glow of the streetlight, so I can finally get a good look at him. And...

Wow.

You know that cheesy thing people say—that they look at another person and get hit by a lightning bolt? I always thought that was absolutely ridiculous until it happened to me about three years ago and I met my first lightning-bolt guy. But that didn't work out, and I had given up hope that it would ever happen again. But now, here it is. That damn lightning bolt once again.

Mystery Man is hot, to say the least. He has thick black hair and coal-black eyes, with a level of intensity that sends yet another lightning bolt through me. His strong jaw makes him seem utterly in control and confident. His face has that pleasing textbook symmetry. He's wearing a black T-shirt that shows off his lean build and makes his dark hair and eyes seem even more intense. There's also no glint of a wedding band on his left hand.

But best of all is the way he's staring back at me. If I got hit by a lightning bolt, he did too. I'd bet my life on it.

"I'm okay," I manage. "Just...you know, shaken."

Mystery Man looks into the distance, making sure that Kevin is really gone. "Is he your boyfriend?"

I shake my head. "We just met tonight. Hooked up on Cynch." My face burns slightly. "I don't mean *hooked up*, obviously. But we had a date for tonight." I add, quite unnecessarily: "It was bad."

"I gathered."

"He doesn't know where I live." I hug my arms to my chest. "I'll report him to the app. They take this kind of thing seriously. I don't think he'll bother me again. But... thanks for helping me."

He flashes a lopsided smile. "Looks like you took him down pretty good yourself. He could barely walk."

I smile at the satisfying memory of how it felt to sink my knee into Kevin's balls. "Thanks."

Mystery Man is staring at me, that half smile playing on his lips. The electricity between the two of us is palpable. Sometimes I'm not sure if a guy is interested in me or not. But from the way Mystery Man is looking at me,

I *know* he's interested. And despite feeling shaken from what just happened, I would happily hand over my phone number right now.

What a great meet-cute. I can already imagine telling the story to our children. *This jerk was trying to kiss me, and that, kids, is how I met your father.*

Okay, I might be getting a little ahead of myself. But when you know, you know.

"Can you make it home okay from here?" Mystery Man asks me.

I look around. In the last few minutes, the streets have become more crowded. It doesn't feel quite as desolate as it did when Kevin grabbed me. "I'll be fine."

"Great," he says.

And then, to my shock, he starts to turn away. To *leave.*

"Um, thank you again!" I call out. "I really appreciate what you did. You're, like, my hero."

That gets a full-on smile out of the guy. And if possible, he's even more handsome when he smiles. He's got to be some kind of actor or model or *something*. I mean, *geez.* "Of course," he says. "I'm just glad you're okay."

We stare at each other for another beat, and I imagine the next words out of his mouth…

Would it be okay if I called you sometime?

Can I take you out on Saturday night?

Can we make passionate love tonight? Are you down for that?

But he doesn't say any of that. He doesn't even ask me my name. He simply raises one hand and says, "Well, good night then."

And then he walks away.

What. The. Hell?

CHAPTER 4

BEFORE

TOM

Daisy.

I can't stop staring at her.

I'm being too obvious. At some point, she's going to start thinking I'm a creep if I keep looking at her from ten feet away and never make a move. But it's hard not to stare. She looks so good today. Her hair is the color of the center of a daisy, and it almost looks like gold glimmering in the sun as she stands surrounded by her friends just outside our high school. Her snug cornflower-blue sweater follows all the soft curves of her body.

Stop staring, Tom. Right now. Don't be a creep.

She looks up, and for a second, I freeze. *Caught.* I wait for her blue eyes to narrow at me, but they don't. Instead, a slow smile spreads across her lips. A couple of her friends notice us looking at each other, and I hear a smattering of giggles. I can make out the words "Tom" and "so cute," both in the same sentence.

"Jesus, Tom. Stop being a wuss and go talk to her already!"

My best friend, Slug, is leaning over me, spouting wisdom in my ear. His breath still smells like cigarettes, despite a healthy spritz of the mint mouth spray he uses to hide the smell from his parents. Unless they're dumb, they must know he smokes and have decided they don't care. Slug is the youngest of five kids, and his parents have pretty much checked out, as far as I can tell. As long as he doesn't take a flying leap off a building, they're happy.

"I'll talk to her," I say.

Except I don't move. My feet feel stuck.

Slug rolls his eyes so dramatically that all I can see between his eyelids is white. "If I had a girl looking at me the way Daisy looks at you, I'd be sticking it to her behind the bleachers as we speak."

Slug drools over every single girl in the entire school, and they all think he's gross. To be fair, he *is* gross. His real name isn't Slug, obviously. He got the nickname when we were in grade school because he used to eat bugs—legit *bugs*. During recess, when we went to the playground and most kids were running around or playing kickball, Slug was chowing down on insects. Mostly ants. But one day, he found a slug squirming its way through the dirt, brought it to the cafeteria at lunchtime, and very theatrically swallowed it in front of our entire class.

After that, most kids didn't want to hang out with Slug. So when I sat down across from him in the cafeteria at lunch once day, he looked amazed. Ten years later, we're still best friends. He stopped eating bugs, at least in front of other people, but he still doesn't have many friends.

What do you say about a guy who is seventeen years

old with a nickname like Slug? Then again, what does it say about *me* that he's my best friend? My *only* friend.

Also, it doesn't help his prospects with girls that even though he shot up to over six feet in the last two years, he's only gained about ten pounds from when he was five feet tall. He looks a lot like a walking skeleton that put on a pair of blue jeans and a T-shirt and got a face full of acne.

He sneers at me. "What the hell are you so scared of? You *know* she likes you."

I adjust the strap of my backpack on my shoulder. "Fine."

His face lights up. "And when you talk to her, will you put in a good word for me with Alison?"

"Sure," I say to make him happy, even though Slug has a better chance of scoring with a Victoria's Secret model than he does with Daisy's best friend.

My heart is thrumming in my chest as I walk over to Daisy and her flock of friends. The girls are standing by the stairs leading to the entrance of the school, in front of a bunch of flyers stuck on the wall. Right behind Daisy's head is a flyer for this year's school musical, debuting in two weeks—*Grease*—and next to that is a black-and-white photo of a teenage girl with the word "MISSING" underneath. I recognize the face of Brandi Healey from our class, who ran away from home way back at the beginning of the school year, which is why the flyer is now crumpled and weatherworn.

"Tom!" Daisy's face glows when I get within earshot. "I thought you were tutoring today!"

I shake my head. I've always had a knack for math and science, so I've been tutoring them since my freshman year. Last semester, I tutored three days a week to make extra money, but this semester, it's only twice a week. I'm pleased Daisy knows my schedule. "Used to."

When she looks at me, her eyes are the color of the Pacific Ocean. I've never seen such a clear shade of blue. I literally can't imagine any girl being as perfectly beautiful as Daisy Driscoll.

But somehow, my eyes are pulled away from her face and down to her slender neck. To the pulsation of her carotid artery, below the angle of her jaw. Most peoples' hearts beat at about sixty to a hundred pulses every minute—I wonder how fast Daisy's heart beats. If I could watch for a minute, I could calculate her heart rate.

"So you're free then, huh?" Daisy says.

"Uh-huh." I scratch at the back of my neck. Daisy's friends are all staring at me and nudging each other. The nice thing for her to do would be to *step away* from them so I could talk to her without being humiliated. But she's not budging. "Do you…um, would you let me…um, walk you home?"

My request warrants a peal of giggles from the peanut gallery. One girl has her hand clamped over her mouth like this is the funniest damn thing she's seen all year.

"Shush." Daisy whips her head around to shoot her friends a look. Then she turns back to me with a serious expression on her face. "I'd *love* to walk home with you, Tom."

I'm so happy, I don't even care if these stupid girls won't quit laughing. Let them laugh. I'm walking home with Daisy.

But before Daisy can step away from her friends to join me, the girl standing closest to her, with pin-straight brown hair and thick glasses, grabs her arm. That's

Alison—Daisy's best friend. I've got Slug and she's got Alison. Both of us could probably do better.

"Daisy," she murmurs.

That's all she says. *Daisy*. Which makes me think she's said a lot of other things about me in the past. And now that one word is a reminder of whatever awful things she said about me when I wasn't standing right here.

Alison doesn't like me. She's made that really clear. And it isn't that she doesn't know me and doesn't understand me. Alison knows me. We are, in fact, lab partners in biology this year. We have spent plenty of time together. And every minute we spend together, she likes me a little less.

"*Shush*," Daisy says, more firmly this time.

Alison releases Daisy's arm, but not before shooting me a dirty look to end all dirty looks. If we were animals in the jungle, she'd be scratching my eyes out right now. I can't believe Slug's got a thing for her.

But I don't care, because a second later, Daisy waves to her friends, and then she and I are walking away from the school in the direction of her house. And when she smiles at me, I forget all about Alison. Alison who?

It's a really great day today. The sun is shining, and after the longest and coldest winter in history, we don't even need our jackets finally. All I can think about is Daisy. She has a dreamy look on her face, and she's almost skipping along beside me. I've known Daisy a really long time, and there are times when she reminds me of that same girl in pigtails that I gazed at from across the playground when I was four years old, even though back then, all I could hope for was friendship. But even when I was four, I knew I wanted to marry Daisy Driscoll.

And someday I will.

"Let me carry your backpack," I blurt out.

She looks at me in surprise. "I can carry my own backpack."

But isn't that what a guy is supposed to do? Carry stuff for the girl? I don't want to screw this up. Daisy is too important. "Yeah, but I want to carry it for you."

She considers my offer for a moment. Finally, she hands over her purple backpack. "You are such a gentleman, Tom."

I'm smiling to myself—I did good. At least I'm smiling until I get her backpack onto my shoulder. The thing weighs a *ton*. What the hell does she have in here? *Bricks?* Jesus.

"You…you have a lot of stuff in here," I gasp.

"I like to carry all my textbooks with me." She squints at me. "Is it too heavy for you?"

"No. *No.* Of course not."

I can't exactly give it back. I didn't have to offer to carry it, but you don't have to be Einstein to realize that I'm not going to score points by telling her that her backpack is too heavy for me to carry. So I suffer silently. I'm focusing most of my effort on not falling over backward from the weight of these two backpacks as we traverse the next several blocks in the direction of her house. Thankfully, it isn't far. We live in a tiny town, about ninety minutes from Buffalo, in upstate New York, where there's only one high school, everyone knows everyone, and you can walk clear across the whole town in an hour.

"You're always so quiet, Tom," Daisy says.

Damn—these backpacks are distracting me. "Am I?"

"Not in class," she amends. "In class, you always have your hand up."

My face gets hot. Does she think I'm showing off in class? I'm not trying to. I just want to get good grades. Next year, we are applying to college, and I want to get into a top school so I can get into medical school eventually. My whole life, I've always wanted to become a surgeon. I think about it a *lot*. I've got an entire shelf full of medical textbooks, and I've read all of them.

I wonder what it's like to cut into a person with a scalpel. To feel their skin separate under my hand. To see their insides.

I can't wait to find out.

"I don't mind," she says. "You're smart. There's nothing wrong with being smart. In fact"—she smiles at me—"it's hot."

That's news to me. "It…it is?"

Daisy stops walking and tilts her head to look up at me. "You know I like you, Tom, don't you?"

I stop thinking about all the weight on my shoulders, and instead, my eyes are drawn to her neck again. She is so slim that I can see her carotid pulse perfectly. I even notice the way it speeds up as she waits to see how I'll respond to her confession.

The carotid artery is the large artery that brings blood to the brain. It's roughly an inch below the surface of the skin. Slicing through the carotid artery would result in death in about ten seconds. The jugular vein is even more vulnerable—it lies just below the jaw line and could easily be sliced with a sharp blade.

I sense, however, that Daisy would not be interested in trivia about the delicate veins and arteries in her neck. So instead, I reach out and take her hand in mine.

She looks very pleased by this turn of events. Much

more so, I suspect, than if I sliced through her jugular with a knife.

Daisy chatters as we walk, talking about her classes and her friends. I listen and nod my head and ask all the right questions at the right times. Although mostly I'm focusing on how sweaty my hand has become. I'm trying to think dry thoughts, but it's hard. Daisy's hand is dry and soft and perfect.

As much as I like being with her, it's a relief when we get to the steps of her front porch and I can hand over her five-ton backpack and also yank my sweaty hand away from hers. I wipe it on my jeans as discreetly as possible. As if she didn't notice my palm had a puddle in it.

Daisy has a nice house—three stories high and freshly painted a pale blue color that matches Daisy's eyes. It's one of the newer ones in the neighborhood instead of being desperately in need of repairs, like mine. Daisy's family has more money than mine, and I'm also willing to bet she doesn't wake up in the middle of the night to the sounds of her parents screaming at each other and dishes shattering as they hit the wall.

"Well," she says. "Thank you very much for walking me home. And thank you for carrying my bag."

"You're welcome."

"You're so *polite*." She giggles, as if pleased and amused by my politeness. I *am* always polite, because at home, there are consequences if I'm not. "Are you *always* such a gentleman?"

There's a slight edge to her voice that makes me think she's looking for something from me. Does she want me to kiss her? We've been holding hands for the last twenty minutes. A kiss would be the natural progression. But it doesn't come easy to me. I've never had a girlfriend before, and I don't think Daisy has ever had a boyfriend before.

Truth be told, I've only kissed a girl once, and I didn't even want to do it. She kissed *me*. Except the only people who know about that are me and her. And now just me.

"Tom?"

Her head is tilted up to mine—she clearly wants me to kiss her. I reach out and run my finger along the base of her jaw. Her lips, puckered in my direction, are shiny with pink lip gloss. They are probably very soft and smooth, and Jesus Christ, why can't I just kiss her already?

"Hey, is that Tom Brewer over there?"

I leap about five feet away from Daisy at the sound of the booming voice coming from the side of the Driscoll house. I am mildly horrified by the thought that if I hadn't been so chicken, Daisy's father would have caught me kissing his daughter. Thank God for small favors.

"Hi, Daddy." Daisy flashes her father an easy smile. "You're home early."

Jim Driscoll steps in front of us, all six foot three of him. He is a solid wall of muscle, and if he had caught me kissing Daisy, he would probably be drop-kicking me as we speak. Daisy has two older brothers, both away in college, so she's the baby and also the only girl. Her father is protective of her.

But maybe he wouldn't have beaten me to a bloody pulp if he caught us kissing. He looks more amused than anything. Besides, I'm not a punk. It's not like he caught *Slug* almost kissing his daughter.

"I've got a late shift tonight," he explains to Daisy. "Just came home to change and kiss your mom goodbye."

Daisy crinkles her button nose. "Yuck, Dad. TMI."

Her father lets out a booming laugh. "Do you find that disgusting? I don't think Tom over here thinks kissing is disgusting." He winks at me. "Do you, Tom?"

If I could disappear into the ground right now, I would do it.

He claps a large hand on my shoulder. I hit five foot ten this year, but Daisy's father still towers over me. So does my own father. "You should come by for dinner some night. Daisy talks about you all the time. My wife and I would love to get to know you better."

"Dad!" I don't know what is more gratifying—finding out the girl I've been fantasizing about talks about me all the time or seeing how mortified Daisy looks when he says it. She flashes me an apologetic look. "I really don't."

He ignores her. "Well, Tom?"

"Yeah, sure," I mumble. "That sounds great."

Daisy's father winks at me. "You tell my wife when you're free, and she'll prepare a feast. You don't even have to wear a tie—although you'll earn extra points if you do."

Daisy's pale skin has turned an adorably pink shade. As her father disappears into the house, she shakes her head at me. "You don't have to come to dinner. Really."

I'm glad she said that, because I have no intention of ever having dinner with the Driscoll family. Even though I think about Daisy every moment of every day, I don't want to get to know Daisy's parents. I don't want to spend time with them. Especially not her father. I'll be happy if Daisy's father and I never have a conversation again for the rest of my life.

After all, the less time I spend with the chief of police, the better.

CHAPTER 5

PRESENT DAY

SYDNEY

As I walk the three blocks back to my building, the depression sets in.

Yes, I just had one of the worst dates of my life. The guy almost *assaulted* me. And I am incredibly shaken from the whole thing.

But it's the other guy I can't stop thinking about. Mystery Man.

He saved me. There was no one else around to come to my rescue, but he was there. And when we looked at each other, there was a spark. I wasn't imagining it. We had a connection.

And yet he didn't want to pursue it. He didn't even ask me my name. Or tell me his.

Maybe this is my fault. He had just seen a man attacking me, and he most likely didn't want to be a creep, hitting on me right after something like that. Maybe he was leaving it to me to make the first move. I should have asked him to escort me home. What's wrong with me?

Well, there's no point in dwelling on it. There are millions of people in this city, and I'll probably never see Mystery Man again for the rest of my life. I blew it.

By the time I reach my building, I am thoroughly miserable. I unlock the front door, glad at least that there is no doorman to make insipid conversation with. I pass through the mail room, where my friend and neighbor Bonnie is sitting on the lone bench, staring down at her phone.

Bonnie lives one floor below me, and she's one year older than I am and just as single. She is also a fan of using Cynch for dating, and over the last two years, she has dated 50 percent of all the single men in New York City. That's a conservative estimate. She says that online dating is a numbers game, so in a given week, Bonnie goes on seven dates, sometimes more. After all, you can have lunch dates in addition to dinner, and who says you can't have drinks with one guy and then dinner with another?

But in spite of the numbers and the fact that Bonnie is very pretty, with silky blond hair, china-doll features, and a cute, curvy figure, she is still single.

"Hey, Bonnie," I say.

Bonnie is smiling down at whatever is on her phone. She's got bright red lipstick on and smoky eyes, and from the looks of her, she's been on a date tonight like me. Hopefully it went better than mine.

"Hey, Syd." She doesn't look up from her phone. "How was your date tonight?"

"On a scale of one to ten? Negative a million."

Bonnie finally lifts her eyes, and her face drops. She clasps a hand over her mouth. "Oh my God."

The look of horror on Bonnie's face makes me uneasy. Why is she looking at me like that? "What?"

"You…" Her fingers fly to her forehead. "You're bleeding—a lot."

Oh no.

I rifle through my purse of mysteries until I come up with my compact. When I finally manage to get a look myself, I let out a gasp. Apparently, when I bumped my head on that garbage can, it did a little more damage than I thought. I have a small cut that has oozed blood all over my forehead. I look like a victim out of a slasher movie.

"Oh God," I mutter. No wonder Mystery Man didn't ask for my phone number. He was probably completely disgusted by my bloody wound. Men do *not* find that sort of thing attractive.

And I should know. I am a bleeder.

I have something called von Willebrand disease, which basically means that if I get a paper cut, I'm going to leave a trail of blood behind me. It was first discovered when I was a little kid, when I kept getting gushing nosebleeds practically every week. As a child, my friends thought it was amusing that I was spurting blood left and right. As a teenager, it was gross and embarrassing.

Thankfully, the nosebleeds are under control. I have accepted that if I get a cut, it's going to bleed more than the average person. I take birth control pills to suppress my menstrual cycles. It's not *that* big a deal.

Well, except when I meet a guy I like and he gets turned off by my bloody wound.

"This is just great," I grumble as I pull out one of the dozens of tissues from my bag and dab at the cut. I'll definitely need some water to get it cleaned up properly. I've got emergency Band-Aids somewhere in the depths of my bag as well.

"Are you okay?" Bonnie asks.

"Yeah, it's not as bad as it looks."

"How did it happen?"

"I fell and clocked my head on a garbage can."

"Ew. Do you need a tetanus shot for that?"

I plop down on the bench next to Bonnie. "Probably not. But don't worry. I'm up to date on my vaccines."

"Good." She winks at me. "I don't want you getting lockjaw or anything."

Of all the people in the building, Bonnie would be most able to sympathize with my awful night. But the truth is I don't feel like talking about it. I want to forget the last two hours ever happened.

"So what are you smiling about?" I ask her. "Hot date tonight?"

Bonnie pats her blond hair, which is pulled back into a purple scrunchie that matches her top. Bonnie is the only grown woman in the twenty-first century who wears scrunchies, but she somehow pulls it off. It's kind of her signature. "Yes, actually. He just walked me home."

Despite everything, I'm happy for her. Besides, if a girl like Bonnie, who is smart and gorgeous and funny, can't find a significant other, there is absolutely no hope for the rest of us.

"I don't want to jinx it," she says, "but I've been dating this guy on and off for a year now—mostly off. He is really hot but a total commitment-phobe. I am basically a booty call for him. I wouldn't even bother with him, but like I said, he's hot, and also he's great in bed." She glances down at her phone again. "But tonight he was talking about being exclusive. He was ranting about how he's sick of dating and wants to settle down."

"I don't know…" I don't want to rain on her parade, but guys like that are trouble. "You really think a guy like that could be serious about commitment?"

"The thing is," she says, "he's a serious guy. He doesn't seem like a player. Honestly, even though we mostly just hook up, I don't think he's hooking up with anyone else. He's super nice, and he's smart, and he's funny. He's actually a *doctor*."

A hot, single doctor who just hits her up for booty calls? She's got to be out of her mind if she thinks this guy is settling down anytime soon.

"Well," I say, "good luck. Are you coming to yoga tomorrow?"

Bonnie, Gretchen, and I have been taking yoga together three afternoons a week for the last year. It's how we got to know each other. "Sure," she says.

"Great," I say. "And you can let me know any updates on Dr. McHottie."

But Bonnie isn't even listening to me. She's back to smiling down at her phone again. Yeah, she's totally gone. I hope Dr. McHottie doesn't turn out to be Dr. McJerkface.

I take the elevator up to the tenth floor, where I've been renting out a one-bedroom apartment since my last live-in relationship fell apart very abruptly. I was dating this great guy, and I honestly thought he might be the One. I mean, we were living together, so it was obviously pretty serious. But then…

Well, I don't like to think about it. Or him.

When I get up to my floor, I walk down the dimly lit hallway on the way to the last apartment on the left. Even though I live in a decent neighborhood and I've got two locks on my door, there's part of me that is always a little apprehensive when I walk into my apartment. Every once in a while, you hear about some single girl in the city getting strangled or stabbed to death in her own place.

But that's unlikely. There are no signs of a break-in. I'm sure there's nobody lying in wait. Besides, what're the chances of being attacked twice in one night?

I fit my key into the lock, jiggling it a little like I always have to. After a few seconds of struggle, the lock turns and the door swings open.

CHAPTER 6

My apartment is silent.

Too silent. A completely quiet moment is rare in a Manhattan apartment, no matter how late it is. Even when I'm stumbling to the bathroom at three in the morning, I can usually hear someone partying right outside my window. That's why the quiet when I open the door unsettles me.

"Hello?" I call out in a hoarse voice.

In response, a siren rips through the silence, tearing down the street right outside my window. I stand there for a moment, waiting for the bleating sound to disappear into the distance before I let out a little sigh of relief.

Everything is normal here. There are no intruders, no signs of breaking and entering. The city is its usual level of noisy. Nothing to worry about.

I enter my small apartment. And by small, I mean *tiny*. An apartment in Manhattan is considered big if you can fit a table in the kitchen. You can't fit a table in my kitchen.

You can barely fit a person in there. My biggest motivation to keep my weight down is knowing I won't be able to fit in my kitchen or bathroom if I put on too many extra pounds. But on the plus side, it's not one of those micro apartments where you can't even stand up straight and your oven doubles as a refrigerator.

I drop my purse in its usual spot on the bookcase next to the front door, which is stuffed with trashy romance novels that have lead characters who look very much like Mystery Man. Romance novels give you an *extremely* unrealistic concept of romance. If I were a character in one of those books, our meet-cute would have quickly been followed by Mystery Man ripping off his T-shirt to reveal gleaming, rock-hard abs and then thrusting his throbbing loins against me.

My apartment is quiet, with no signs of anyone lying in wait to murder me. The living room is sparsely furnished with a sofa from IKEA, a wide-screen television, and a desk with my laptop on it that I have been using with increased frequency since I started mostly working from home during the lockdown.

My first stop is the bathroom, so I can check out the damage to my forehead. The cut itself is small, but thanks to my faulty clotting factors, it's bleeding quite a lot. I look quite frightening. No wonder Mystery Man hightailed it.

Since this is a frequent occurrence, I have a well-stocked first aid kit. I grab some gauze and keep pressure on my forehead. After I sop up most of the fresh blood and clean up what has already dried, I tape a pressure dressing in place. Hopefully by tomorrow it will have stopped bleeding enough that I can make do with a Band-Aid.

Stupid Kevin. I'm going to write a lengthy complaint to Cynch. I should have called the police after all.

After the dressing is secured, my eyes drop down to the rest of my face. I look pale and tired. I recently turned thirty-four, although most people think I'm in my mid twenties, but right now, I could pass for forty. I'm not beautiful the way Bonnie is, but a lot of men find me attractive. My brown hair has natural blond streaks, my eyes are an intriguing gray color, and a little mascara is enough to make my usually invisible light-brown eye-lashes stand out. When I smile, I have a hint of dimples, and my teeth are the pleasing result of three years of braces from ages eleven through thirteen.

And yet I can't manage to find a decent guy.

I get the feeling that Bonnie is picky, but I'm not. I'm not looking for the most gorgeous guy on the planet. I'm not trying to marry a millionaire. All I want is a decent man who doesn't have a drinking or a gambling problem, who is fun to talk to, who has a nice smile, and who likes me as much as I like him.

Is that really such an impossible dream?

I suppose it must be, or else I wouldn't be alone right now.

While I am busy feeling sorry for myself, my phone rings in the other room. I retrace my steps back to where I left my purse on the table next to the front door and dig my phone out from inside. For a split second, I get excited that maybe Mystery Man tracked down my phone number and is calling to ask me out on a date.

But no. It's the worst possible alternative to that—it's my mother.

I can't think of anything I am less excited to do right

now than talk to my mother, but it would be cruel not to pick up the phone. She worries a lot about me going out on dates, even though I assure her that I always meet men in public places and that they don't know where I live. Of course, given what happened tonight, her concern isn't unjustified.

She's worried even more the last few years, since my father died suddenly from a heart attack. He used to keep her calm, but now that she's retired from her teaching job and is living all alone, I'm pretty sure all she does is sit in her house and worry about me. If I lived anywhere besides Manhattan, she would surely sell her house in Connecticut and move in right next door to me. But she finds the city intimidating, so I'm safe from having my mother as my next-door neighbor—for now. Although if I told her about Kevin, she would probably put her house on the market tomorrow.

"Sydney!" she cries before I can even say hello. "Did you have a date tonight?"

"Yes." I take my phone into the kitchen to grab that glass of wine I was craving at dinner. "But it's over."

"Oh." I can't tell if she sounds relieved or disappointed. Probably a little of both. "How was it?"

"Eh."

"Is that good or bad?"

I tip about half a cup of red wine into a plastic glass—no point in being fancy if I am all alone. Hey, at least I'm not drinking straight out of the bottle. "I don't think there will be a second date."

The understatement of the century.

"I just don't understand it," my mother says. "You are such a beautiful girl. The boys should be lining up for second dates with you!"

I wonder how old I will have to be before my mother stops calling the men I date "boys." I imagine if I'm single when I'm fifty—which is starting to feel increasingly likely—she will still be referring to them as boys. By then, she'll probably be living with me. We'll probably be sharing the same bed.

"It's a mystery," I mutter as I take a long drink of wine.

"Oh, but I have some good news!"

Please not a setup. Please not a setup. "Um, what?"

"My friend Susan's daughter just had a baby!"

I take another swig of wine. "Wow. Fantastic."

"No, you don't understand," my mother says. "She's thirty-eight! She is thirty-eight, and she was still able to have children. And you're only thirty-four, so you've got at least four years of fertility. More if you freeze your eggs."

"Wonderful." I drain the rest of my wineglass. "Listen, I'm kind of tired, so I'm going to go now."

"Don't be mad at me, Sydney. I'm just trying to show you that you have options!"

"I'm not mad. I'm just tired."

It takes another minute of reassuring my mother to get her off the phone. Even though talking to her gives me a slight headache, when I hang up, the apartment seems deafeningly silent again.

Why is dating so hard? Why can't I just find a great guy, marry him, and live happily ever after? Is that really too much to ask for?

CHAPTER 7

Yoga is over at 4:30.

Arlene's hatha yoga class in the late afternoon can get pretty crowded, but I got there early enough to snag a spot next to my friends. I mean, I get that yoga is about pranayama and shatkarma, but it's also about shooting your friends agonizing looks when the teacher suggests a ridiculously difficult pose and keeps telling you to *breathe* when all you want to do is freaking collapse.

Arlene ends her guided meditation, which is how we spend the last fifteen minutes of every class. I glance over at Gretchen on my right, who is already back in a seated position, her palms pressed together. "Namaste," Gretchen says in unison with the other women in the room.

Bonnie snickers like she always does. She doesn't take the whole thing as seriously as Gretchen, but she likes to keep herself flexible for...well, you know.

"Okay, guys," Gretchen says as she scrambles back to her feet. "Time for coffee, right?"

I look over at Bonnie as I roll my mat back up. It usually takes me at least two tries to roll it tight enough to fit back in the bag. "Unless you need to get ready for another date with the hot doctor?"

Bonnie laughs, and Gretchen arches an eyebrow. "Hot doctor? What is that all about, young lady?"

I adore Gretchen, but she is super nosy when it comes to hearing about our dating lives. Especially since she became exclusive with Randy and doesn't have her own dates to get excited about. She says she has to date vicariously through us, although I find it a little offensive, because I would love to have a serious boyfriend like she does.

Well, maybe not like *Randy*. But someone I like as much as she likes him.

I'm not *too* jealous of Gretchen though. When we first met, she was still hung up on some guy she'd been dating who broke her heart, but now it seems like she's over it. That's what a good relationship will do for you. It gives me hope for my own future.

Bonnie pulls her blond hair out of her green scrunchie, shakes it out, then secures it again. "Let's get coffee and I'll fill you in."

Fifteen minutes later, the three of us are squeezed into a table at the coffee shop next door to the yoga studio. The shop has notoriously bad service, but we are too lazy to wander any farther away. Gretchen tries to flag down a waitress, waving her hand frantically to get the woman's attention.

"Don't forget," Gretchen says, "it's my treat."

"How come?" Bonnie asks.

"Because Gretchen was too busy having hot sex with

her boyfriend and she abandoned her escape-call duties," I explain.

"I feel *so* bad about that." Gretchen gives up on the waitress and turns to look at me, her lip jutting out slightly. Between my two friends, Bonnie is objectively prettier. She has the silky blond hair and curvy body. But Gretchen has a very sweet face, with big anime eyes and a button nose that has a smattering of pale freckles across the bridge. Plus, she looks pretty good in yoga pants and her snug flower-printed V-neck T-shirt. "Do you hate me now?"

"A little," I say.

"I would have given you an escape call, Syd," Bonnie says.

I shake my head. "Weren't you too busy on your date with Dr. McHottie?"

"Oh right!" Gretchen's eyes light up. "What's that all about? I didn't know you were dating anyone seriously."

"I'm not." Bonnie squirms in her seat. "I mean, it's not official yet. He is still very skittish, but…" A secret smile touches her lips. "I really like him. Really *really*."

"Is he hot?" Gretchen asks.

"*So* hot," Bonnie confirms. "He's honestly just… He's perfect. He's the kind of guy who makes me glad I never settled."

I can't help but notice that she looks directly at Gretchen when she says the word "settled." Hopefully, Gretchen doesn't notice.

"That's awesome, Bonnie." I reach out to give her hand a squeeze. "I hope he doesn't turn out to be a jerk."

Bonnie makes a face at me. "Gee, thanks."

I wince at what I now realize was an unnecessarily bitter comment. Bonnie met a great guy. Why am I trying to plant doubts in her head? I should be happy for her. But it's hard not to be skeptical after all my dating experiences in the city, culminating with last night's Worst Date Ever.

"I'm sure he's great," I say. "There are just a lot of jerks in this city."

"Right, and I've dated pretty much all of them," Bonnie points out. "He's not one of them—I promise you. I deserve a decent guy after all my crappy dates."

"You totally do!" Gretchen says. "I bet he's amazing. I hope you'll be as happy as Randy and I are."

Bonnie's lips tighten at that statement, but thankfully, she keeps her mouth shut. If Gretchen knew what Bonnie really thought of Randy, she would be crushed.

"Anyway," Gretchen says, "to change the subject slightly, the new exhibit I've been working on at the museum is opening tomorrow. If you guys are free, I'd love you to come see it!"

Gretchen works at the museum, presumably earning next to nothing. She also has one of those micro apartments downtown, and I can tell she is eager to move in with Randy, who has a decent-size apartment supplied by our landlord. I can't blame her.

"I'd love to come!" I say.

"Yes, totally," Bonnie says without enthusiasm.

While Gretchen returns to her task of trying to flag down the waitress, my phone buzzes in my purse. I pull it out, and sure enough, there's a message from Bonnie waiting for me:

Do we really have to go to this museum thing?

I shoot her a look. Bonnie is notoriously unexcited

about Gretchen's natural history museum exhibits, but I think they are pretty cool. Gretchen has a job that she loves, and I give her kudos for that. Not that I don't love being an accountant, but... Well, being an accountant isn't anyone's dream job. It was one of those practical things my parents told me to do.

It's a great job that you can do anywhere. And you can still work after you get married and have children.

Yes, even in college, I was preparing for the eventuality of getting married and having children. Pathetic, right? I never dreamed that ten years later, I'd be no closer to that goal. I haven't had one decent date in the last year.

And even though I am happy for them, it's hard to watch Gretchen with her boyfriend...and even Bonnie now settling into an exclusive relationship with Dr. McHottie. I miss having a boyfriend. I miss cuddling on the sofa. I miss having a warm body next to me in my bed every night as I drift off to sleep. I miss...

Well, you know. *That.*

God, why couldn't things have worked out with Jake?

But when I close my eyes, I don't see Jake. I see that mystery man from last night, who I can't seem to get out of my head. I haven't had a jolt like that in a really long time. I blew it last night with my bloody forehead, but part of me wonders if there's still a chance for something to happen. If only I could find him again.

"Hey," I blurt out. "How can you find a missed connection?"

"A missed connection?" Bonnie asks.

Gretchen turns to look at me, and at this point, I tell the two of them the whole dramatic story. Gretchen clutches her chest, now doubly sorry that she didn't come through with her rescue phone call. But when I tell them about the guy who saved me, they look so excited. Gretchen probably would have spit out her coffee if our waitress had shown up by now.

"That's so romantic!" she cries, her big eyes practically circles. "So what happened?"

"Unfortunately"—I grimace—"as Bonnie can tell you, I had a big ugly gash on my forehead, and he took off."

"It wasn't that bad," Bonnie says, although her cheeks turn slightly pink like they always do when she's lying.

"Still," I say, "I wonder if I could find him again, and I can look more...presentable this time."

"Totally!" Gretchen bobs her head. "I heard a story about a guy who met a woman on a plane and he never got her last name or her phone number before the end of the flight. So he launched a Twitter campaign to find her. And he did!"

"That sounds awfully elaborate," I say. "I don't even have a Twitter account."

"What about Craigslist?" Gretchen says. "Don't they have a whole missed-connection page?"

"Craigslist?" Bonnie shakes her head. "Do you want her to get *murdered*?"

Gretchen ignores her. "Or maybe you can check Cynch and see if he has a profile? If you met him around here, I bet you can narrow down your searches to a few-miles radius."

That's not a bad idea. It seems like every single person in the city has a profile on Cynch. If he is single, I bet he's on there.

"Would I seem like a stalker if I messaged him through Cynch?" I ask.

"No way," Bonnie says. "Dating is cutthroat these days. You do what you have to do to survive, you know? And if he's a decent guy, it's worth it."

"Totally," Gretchen agrees.

Bonnie and Gretchen almost never agree on anything, so the fact that they both think I need to find this guy seems like some kind of sign. I'm going to find Mystery Man.

Although even as I'm strategizing with my friends about finding this guy, I can't help but wonder if maybe I shouldn't. Maybe it's not such a good idea to get involved with a random guy I found wandering around my neighborhood late on a Tuesday night.

But I'm sure it's fine. After all, he rescued me.

CHAPTER 8

BEFORE

TOM

Daisy is busy after school today, volunteering at an animal shelter. She's always volunteering for something. I, on the other hand, am still scrambling to fill that tutoring slot that I lost this semester, because it's the only way for me to get spending money. In any case, she's not around to let me walk her home, so I end up walking with Slug.

"So did you score with Daisy yesterday?" Slug asks me as he kicks some dirt on the sidewalk with his size-13 shoes.

"I can't talk about that."

He grins at me. "That means no."

"It means *I can't talk about it*," I say, even though he's right. It does mean no.

"Maybe you and Daisy could double date with me and Alison."

"Um, Alison doesn't like either of us."

Unfortunately, it's true. When I talked to Daisy at her locker after school, Alison hovered nearby, shooting me dirty looks. The only person she seems to hate more than me is Slug. But it's a close call.

I hope she doesn't trash-talk me to Daisy. If she does…

"Come on. You gotta help me out, Tom," Slug says. "All the girls like you. It's not fair."

"That's not true."

"Bullshit. It *is* true, and you know it."

Okay, he's not entirely wrong. After I had my growth spurt, I started getting a lot of looks from girls. My mom is really pretty—she even did some modeling when she was young—and she always says I take after her in looks. But really, I couldn't care less about girls liking me. There's only one girl that I care about.

"I'll see what I can do," I lie. I can't get Slug a girlfriend. I would if I could, but I can't. He's actually a really good guy, but something about him makes girls nervous.

"Thanks, buddy." He pauses on the sidewalk, looking down at a particularly busy anthill. Anything insect related fascinates him. "Now that the winter is over, I bet the queens are laying eggs again."

Slug is a wealth of information about anthills. For example, did you know that the surface of an anthill is actually covered with small entrances that the ants open and close like doors? And did you know that anthills can reach heights of eight feet tall and be hundreds of years old?

If you destroy an anthill in front of Slug, you should just get out of town right now. In his eyes, that's an unforgivable offense. The one time he got suspended from school was when he gave Johnny Calhoun a black eye after he kicked apart an anthill. The whole time Slug was whaling on Johnny, he kept shouting, *You're committing genocide!*

And he wonders why he can't get a girlfriend.

"Do those ants look delicious to you?" I ask him. Despite his fury at Johnny when he kicked apart the ant-hill, which was *needless* destruction, Slug believes that eating insects is perfectly okay. Sort of the natural circle of life.

He laughs. "I don't know why everyone is so against consuming insects. They're animals, just like all the other meat products we eat. Is it really so much worse than eating a cow or a duck? Or a *pig*?"

"Um, yes. It really is."

"One day, I'm going to make you a cake entirely made from crickets. And it's going to be the best cake you ever ate."

"It'll probably be the *last* cake I ever eat."

He punches me in the shoulder, although not hard enough to hurt. "Hey, can I come over to work on math homework?"

What he *really* wants is for me to do the work and then he'll copy my answers. I've known him long enough to know the routine by now. And after he copies my answers, he'll stick around for dinner and eat every scrap of food in our kitchen.

"You know," I say, "if you keep copying my home-work, you're never going to be able to pass the exams."

"So what? It's just math."

"You still need to pass."

"Nah, it's not important to my future career." He shrugs.

Slug only recently discovered that studying bugs is an actual job that people can have, so now his biggest career aspiration is to become an entomologist. But who knows how long that will last. Before that, he wanted to be a mailman. And before *that*, he wanted to be a cop after Chief Driscoll invited our class on a tour of the police station.

"Fine," I say. "You can come over."

He grins again. Even though he's only seventeen, his teeth are already yellow. It's probably from the cigarettes. "You're the best, Tom."

Yeah, yeah.

When we get to my house, I discover the door is already unlocked, which means my mom is home. Half the time, she leaves the door unlocked, because it's that kind of neighborhood, so it doesn't surprise me. But I *am* surprised to find my father standing in the hall, yanking on a jacket.

"Dad?" I say.

My father, like Daisy's father, towers over me. He is forty-five years old, but the spiderweb of purple veins on his nose and cheeks makes him look at least ten years older. I know how genetics work from biology class, but I could swear I didn't inherit any genes whatsoever from this man. He is tall and burly, while I am medium build and lean. Even if I grow another inch or two, I'm never going to look like him. We're nothing alike.

Nothing.

"What are you doing home so early?" he grumbles.

"School is over," I remind him.

There are alcohol fumes emanating from his skin. It's not even four in the afternoon and my dad is already sloshed. Great.

His face is pink from the blood close to his skin. Did you know there are about twelve pints of blood in the average male body? If you lose more than 40 percent of that blood, you will die. For a man my father's size, that means he is about five pints of blood away from death.

"And you brought your loser friend—Cockroach," my father observes. "Fantastic."

I consider reminding him of Slug's actual nickname, but there's no point. I'm not sure a slug is any better than a cockroach anyway.

"I'll be home late," my father mutters under his breath. "Don't bother your mother, okay, kid?"

Before I have a chance to answer, he pushes past me. He marches out of the house, slamming the door behind him. I never liked my father, even when I was a little kid. Frankly, it's a relief when he takes off like that. Hopefully, he won't be home for dinner.

Or maybe he'll crash his Dodge and he'll never be home again.

As my father's car revs up in the garage, I lead Slug into the house. Naturally, he makes a beeline to the kitchen. Slug is always eating. *Always*. He weighs less than Daisy's backpack, and yet he's always stuffing his face.

My mother is in the kitchen, washing dishes in the sink. Her hair is loose, running halfway down her back. When she was younger, she used to have jet-black hair like mine, but now it's threaded with lots of gray strands. She doesn't bother to color them.

I don't know if it's my imagination, but my mother's body seems to stiffen when we walk into the room. She drops her head so that her gray hair becomes a wall around her face.

"Hey, Mrs. Brewer," Slug says.

My mother murmurs a hello without turning around. I stare at the back of her head, my heart thumping in my chest. I have a bad feeling I know what's going on here. It's happened before after all.

"Mom?" I say.

It takes her a few seconds, but she finally turns around. The expression on her face is apologetic, even though *she* is the one with the split lip. I stare at her, my hands balling into fists until my knuckles turn white.

"Mom…"

"I opened the cabinet in my face." She gingerly touches the open wound on her lower lip, which definitely wasn't from some kind of *accident.* "It looks a lot worse than it is."

I glance at Slug, who has already got our refrigerator open and is scavenging for food. I don't know if he saw my mother's face, but he's decided to stay out of it.

"Tommy," she says softly. "Don't make a big thing of it. I'm fine—really."

It's been six months since the last time I saw my mother with bruises on her face. Six months since the last time I wanted to take my fist and smash it into my father's face. I thought things were better. He stopped drinking as much. I thought…

"I'm fine," she says firmly. She looks over at Slug, who has grabbed an entire wedge of cheese and some chips from the pantry. "You and Slug go on up to your room."

"Mom…"

"Tom, let it *go.*"

Her jaw is tight. Maybe she used to be a model when she was younger, but those days are long over. Like my father, she looks about ten years older than she really is. Although she is still pretty enough that Slug will sometimes look at her in a really inappropriate way.

I don't want to let this go, but what can I do?

Still, I can't stop thinking about my mother's battered face, even when Slug and I are up in my room. We're sitting together on my bed, and we're supposed to be doing math homework, but I can't focus. I just keep thinking about my father's fist smashing into my mother's mouth.

My father is so much bigger than I am. If I ever stood up to him, it wouldn't turn out very well for me. Especially if he were in one of his whiskey-fueled rages, when he looks like he could lift an entire car and spin it around over his head. If it were me against him, he would win.

Unless I had a way to even the fight…

"I can't believe he did it to her again," I blurt out.

Slug is sitting at the other end of my bed, crunching on a Dorito. "You okay, man?"

"No." I throw my number-two pencil across the room. It hits the wall, leaving behind a gray smudge. "I hate my father."

Slug grunts. "I know."

I called the police on him once. I got sick of his tantrums and thought maybe I could help my mother, even though she told me not to. I still remember the stunned expression on his ruddy face when the cop showed up at our front door. I was pleased by how scared he looked until my mother went and denied the whole thing. She *defended* him. She went along with his bullshit story about how she fell down the stairs. After that, there was nothing the police could do.

"I'd like to kill him," I blurt out.

Slug looks up from the spiral notebook on his lap. Slug and I have been friends for ten years, and I've never said anything like that to him before. I've never let on the sorts of wild thoughts that run through my head sometimes. I've been careful about it. Even though Slug is my best friend, I don't expect him to understand. I don't know why I said it now, except I can't stop thinking about it.

I expect his face to wrinkle in disgust, but weirdly, it doesn't. Instead, he says, "Well, why don't you?"

What?

I stare at him. "What did you say?"

He lifts a shoulder. "Nothing wrong with killing someone if he deserves it."

"Actually, there is."

"Not really."

"It's illegal. I would go to *jail*."

"Only if you get caught."

Slug fingers a zit on his face which has turned bright white and is on the verge of popping. He's joking. I mean, it's not like this is a funny joke or anything, but he has a pretty twisted sense of humor. He's not seriously suggesting that I should really kill my father.

At least I don't think he is.

For a moment, I allow myself to imagine it. I imagine those five pints of crimson liquid oozing out of my father's body until he finally crumples on the floor, his eyes rolling up in his head. And for a split second, it feels so real that I almost think I'm going to be sick.

CHAPTER 9

PRESENT DAY

SYDNEY

After we *finally* get our coffee, Gretchen heads to the museum to take care of a few things for her exhibit, which is opening tomorrow. Bonnie and I walk back to our building, and the whole time, she's got that same secret smile on her face. Boy, she's really gone. I've never seen her like this.

We are about three blocks from the apartment building, at the exact same spot where Kevin attacked me last night, and as we approach the building where I pretended to live, I see a man sitting on the steps. When he notices us, he leaps up.

"Sydney!" he cries.

Oh no. It's *Kevin*, his thinning hair tied into another messy ponytail. Didn't he get the message when I kneed him in the balls last night? I felt like it was pretty clear. But he's coming toward me with open arms, like we're long-lost lovers.

Bonnie shoots me a questioning look, obviously

wondering if this is Mystery Man. I shake my head emphatically at her.

"Sydney," he says again, "can I talk to you?" He glances at Bonnie. "Alone?"

I fold my arms across my chest. "No, you may not. You attacked me last night."

Bonnie's eyes widen. "This is *that* guy?"

"Yes, he is," I say tightly. "And I'd like you to leave, Kevin."

He's wearing a pair of frayed blue jeans that are sagging slightly on his narrow waist, and he grabs the waistband to haul them up. "We had a misunderstanding. I was just trying to say good night, and you took it the wrong way."

"I promise you, I did not."

"Sydney," he says pleadingly, "you're my perfect woman. Don't let something great slip through our fingers."

His perfect woman—except for my monster arms. "Sorry. Not interested."

Kevin nods in the direction of the building where he thinks I live. "Could we go inside and talk about this for five minutes?"

Bonnie has been listening to this whole exchange, and when I glance over at her, she looks furious. "Oh my God," she pipes up. "Sydney obviously doesn't want to talk to you!" She reaches into her purse and pulls out her phone. "Either get out of here right now, or I am dialing 911 to tell them a creepy guy with a ponytail is harassing us."

Kevin looks between the two of us as if debating what to do. Finally, he takes a step back, his hands in the air. "Okay, fine. But you're making a mistake." His eyes darken as they bore into me. "A *big* mistake."

I cringe as I remember the way he grabbed me last night. I was lucky enough to be saved, but I might not have that kind of luck next time he corners me.

"No, *you're* making a big mistake if you ever go near my friend again!" Bonnie snaps. She punches 9 and 1 into her phone, then holds it up. "Do you want me to dial the last 1? I'm happy to do it."

Kevin gets the message this time. He scurries away, his ponytail bouncing behind him. It's only when he's out of sight that I nudge Bonnie. "Nice job. You are seriously kind of a badass."

"Yeah, well." She buffs her fingernails on the sleeve of her shirt. "I'm much better when the guy isn't fixated on *me*. If he came here looking to harass me, I'd probably be inviting him up for coffee now."

When I'm certain Kevin is definitely gone, we continue on our way back to our actual building, a few blocks away. When we reach the inside of the lobby, we find Randy standing on a step stool, swapping out one of the light bulbs overhead. He barely needs the stool though, since he's freakishly tall. Even taller than Kevin—definitely well over six feet, with baggy eyes and dirt that seems permanently ground into the ridges of his fingers. He's not my taste, but I can see what Gretchen likes about him—he's scrappy.

"Hey." He winks at us as the door behind us swings shut. "Where's my lady?"

"She went back to the museum," I tell him.

"Ah. I miss her already."

Bonnie rolls her eyes at me, and I elbow her in the ribs. "She said she'll be back in an hour or two," I say.

"By the way," Bonnie says, "my toilet is making that

59

strange noise when I flush it again. Can you come by to take a look?"

"Sure." Randy finishes with the light bulb and steps off the stool, dusting off his hands on his jeans. "Is it okay if I come by tomorrow morning? A bunch of people are having problems with their air-conditioning, and they're going to give me hell if I don't come by today to fix it."

"I guess so." Bonnie narrows her eyes. "Tomorrow morning? Like, what time?"

"How's nine?"

Bonnie works from home like I do, so she nods. "Perfect."

Randy sets about changing another light bulb while Bonnie and I head over to the elevators. It's only after the door swings shut that Bonnie drops her voice and says, "Will you come over to my apartment at nine tomorrow?"

"You're joking."

"I'm not." She adjusts the scrunchie in her hair. "I don't want to be alone with Randy. He gives me the creeps."

"Bonnie, he's totally harmless. I mean, Gretchen is *dating* him."

She arches an eyebrow. "He seriously doesn't make you *at all* uncomfortable?"

Honestly, Randy seems perfectly nice. He's been the super in our building since I moved in, and every time he has been in my apartment, he's been extremely respectful. He's never done anything I would consider threatening in the least.

And yet...

There's something about the way he looks at me sometimes. Not all the time, but sometimes. He stares just a little too long. And it doesn't exactly feel like he's checking me out, like some guys do. It's something else. I can't quite put my finger on it, but I can't pretend I don't know what Bonnie means when she says he's creepy.

"You know," I say, "my toilet sometimes makes weird noises too. Usually I just take off the top of the tank and there's a little handle inside that I jiggle, and—"

"No, thank you!" Bonnie interrupts me. "I'm going to let the super take care of my toilet needs. Will you come or not?"

"Fine," I say. "Nine o'clock?"

"Make it a quarter to nine," she says. "I'll brew some coffee."

Ninety percent of my social life these days consists of drinking coffee with friends. But oh well. There are worse things.

And hey, maybe Bonnie can help me track down Mystery Man.

CHAPTER 10

I've got to be at Bonnie's apartment in fifteen minutes.

I woke up about an hour ago. I showered and nearly put on the pair of sweatpants that I have been wearing with increasing frequency during the week. Working from home has its advantages, but I'm starting to look like a slob. Instead, I put on a pair of yoga pants, which are ever so slightly better.

Bonnie said she would make coffee, so right now I'm drinking some pre-coffee coffee. I have spent the last half hour scrolling through Facebook while contemplating deleting Facebook. I used to enjoy it, but every single one of my friends' posts now seems to consist of babies upon babies. Is anyone besides me *not* procreating right now?

These women who I used to call my friends seem to be charting every insignificant milestone in their babies' lives and posting them online. What if the babies want some privacy? *I* wouldn't want eight different perspectives on my eyelashes posted to the internet.

And then, of course, the baby bumps. Do I really need to see a profile photo of your stomach every single week for nine months?

And yes, I can judge them, because at this rate, I am *never* going to have children of my own. I can't fathom the situation in which this would possibly happen.

Last night, I wasted a good hour on Cynch. Over the last year, it has become by far the most popular dating app in the city, possibly because it touts itself as being "exclusive" to New Yorkers. An NYC zip code is required to join, which of course makes it irresistible. Jersey girls need not apply.

Other than being New York exclusive, it's a fairly standard dating app. Each profile contains a photo and the usual stats: single or divorced; has kids or want kids; investment banker or janitor. But one advantage it offers is the capability to search all profiles within a given radius.

That's how I attempted to find Mystery Man.

I searched all the guys in Mystery Man's approximate age range living in a two-mile radius. I extended it to three miles and then five. I looked through every damn profile, and there was not one guy who resembled Mystery Man living within a five-mile radius of this building.

(Yes, I am that desperate.)

In any case, I am left with four options:

1. Mystery Man is single and the one guy in the city who is not on Cynch.

2. Mystery Man is single but doesn't live in my neighborhood.

3. Mystery Man is not single.

4. Mystery Man is gay. (That's a different search term.)

The first option seems like the most likely. Maybe he's single, but he doesn't believe in internet dating. That's fair.

The second option leaves me feeling a little perplexed. If he is single and he doesn't live around here, what was he doing in a residential area all alone in the middle of a Tuesday night?

And that's when a wild thought suddenly occurs to me.

Bonnie was in the lobby when I got home, having just finished her date with Dr. McHottie. And then, by chance, I ran into an attractive guy only a few blocks away from our apartment building.

Is it possible that Mystery Man and Dr. McHottie are one and the same?

No, I don't think it's possible. That would be a strange coincidence, wouldn't it? Anyway, Bonnie said her doctor boyfriend has blond hair, and Mystery Man has very dark hair.

Wait, she did say that, didn't she? I think she did.

While I'm contemplating this possibility, a message pops up on my phone from the Cynch app. While I was searching for Mystery Man last night, another guy named Chad requested to connect with me. He looked pretty cute in his profile—all sparkling green eyes and dimples—and he seemed nice enough, so I accepted the connection. And it seems like Chad wants to talk.

See? I don't need Mystery Man. There are plenty of guys out there, and I'm ready to get back on the horse, as long as we stick to crowded areas this time.

I grab my phone to check the message, expecting that Chad wants to set up a time to get drinks. He hasn't done anything heroic for me like Mystery Man, but I don't need a hero. I just need a decent guy.

Except then I read his message. And my heart sinks.

Hey Sydney, sorry about the ruse, but it's Kevin. I really want to talk to you about the other night. I really feel like we had a lot of chemistry, and I don't want you to blow it because of a misunderstanding.

He doesn't want *me* to blow it? Is this guy for real?

I block his profile and report it to Cynch. I'm irritated that he was even allowed to sign up under another profile. Don't they have any quality control? The man is *dangerous*. I wonder if I should go straight to the police this time. Does this constitute harassment?

In any case, I don't have time to call the police right now. I've got to get over to Bonnie's apartment. She told me to be there at 8:45, and she is a sucker for promptness. Besides, Cynch is starting to depress me. Is it possible there are no decent men left in the entire city? I'm starting to think half the guys on Cynch are just Kevin in disguise.

I take the stairs down one flight to Bonnie's apartment, which is almost directly below mine. I get there at 8:46 and press my thumb against the doorbell, waiting to hear her footsteps after it echoes through her apartment.

But after thirty seconds, there are no footsteps. Bonnie hasn't thrown the door open. There's no sign anybody is even home.

Great.

I ring again, letting my thumb linger on the doorbell longer this time. Bonnie told me to show up at this exact time. She wouldn't stand me up at her own apartment, would she? But then again, emergencies happen.

I reach into the side pocket of my yoga pants and pull out my phone. I check my text messages, but there's nothing from Bonnie telling me not to come. I shoot off a message to her:

Hey, everything ok? I thought we were meeting at your apartment at 8:45?

I wait for bubbles to appear on the screen indicating she's typing in a response. But there's nothing.

After another minute, the elevator doors for the floor swing open. *Finally*—she must have gone out to grab more coffee or something. Except it isn't Bonnie who steps out of the elevator. It's Randy, wearing his usual worn blue jeans and a T-shirt hanging loose on his skinny frame.

He raises his hand in greeting. "Hey, Sydney. What are you doing here?"

Bonnie told me to come because she finds you too creepy to be alone with. "Bonnie invited me over for coffee, but she doesn't seem to be home."

Like me, Randy rings the doorbell. Once again, we wait for sounds of her footsteps behind the door, but once again, the apartment is silent.

This is really strange. It's not like Bonnie at all.

He glances down at his Casio watch. "I've got a busy day. I can't wait around for her."

"But you have the key, don't you?"

Randy's spidery fingers fly to the oversize key ring hanging off his jeans. He has the key to every apartment in the building. He has been in my apartment several times when I wasn't around—with my permission, of course.

"So you can get in, right?" I press him.

"I guess." Randy's Adam's apple bobs slightly. He is so skinny that his Adam's apple is painfully large and sharp. It almost looks like you could slice a finger touching it. "But Bonnie doesn't like me to come into her apartment when she's not there."

It hits me that Randy is aware that Bonnie doesn't like him. I wonder if he has any idea exactly what she says about him when he's not around. More importantly, I wonder if *Gretchen* has any idea. Gretchen is one of those people who is obsessed with being liked by everyone, and I'm sure she wants everyone to like her boyfriend as well.

"I'm just worried about her," I admit. "This isn't like her."

"Maybe something came up?"

"Look," I say, "you don't have to fix her toilet, but can we at least just go inside and check on her? Like, for one minute?"

"I don't know…"

"Please? I'm worried about her." When he hesitates, I add, "I'll tell her I made you do it."

He looks down at his watch again and sighs. "Okay. Just real quick though."

Randy takes what feels like forever sorting through every key on the giant ring until he finds the right one. I keep glancing over at the elevators, hoping that Bonnie will suddenly materialize carrying a bunch of coffees from Dunkin' Donuts. I mean, I'm sure she's fine. She probably had a date last night with Dr. McHottie and is currently cuddled up in his big bed with his million-thread-count sheets.

I'm happy for her—I swear.

Randy finally gets the door open, but he lets me enter first. As I step into Bonnie's apartment, I half expect to see her racing into the living room with a towel wrapped around her midsection, furious with the two of us for busting in while she was trying to shower.

But no. It's completely silent.

Bonnie's apartment is almost identical to mine in its arrangement, but it looks so different. Bonnie likes nicer things. I have my bare-bones sofa and desk and book-case, but she spent a lot more time picking out an expen-sive leather sofa, a chestnut coffee table, and an antique armoire. Her apartment looks like something out of a magazine article on Manhattan living.

"Bonnie?" I call out.

No answer.

"I don't think she's here," Randy says.

He's right. It doesn't seem like she's here. Undoubtedly, she's out with her sexy doctor boyfriend. I get what it's like to be snuggled in somebody's bed and not want to grab an Uber home at two in the morning. But for God's sake, she could've at least called me to tell me she wasn't going to be able to make it.

"I may as well check the toilet while I'm here," he says.

Randy wanders off in the direction of the bathroom. I stay behind in the living room and reach for my phone again. There are still no messages from Bonnie. Seriously, this is kind of rude. I would understand if she canceled at the last minute, but to not even call at all?

Finally, I select Bonnie's name from my list of contacts. I'm going to at least let her know that I was waiting for her as promised and that now she owes me a coffee like Gretchen did.

Except when I connect the call, I immediately hear her ring tone. Coming from inside the apartment.

Okay, that's strange...

I turn my head in the direction of the ringing sound. It's coming from the kitchen.

I step into Bonnie's kitchen, which is about as tiny as mine, so it takes roughly five seconds for me to spot her cell phone sitting on the kitchen counter, next to a black scrunchie. Bonnie's phone is still in her apartment.

And that's not all.

My gaze drops down to the linoleum floor. As a rule, Bonnie is a stickler for cleanliness. But right now, her floor isn't clean. It is stained with dark-brown circular droplets forming a trail that I now realize leads out of the kitchen and down the hallway to Bonnie's bedroom.

Oh my God.

"Randy?" I croak.

"Hang on!" he calls back. "I'm just trying to fix the toilet."

I follow the trail of droplets down the hallway, my heart pounding. I pass the bathroom, where Randy is fiddling with something in the toilet tank, oblivious to the blood stains on the floor. The trail leads directly to Bonnie's bedroom door, which is closed.

Maybe she's okay. Maybe she had a minor accident and is just sleeping in to recover.

Of course, Bonnie isn't the bleeder. I am. Aside from me, most people don't track blood all over their apartment without noticing.

I reach out and rest my hand on the doorknob. The thought occurs to me that maybe I should call the police instead of investigating on my own. But then again, I'm already here. I don't want to call the police over nothing. Maybe Bonnie is fine. Maybe everything is totally fine.

Slowly, I turn the doorknob. I push the door open, revealing Bonnie's queen-size bed with the lavender bedspread.

And when I see what's on the bed, I can't stop screaming.

CHAPTER 11

TOM

Today is the day I am going to kiss Daisy.

Maybe.

It's the third time I have walked her home from school. When I parted ways with Slug, he warned me not to chicken out. I'm determined to do it today.

Daisy and I are holding hands again, and I'm doing a great job of not being sweaty. I'm focusing all my energy on it. Daisy keeps smiling at me as she talks about the health fair she's volunteering at this weekend. She's always volunteering somewhere. She's so *good*. And I am so…

"Will you come, Tom?" she asks me.

"Come?" I say blankly.

She laughs. "To volunteer at the health fair! They can always use more hands. And you want to be a doctor, so it would look good on your college application."

"Sure." It probably *would* look good on my college application, but I don't care about that. If Daisy asked me to eat garbage, I would do it.

She claps her hands together. "Wonderful! What about Slug? Will he come?"

"Doubt it. Unless he thinks he can find a girlfriend there."

She giggles. "Does he still eat bugs?"

Even though he won't do it publicly, I would be very surprised if Slug didn't at least occasionally pop a beetle or two in his mouth. He seems to genuinely enjoy them. But it won't help his prospects if a rumor spreads that he's still eating bugs, so I just say, "Nah."

"Anyway," Daisy says, "let's meet outside the community center on Saturday afternoon before it starts."

"Or we could have lunch first?"

Daisy pulls a face. "Sorry, I can't. There's so much I have to do!"

Rejected. Maybe Daisy is having second thoughts about me. Maybe this will be the last time she'll ask me to walk her home. Maybe I *shouldn't* try to kiss her...

"How about on Sunday?" she suggests. "We could meet after church?"

I smile and nod, not bothering to mention the fact that my family doesn't attend church. My mother used to go when she was young, but my father thinks the whole church is "a bunch of swindlers," and he won't let either of us go. Not that I would go even if I were allowed. There is something about walking into a church that makes me very uneasy.

As we're walking by somebody's backyard, I spy a flower growing out of the grass with a yellow center and soft white petals. A daisy. Naturally, daisies are Daisy's absolute favorite flower. Before we can walk past, I pluck the flower from the ground and hold it out to her.

"For you," I say.

I thought she'd get a kick out of it, but instead, her face falls.

"I thought you liked daisies," I say.

"Yes, but..." She scrunches up her face as she looks down at the flower still in my hand. "You *killed* it. It was growing happily in the ground, and now it's going to *die*."

"Oh." It never even occurred to me that she would think that way. "Is there a way to save it?"

She shakes her head sadly. "No, there isn't." She tugs the stem out of my hand. "But I'll put it in water when I get home. At least it will last a few days that way."

Great. Now I'm a flower murderer.

"It's okay, Tom." She squeezes my hand. "You didn't know."

I lay my palm on my chest. "I will never kill a flower ever again."

And I mean it. I will never kill a *flower* ever again.

My declaration has brought a smile to Daisy's face. She tugs on the hem of my T-shirt, bringing me closer to her. I realize now we're only about six inches apart, and she's looking up at me with her clear blue eyes. I can barely think straight, but there's one thought in my head that is very, very clear:

Kiss her!

So I do it. I dip my head down and press my lips against hers. And they are just as soft and perfect as I imagined. She's so delicate. I'm not a big guy, but she's a lot smaller than I am. If I grabbed her head and gave it a solid twist to the left, I could break her neck. It wouldn't even be hard to do.

"You are a *very* good kisser, Mr. Brewer," Daisy breathes when our lips finally separate.

"Thank you," I say.

She winks at me. "Your first time?"

I hesitate for just a moment before deciding to lie. "Yes."

"Mine too." She runs a finger playfully down my chest. "I always knew you were going to be my first kiss."

And now I'm doubly glad that I lied. It's not like there's any way she could find out the truth. Nobody else but me is around to tell her.

"I'd like to do it again very soon," she tells me.

"As would I," I say awkwardly.

It's only when she pulls away from me that I realize that while we were kissing, the daisy fell from her fingers. When I look down, I see it under my sneaker, the white petals smashed into the pavement.

CHAPTER 12

PRESENT DAY

SYDNEY

I can't stop shaking.

The police are here. Officers wearing paper boots and gloves are tromping in and out of Bonnie's apartment, doing whatever police officers do at a homicide scene. I have been sitting on Bonnie's expensive leather sofa, which she was so excited to get a great deal on, and I have spent the last twenty minutes rocking back and forth and hugging myself. Nobody has asked me to step outside, which is a good thing, because I don't think I could walk right now.

Randy was the one who called the police. I can still hear his voice echoing in my head. *Her name is Bonnie Griffin. She asked me to come over to fix her toilet, and we found her in the bedroom. And she...she's dead.*

I will never get the image of Bonnie lying in that bed out of my head—not for as long as I live. This wasn't a woman who just went to sleep and never woke up in the morning. She wasn't *that* kind of dead. I don't think I've ever seen that much blood in my entire life, and I have seen quite a lot of blood.

A female officer comes over to sit down beside me. Her hair is pulled back into a tight bun, but she has a kind face. She rests a hand gingerly on my shoulder, as if she's worried I might break.

"How are you doing, Ms. Shaw?" she asks.

I can't quite manage a response. I suppose that's an answer in itself.

"We have a detective being briefed outside," the officer tells me. "He'd like to ask you a few questions if that's okay? Do you think you're up for it?"

Again, I can't get my vocal cords to function.

"I know it's hard," she says gently. "But you want to find out who did this to your friend, don't you?"

I do. I really do. Whoever the monster was who did this to Bonnie, I want them to pay. Because she did not deserve that fate. Nobody does.

And whoever did that to her is a sick, sick individual. They need to be locked up with the key thrown away.

"Okay," I croak. "I'll do my best."

My head jerks up at the sound of the front door opening. Presumably that's the detective who has been assigned to find out what happened to Bonnie. Despite how awful I'm feeling at this moment, I have to put my big-girl pants on right now. It's the only way to help my friend get justice. Hopefully they assigned one of their best detectives, and he will track down the killer ASAP.

And then the detective steps into the room, and I get a look at his face.

Oh no.

The female officer leaps to her feet and darts over to

talk to him. "Detective Sousa," she says. "This is Sydney Shaw. She's a friend of Bonnie Griffin. She was the one who discovered the body."

The detective is staring at me. He doesn't introduce himself, but it's unnecessary. I already know his name is Jake Sousa.

I know because we lived together for an entire year.

"I know Ms. Shaw," he manages. "We, uh… Anyway, I'll take it from here, Morales. Thank you."

I can't imagine how many detectives there are in the NYPD. Hundreds? Thousands? Why did *Jake* have to be the one assigned to this case? Couldn't it have been a detective who *doesn't* bring back painful memories?

Jake takes a few tentative steps toward me, like he's not sure if I might jump up and bite his head off. It's a distinct possibility. I take the opportunity to give my ex-boyfriend a once-over. Sadly, he still looks great. Pushing forty, with just a hint of gray in his temples. He's just as tall as Real Kevin, but instead of being bone thin, he's muscular and still does a hell of a job filling out a suit. My eyes are on his left hand—no wedding band, but that isn't a surprise. He'll be single till the day he dies.

Jake offers me a strained smile. "Sydney," he says. "It's been a while."

"Yes," I say tightly. I don't believe it's a coincidence he's here. I refuse to believe that my former boyfriend was assigned the case just *by chance*.

"When I heard the address, I asked for the case," he finally says. "I remembered this was where I was forward-ing mail the year after you moved out."

"I see."

I really wish he weren't here right now. This is hard

enough as it is without having to face my ex for the first time since our breakup.

Jake settles down next to me on the sofa, his brown eyes leveled at me. "Look, Sydney. I'm not going to pretend this isn't awkward. But I've got a job to do here."

I don't respond, but I recognize he has an excellent point.

"I need your help," he says in that firm, deep voice of his. Jake has this way of making you believe that he's got everything under control. It's something I used to love about him. "We need to find the monster who did this to your friend."

I swipe at the tears forming in the corner of my right eye. He's right. I need to let go of my angry feelings at Jake, because the most important thing is getting justice for Bonnie. "Fine."

"First off," he says, "tell me everything that happened this morning."

My voice is trembling slightly as I recount all the events of the morning, including coming down to Bonnie's apartment, meeting Randy at the door, and then discovering her body, sliced to pieces in her bedroom. This wasn't a crime of passion. Bonnie was *tortured*. She was *mutilated*.

Jake listens the whole time in that quiet, intense way he always does. Of every man I have ever met, Jake is the most skilled at listening. He makes you feel like he's tuned out everything else and like you are the only person who exists in the entire universe.

"I'm so sorry, Syd," he says when I finish my story. "That sounds terrible. But you have my word." He places a hand over his heart. "I am going to find the person who did this and make him pay."

"Thank you," I say softly. And I actually believe him.

"Now tell me." He clears his throat. "Do you know anyone who would have wanted to harm Bonnie?"

"No, she was awesome. Everyone liked her."

"Was she dating anyone?"

She was dating *everyone*. But I don't want to say that. It will sound like I'm posthumously slut-shaming Bonnie, and anyway, she was trying to be exclusive with someone. "She dated a lot. She used the Cynch app. Do you know it?"

"I know it."

"Can you look up who she was dating on the app?"

"Yes, we are looking into that. There was no sign of forced entry, so whoever did this was someone she knew and allowed inside."

I'm not telling Jake anything he didn't already know— he's the sort of person who is always one step ahead. Still, I want to give him a piece of information he might not already know. Something that could be important. "There was someone special though," I say.

"Oh yeah?" He looks at me with interest. "Who is that?"

"This guy she's been dating for the last year," I explain. "But they recently decided to be exclusive."

He nods slowly. "What's his name?"

I open my mouth, but no sounds come out. What the hell was his name? She told us his name, didn't she? I could have sworn she said it at some point. Something starting with…a *J* maybe? Or was it a *G*?

Maybe she didn't tell us. She was always very tight-lipped about guys she really liked, because she didn't want to jinx it. And the truth is I was so jealous of her newfound happiness that I didn't push her too hard for the details.

"I don't know," I admit. "But she told me he was a doctor."

"What kind of doctor? Did she say where he works?"

No and no. "I'm sorry."

Jake is looking at me like I'm the most useless person ever. And I can't blame him. Bonnie was one of my best friends, and I know absolutely nothing about this guy she was so wild about. Why oh why didn't I make her tell us his name?

"She was texting him the night before last," I recall. "They went out on a date, and then they were texting each other afterward. You can check on her phone and see who she was texting."

He rubs his jaw as if debating whether to tell me something. Finally, he sighs. "We saw the text messages on her phone from what seemed like a boyfriend. But they were all coming from a burner phone."

A chill goes down my spine. The sexy doctor that Bonnie was crushing on the other day had been texting her from a *burner* phone. Of course, he probably wasn't even really a doctor. Everything he told her was probably a lie. Even if he had told her a name, it probably wasn't his real name.

Is it possible that the man planned to kill Bonnie from their very first encounter?

"So it's him then." I swallow down a lump in my throat. "This guy she had been seeing was the one who killed her."

"It's a possibility we are exploring," he admits. "But it's not the only possibility."

It seems so obvious, and yet he's right. There are other possibilities. For example, there's a man who has a key to

Bonnie's apartment. A man who could have let himself in without any struggle at all. A man who Bonnie herself was afraid to be alone with.

But could I really point the finger at Randy? He's the boyfriend of one of my closest friends, and I've known him for years.

Then again, if he is capable of doing this to Bonnie, it's my responsibility to let somebody know.

"Listen," I say. "Our super, Randall Muncy…he has the key to Bonnie's apartment and…"

Jake nods slowly. He doesn't look at all surprised to hear this. "Mr. Muncy has an alibi for last night. His girlfriend was with him the entire time."

Of course. It doesn't surprise me that Randy and Gretchen spent last night cuddling, since that's what they do every night. I'm relieved to know Randy couldn't have done this though. But there's one other potential suspect I need to mention.

"Also," I add, "I went on kind of a bad date a couple of nights ago with this guy I met on Cynch who you should probably look into."

"You're dating?" he blurts out.

I look at him sharply. "*Yes*. Anyway, the guy sort of…" I don't want to tell Jake exactly what went down between Real Kevin and me, because I can't face the judgmental look in his eyes, but I also have to make sure he takes it seriously. "The date didn't go well, and he showed up again yesterday to try to talk to me. Bonnie… She stood up for me…"

I can't talk anymore because of the lump in my throat. I want to burst into tears when I remember the way Bonnie told off Real Kevin yesterday. She was a true friend. If there's any chance that she was killed because of me…

"Listen, we are going to find the guy who did this," Jake assures me. "Believe me, we have a lot of resources dedicated to this, and I want to give you my personal assurance that I am going to find him. We are going to look into this Cynch guy and every other possible suspect until we find the killer." A crease forms between his brows. "You believe me, right, Syd?"

I do believe him. There is nobody more dedicated to his job than Jake Sousa. That is, in fact, why his first marriage ended in divorce. It's also the reason why I finally called it quits on our relationship when I realized I hadn't seen my boyfriend for even one meal in the last two weeks because he couldn't stop working. *What's the point of being in a relationship with somebody you never see?* was what I yelled at him while I was packing my belongings.

He never even promised to try to cut back on work. He told me in that sincere voice of his that his job was the most important thing in his life and that any woman who was with him needed to understand and respect that.

And that, ladies and gentlemen, is the story of the first man I ever loved.

I don't love Jake anymore. For a while, I hated him, but right now, I'm glad he's here. If anyone can find out the truth about what happened to Bonnie, it's this man.

CHAPTER 13

TOM

My mother insists on giving me a ride to the community center for the health fair because it's all the way across town.

At first, I tell her no. She's got a crummy, beat-up Chevy that looks like something out of the junkyard. It's embarrassing to be seen riding around in it. But then she offers to let me get behind the wheel, and I'm sold. I got my license over the summer, and I've barely even gotten to use it.

"Are you checking your mirrors?" Mom asks me for the five millionth time as I change lanes in preparation for making a left turn.

"Yes, of course I am."

"Just checking."

"Ugh. Mom, I know how to drive."

Finally, she stops quizzing me about my mirrors and turn signals and lets me just drive. It's only about fifteen minutes by car, but I enjoy every minute of it. Maybe next year, she'll let me drive to school in the morning. A lot of the seniors take their cars to school. I've saved up some money from tutoring, and I could probably get a car at least as good as this one.

"So is your girlfriend going to be there?" my mother asks me.

Good thing we are stopped at a red light, because if we weren't, I definitely would've crashed into something. "*What?*"

"Daisy Driscoll. She's your girlfriend, isn't she?"

How does she know that? My face gets extremely hot. "Sort of. I guess. I don't know."

Daisy and I have never talked about whether we're boyfriend and girlfriend. I'm not sure if she thinks about me that way. But then again, why not? We did kiss. And it's not like I'm going to be dating anyone else.

Still, I don't want to *assume*.

My mother smiles as she watches my expression. When she smiles, the creases on her face grow deeper. I don't know how my mother got so old looking recently. It makes me sad sometimes.

"Daisy is a nice girl," she says. "I'm glad you finally worked up the courage to ask her out."

I don't know what to say to that. *Thank you?* So I just grunt.

"If you ever need any advice, Tom—"

"I don't."

"Make sure you don't forget her birthday or Valentine's Day," she says. "And all girls love flowers."

Not Daisy. She nearly started to cry when I plucked that daisy out of the ground. Maybe I can get her a flower in a pot or something. Anyway, I don't feel like discussing it with my mother. Instead, I focus all my energy on not crashing the car.

We arrive at the parking lot of the community center ten minutes early. I give my mother a quick peck on the cheek, then I hurry around to the entrance, hoping to get to spend a little time with Daisy. Unfortunately, when I arrive, Alison is the one waiting in front of the doors.

I'm not in the mood for Alison. I didn't sleep well last night. I woke up at two in the morning to the sounds of my parents shouting at each other. Well, my father was shouting and my mother was crying. Then I heard a loud crash, and I came running down the stairs. But by then, my father had already retreated into the basement, and my mother was sitting on the sofa, pretending she wasn't sobbing.

It's hard to go back to sleep after something like that. But on the plus side, I didn't see any bruises on her face. I don't know about the rest of her though.

I try not to think about it. It just gets me angry.

When Alison sees me approaching, she gives me one of her classic scowls. "Oh," she says. "It's *you*. I didn't know you were coming."

"Daisy asked me to come," I say, trying not to sound defensive. Do I really need to justify volunteering at a health fair?

"Wonderful," she says in a flat voice.

Alison has never said a nice word to me in all the time I've known her. Part of me wants to ask her why she dislikes me so much. But there's another part of me that already knows why and doesn't want to hear her say it.

"Well," she finally says, "Daisy will be glad you're here."

"Uh, yeah."

A thought occurs to her, and she scrunches up her entire face. "Slug isn't coming, is he?"

"Nah." Slug wouldn't come to something like this if his life depended on it. Even if he had a chance to score with Alison, which he definitely doesn't.

She shudders, emphasizing the pointlessness of Slug's crush on her. I really don't get why he likes her. He keeps saying she looks like a sexy librarian, although I don't understand what's appealing about that, especially to a guy like Slug.

We're standing in front of a large bulletin board. There's a giant flyer advertising guitar lessons. I wonder if Daisy would like it if I learned to play the guitar. Don't girls dig stuff like that? I would do just about anything to impress her.

Alison swivels her head to follow my gaze. At first, I think she's looking at the guitar flyer, but then she says, "They never found her, did they?"

"Who?" I start to ask, but then I notice what she's looking at. It's one of those old missing signs for Brandi Healey—the runaway. "Oh. Guess not."

"How long has it been?"

I shrug. "I don't know. Four or five months?"

"You knew her, didn't you?"

A weird, cold sensation runs down my spine. "Well, yeah. She was in our class at school."

Alison's mud-brown eyes are trained on my face. "Right. But you used to tutor her in math, didn't you?"

An alarm bell is going off in the back of my head. She's right—Brandi was one of my students until she disappeared. But so what? It's not like anyone blamed me for her running away. I was just the dorky guy helping her pass geometry. The police barely talked to me.

I open my mouth, although I'm not sure what I'm going to say. But I get interrupted by Daisy rushing over to us, her pretty face flushed and happy.

"Tom! Alison!" she says breathlessly. "You came!"

"Of course I came," Alison snips.

Despite Alison's attitude, Daisy wraps her arms around her in a warm hug. After she's done hugging Alison, I get hugged next. And our hug lasts longer. A *lot* longer. Long enough that I'm grateful when Daisy hands me a volunteer apron to cover up the growing tent in my pants.

"So," Daisy says to me, "I've got to find a job for you, Tom. Do you know how to check blood pressures?"

I don't. "I could learn."

She considers this but then shakes her head. "Alison, why don't you do the blood pressure checks? I'll have Tom take blood."

Take…*what*?

When we enter the building, Daisy snatches up my hand in hers and leads me to a middle-aged woman holding a clipboard. "Hi, Elise," she says to the woman. "I've got a new volunteer to do the diabetic screening."

Elise smiles at me, her pen poised on the clipboard. "That's wonderful. Who do we have here?"

"This is Tom Brewer," she says. "He's my boyfriend."

The smile on my face freezes. Did Daisy just call me her *boyfriend*? Am I really her boyfriend? Did I actually make the cut? I'm suddenly doing jumping jacks in my head.

After Elise signs me in, Daisy leads me over to a table with a sign above that says "diabetes screening." There's a set of chairs around the table and a few small blood sugar monitors.

"So what you need to do," she explains in a weirdly stiff voice, "is you use the Accu-Chek lancing device to stick people, and then you put a drop of blood on one of the test strips to find out the blood sugar level."

"No problem," I say.

I don't let on how excited I am to embark on this task for the afternoon. I assumed I would be doing something like handing out pamphlets on proper diet and exercise. I never imagined I would be sticking *needles* into people. I never thought I'd get to do anything like this before medical school.

I've got to start volunteering at health fairs more often.

She grins at me. "I figured you could handle it. Alison gets squeamish, but I know you won't."

"Definitely not."

"Perfect. Just don't tell anyone that you're under eighteen, because technically minors aren't supposed to do blood sugar checks."

It's the first time Daisy has ever suggested doing something immoral like lying, and somehow, it makes me like her even more, and I didn't know that was possible. I can't stop thinking about her, and when I'm with her, it's almost too much. I like her so much, sometimes I feel like I'm choking.

"By the way, I hope what I said before was okay," she adds, her voice hesitant.

"What you said?"

She shifts between her sneakers. "You know, about you being my boyfriend. I know we never talked about it." She takes a shaky breath. "I just... I don't know, it popped out. But you don't have to be my boyfriend if you don't want to be. Like, it's no big deal."

"No," I say quickly. "I want to be your boyfriend."

Her blue eyes light up. "Really?"

She has no freaking clue. "Really really."

Daisy looks so happy after I say that. She starts humming to herself as she shows me the package of sensor pads and explains how to load them into the monitor. I watch her carefully, partially because it's hard for me to take my eyes off her and partially because I need to figure out how to do this thing.

After Daisy has shown me everything, she asks, "You got it?"

"Got it." It's not rocket science or anything.

She cocks her head to the side. "Want to practice on me?"

My heart speeds up. Sticking a needle into Daisy's finger? Somehow, that doesn't seem like a great idea. I've been doing everything in my power to avoid thinking about stuff like that. "I don't know…"

"Come on. I can't release you on the public without one practice session."

Except couldn't it be on anyone but Daisy Driscoll?

But no, this is happening. Daisy sits down in one of the plastic chairs, and she isn't satisfied until I'm sitting next to her. She places her soft hand on the table, and I can only just barely make out the pulsations of her radial artery in her wrist.

"You need to load the lancet in the device," she explains. "You can't reuse them, obviously."

"Uh-huh…"

Daisy instructs me as to what to do, but my hands

are shaking so badly it takes me about four tries to load the lancet. It's embarrassing. She actually starts to laugh. "Why are you shaking so much? Don't you want to be a surgeon?"

When I finally get the device loaded, Daisy offers me her index finger. I press the head of the device against the soft pad of her finger. I press the button on the side, and the device jerks as the needle thrusts forward. When I pull it away, a tiny red droplet oozes out of her fingertip.

"Is that enough blood?" I ask.

"You may need to squeeze a little more out. I'm not much of a bleeder."

I hold Daisy's finger between mine, kneading out enough blood to fill the sensor pad. I watch in fascination as the crimson dot grows in size. It's amazing how even though Daisy is the most beautiful girl I've ever seen, her blood looks like everyone else's. The same color, the same consistency.

And if she bled out five pints, she would be dead like anyone else.

Actually, she would probably be dead after even less than five pints. Maybe just three or four. I can just imagine the color draining out of her soft cheeks, the way her body would go limp. Well, she would be limp at first. But then she would eventually stiffen in rigor mortis. I've read all about it.

Daisy would be so easy to kill. It would barely even be a challenge.

"Tom?" Daisy's voice is heavy with concern. "Are you okay? You look really pale."

"I'm fine."

"You're kind of hurting my finger."

As quickly as I can, I get Daisy's blood on the sensor pad. She pulls her hand away from me, a slightly troubled look on her face. The glucose monitor counts down, analyzing the sample of her blood for the sugar level. Thirty, twenty-nine, twenty-eight…

"Do you need a Band-Aid?" I ask her.

She stares at me for a second, then shakes her head. "I'll do it."

She grabs a Band-Aid from the box on the table and uses her other hand to get it in place. It's a bit of a struggle for her, but when I try to help, she pushes me away. I really messed up. I should've lied and said I knew how to take blood pressure. I would've figured it out.

Blood pressure would have been much safer for me.

"Are you sure you feel comfortable doing this station, Tom?" she asks me.

"I'm comfortable."

"Are you sure?"

"I'm *sure*."

The glucose monitor beeps. Daisy's reading is back: 120.

"That's normal if they're not fasting," she explains. "There's a table of numbers right here that you can refer to. If their blood sugar is high, you just refer them to see their doctor as soon as possible."

"Got it." I manage a smile. "It was just first-time jitters. I got it though. I promise."

Daisy looks at me for a long moment, but then her face relaxes. She reaches out to squeeze my arm. "I believe in you."

I wonder if she would still feel the same way if she knew the thoughts that were going through my head as I squeezed the blood out of her finger.

CHAPTER 14

PRESENT DAY

SYDNEY

Gretchen and I have gone through an entire box of tissues tonight. And a bottle of wine.

After each glass of wine, our reminiscing about Bonnie has gotten more and more tearful. Gretchen's eyes and nose are red and puffy, and I'm sure I would look identical if I checked myself in the mirror. It's getting late, but she doesn't seem to want to leave. And I don't want her to leave.

"Did you ever see Bonnie practicing smiles?" Gretchen asks me.

"Practicing smiling?"

"Yes!" She manages her own smile through her tears. "I caught her doing it once in the mirror. She told me she liked to practice different smiles for different situations so she didn't look weird to people. Like, she had one smile if she was happy, obviously. And a different smile if she was trying to impress a client. And a different smile if someone was being silly."

"Wow," I say, "I had no idea! What smile do you think we were getting?"

Gretchen looks affronted. "The *real* smile, of course."

"Maybe…"

Although there's part of me that wonders if Bonnie had a side we didn't know about. Even though I got to know her pretty well, there was a part of Bonnie that I could never quite reach. Like, she was in love with Dr. McHottie, she wanted to be exclusive with him, and yet she never even told us his name or introduced him to us.

If she had, everything might have been different. Maybe he wouldn't have risked killing her if he knew her friends could identify him.

The thought of it makes me tear up all over again.

"Oh, hey." Gretchen digs around in her purse. "I brought something."

I grab another tissue and dab at my eyes. "What?"

Triumphantly, she pulls out two scrunchies. "Bonnie left these at my apartment. I thought we could wear them. In her honor, you know?"

I solemnly accept the scrunchie, lacing my hair through the fabric. Gretchen does the same. Of course, we both look ridiculous. Only Bonnie was able to rock a scrunchie.

Gretchen grabs her wineglass off my coffee table, which contains the remainder of the bottle of red wine that had been full this morning. "To Bonnie."

I tap my own wineglass against hers. "To Bonnie."

On that note, we both drain the rest of our wine. I wish we had another bottle. I need to keep another in the house, just in case any more of my close friends are murdered in the near future.

Gretchen takes a shaky breath. "I better get home. It is getting really late."

I don't want her to go, but I can't deny that it's close to midnight. I should try to go to bed, but I'm sure I'll just toss and turn. "Do you need to call an Uber?"

She shakes her head. "I'm going to spend the night at Randy's apartment."

Right, Gretchen doesn't have to spend the night alone like I do. "How is he doing?"

I still have mixed feelings about him, but I have to admit, Randy was a champ this morning. Once I started screaming, he was instantly at my side. I was ready to pass out, but he took charge. He led me into the living room, shutting the door to the bedroom behind him, and then placed a call to 911. I was practically hyperventilating at that point, but Randy was utterly calm. I was grateful at the time, although he must have been shaken.

"He's okay," Gretchen says. "He takes this kind of thing in stride."

He takes finding a mutilated dead body in stride? Okay…

"Anyway…" Gretchen rubs at her swollen eyes as she gets to her feet. "I'm going to head out, but let's talk tomorrow, okay?"

As I walk her to the door, all I can think is that I don't want Gretchen to leave. It's late, but I'm sure we can track down another bottle of wine. All I want is for Gretchen to stay in my apartment and reminisce with me more about Bonnie until my eyes finally drift shut.

But I can't stop her from going. She gives me a hug at the door, then I watch her make her way down the hallway to the elevator. I keep the door cracked open until she's gone.

And now I'm alone.

There are times when I love having an apartment all to myself. I've had some pretty bad roommates in the past, and I'm the sort of person who appreciates my solitude. But right now, I hate it. The apartment feels so empty. I feel absolutely and utterly alone.

Since the wine is gone, I go into my kitchen and locate the next best thing: a pint of ice cream. I check the flavor: mint chocolate chip. I hate mint chocolate chip. Considering I live alone, I'm not sure why the only ice cream I have in the freezer is a flavor I don't even like, but then I remember that Bonnie brought it over. We were having dinner together. I was the one cooking, and she was responsible for dessert. I gave her a hard time about bringing my least favorite flavor of ice cream, but her response was, *It's ice cream, Sydney. Every flavor is good by definition.*

Apparently, I will be wearing a scrunchie and eating mint chocolate chip ice cream in her honor.

I plop back down on the couch with my ice cream. It may not be my favorite flavor, but it still tastes pretty damn good. I mean, it's ice cream. You really can't go wrong.

As I'm stuffing myself, I reach for my phone. The first thing I do is bring up the Cynch app. This morning, I was looking for the Mystery Man—that feels like one hundred years ago. He is the furthest thing from my mind right now.

This time, I type something very specific into the search bar. I type in the name Jacob Sousa.

And there he is.

CHAPTER 15

If I ever needed confirmation that Jake was still single, now I have it. He's still on Cynch. He's still looking for the One, after we definitively determined that I was not the One.

Jake looks good in his photo. It's not a fake photo like Kevin's. It looks more like him than most people's photos do, but that doesn't surprise me. Jake was never the kind of guy who felt like he had something to hide—what you see is what you get. He's dressed in the same shirt and tie he usually wears to work, and he's sporting his perpetual five-o'clock shadow. I swear, five seconds after he shaves, his beard instantly grows back. It also hides some acne scars left over from his teenage years, although it's hard to imagine Jake ever being a skinny teenager. It seems he emerged into the world already thirty-five years old.

I read through the details Jake lists on his profile. *Doesn't have kids. Wants kids. Nonsmoker. No political affiliation. Favorite hobby: Watching football.*

Well that's a lie. Jake doesn't have time for hobbies.

Under what he's looking for, he wrote: *I want to find a woman I can come home to at the end of a long night of work, enjoy a hot dinner together, and watch a movie on the TV.*

More lies. Jake doesn't want a woman he can come home to. He doesn't want to come home at all.

But despite my simmering resentment, when I look down at his photo, I remember that tug I used to feel when I was with him. We first met through Cynch, years ago, after we had both been on a ton of bad dates, and the second I saw him... Well, it was that lightning bolt. I knew that I wasn't going on any more bad dates for a long time.

Why couldn't it have worked out? Jake and I should be married by now. We should be having children and posting obnoxious baby pictures all over Facebook.

I scroll through the contacts on my phone, and sure enough, Jake's name is still there. A smarter woman would have deleted him after we broke up, but I didn't. As long as he hasn't changed his number, I still have it programmed into my phone.

Before I can stop myself, I click on his name.

The odds seem small that Jake will actually pick up the phone—after all, it's midnight and he's working a case—so I'm surprised when I hear his deep voice on the other end of the line. Well, I'm surprised until I remember that the man never, ever sleeps. "Sydney?"

"Hey."

He doesn't ask me why I'm calling, but the fact that he didn't delete me from his phone says a lot. "Hey."

Despite the fact that I'm just as alone as I was a minute earlier, I feel better now that I've got Jake on the line. He always had a way of making me feel secure. His presence can fill a room, even over the phone.

"So how is the case going?" I ask him. "Did you find that boyfriend?"

"You know I can't talk to you about that, Syd. It's an ongoing investigation."

Jake was always such a stickler for the rules. "Right. I see."

He lets out a long sigh. "I can tell you that we haven't made any arrests yet."

"Do you have a person of interest?"

He hesitates. "No."

Great. So the guy who killed Bonnie is still out there while she is lying in the morgue. "I don't get it. Don't you guys have all this amazing fingerprint and DNA technology? How is it possible that you don't have the killer in custody?"

"It's not that simple, Sydney. We have DNA and fingerprints but no matches in our database." He pauses. "Well, except for Randall Muncy, but we know he's not our guy."

"Great."

I called Jake to get comfort and maybe find out that they caught the bastard who did this. But the revelation that they don't even have any suspects… Well, I'm astonished. How is it possible that they can't track down Bonnie's boyfriend?

"Listen," Jake says, "are you still living alone?"

I bristle. "*Excuse* me?"

"No, I mean…" He clears his throat. "You should just be careful. Make sure you lock your door. Do you have a dead bolt?"

"Yes."

"Well, use it. Are you still on Cynch?"

"Yes."

"Think you could take a break from it for a while?"

I grit my teeth. "One of my best friends was murdered last night. I'm not exactly thinking about my next date."

"Okay, well, good."

This talk is making me uneasy. "Is there a reason that I should be worried, Jake?"

He's quiet for a long time, and if he were sitting beside me, I would want to wring his neck. "Okay," he finally says, "I'm going to tell you something that we haven't leaked to the press yet. But I think you should know."

"Know *what*?"

"You swear this is just between us?"

"Yes!"

"I wasn't being entirely honest with you before." Jake takes a breath. "We actually do have a fingerprint match."

I suck in a breath. That's *great*. That means they must be close to making some sort of arrest. "So how come you haven't arrested the guy?"

"Because we don't know whose fingerprints they are."

I frown. "I don't understand. What do they match with then?"

"Another crime scene."

My stomach sinks as I absorb what he is trying to tell me. The fingerprints in Bonnie's apartment match fingerprints found at another crime scene. Does that mean…

"It was another woman about Bonnie's age," he says. "Looked sort of like her too. And there were other details that were similar. Like what was done to the body before and after death."

I overheard one of the police officers saying that they

thought Bonnie was tortured before she was actually killed. It's the kind of thing that's very hard to get out of your head. "Something in particular that was similar?" I ask.

"Yes," he confirms. "But you have to swear you won't tell a soul, Syd. This is not public information, but you deserve to know."

The way he's saying it, I'm not even sure I want to know any more. And yet I won't be able to sleep tonight if he doesn't tell me. "What is it?"

"Both women…they had a large chunk of hair snipped from their heads very close to the scalp—at exactly the same spot. And we couldn't find the hair anywhere in the apartments. So it seems like the killer may have taken it… as a souvenir."

And now I'm imagining some lunatic storing Bonnie's hair in a jar in his basement.

"The other victim also dated a lot of men on Cynch," Jake says. "They were able to locate several of her recent dates and eliminate them as suspects, but there were fingerprints in the apartment as well as DNA that could not be identified."

"When was this?"

"About eighteen months ago."

Bonnie told me she had started dating that guy about a year ago. So apparently he murdered a woman, took a break for six months, then found his next victim.

My head is spinning, and it's not from the wine. I'm sorry I ate all that mint chocolate chip ice cream, because I feel like I'm going to throw it all up.

"Sydney," Jake says firmly, "we are going to find this guy. I promise you that."

"You haven't found him yet."

"Look, if this wasn't a crime of passion, it might take more time." I can envision that sexy crease he gets between his dark eyebrows. "A serial killer who planned this in advance would have covered his tracks better. He was obviously careful not to be seen with her publicly or allow himself to appear on social media with her. Who knows if she even knew his real name? But don't worry. We *will* find him—sooner or later."

I'm not sure I believe him, but what choice do I have? It's not like I have any control over this case. But I do think that if they truly believe there's a serial killer roaming the city targeting young women, they are going to do everything in their power to find him.

"Syd," he says. "Are you okay?"

I look over at my empty bottle of wine, empty tissue box, and melting ice cream. "I've been better."

"Do you want me to come over?"

My face burns. "Are you asking for a *booty call?*"

"No! Christ, no." He sounds flustered in a way I used to find very endearing. "I just thought maybe tonight you wouldn't want to be alone. And I could, you know, be there. On your couch, obviously. If you want."

"Don't you need to get some sleep?"

"Sleep? What's that?"

Despite everything, I let out a snorting laugh. Jake did seem to exist on only a couple of hours of sleep every night.

"It's fine," I say. "My friend Gretchen was here all night. And now I'm going to sleep. Besides, it would be weird if you came over."

"I wouldn't let it be weird."

"I don't know if you have any control over it." I let out a yawn. "Anyway, I guess I'll attempt to go to sleep now."

"Okay," Jake says. "Just make sure you throw that dead bolt."

"Jesus," I mutter. "Don't worry so much. Nobody is going to break into my house tonight and murder me. That seems really unlikely."

"Just do it."

"Yes, Mom," I grunt. "Anyway, good night. Thanks for the terrifying update."

"Good night, Syd."

We hang up, and for a moment, all I can do is sit there, staring at the black screen of my phone. And then I get off the couch, walk over to the front door, and make sure the dead bolt is in place.

CHAPTER 16

BEFORE

TOM

I wake up covered in sweat.

I was dreaming about Daisy. *Again.* Every other night, I dream about her. And every time, I wake up with my heart pounding and my bedsheets soaked.

In this dream, Daisy and I were in the kitchen together, cooking. I used to love cooking with my mom when I was a little kid, and I still enjoy it, even though my father says cooking is "women's work." I learned how to sharpen knives using the rim of a ceramic mug, so all the knives in our kitchen are very sharp. Too sharp.

Daisy was slicing some green beans when she let out a yelp. In real life, all she could have possibly done was nick the tip of her finger, but in my dream, she had managed to somehow slice off her entire hand. The severed hand lay on the table, the fingers twitching. And Daisy looked up at me with her liquid blue eyes. *I had an accident, Tom.*

What should I do? I asked helplessly as I watched the blood gush from the stump of her left arm.

Well, Daisy said, *now I am uneven. So you'll have to cut off the other hand so I'll be symmetrical again.*

Even in my dream state, I recognized this wasn't a good idea. But I obligingly took the carving knife out of the knife block while Daisy lay her right hand down on the kitchen counter. I held the knife over my head and brought it down hard on her right forearm. It sliced cleanly through the bone, severing her right hand.

That's when I woke up.

About three or four times a week, I have a dream in which I am stabbing or strangling my beautiful girlfriend. On two occasions, I imagined myself holding her under water until she drowned. And every time I wake up, I feel a rush of relief.

I didn't do it. I didn't hurt her. Daisy is okay.

My relief tonight lasts only a few seconds though. That's how long it takes to realize what woke me up. It's the sound of screaming.

My mother is screaming.

I jump out of bed, not bothering to throw on any clothes, so I'm just in my white undershirt and boxers. I haven't heard her scream like this in a long time. For a while, when I was a little kid, it used to happen all the time. My mother instructed me not to leave my room if I heard scary noises. *Hide in the closet, Tommy,* she told me. *Promise me you won't come out until I say so.*

When I get downstairs, I realize the noises are coming from the kitchen. The sound of my father's booming voice echoes through the house. "It's none of your damn business what I do when I go out!" he shouts at her. "Your job is to look pretty and have dinner on the table every night! And you're doing a shitty job at both!"

Something else shatters in the kitchen—he's throwing more dishes at her. My body fills with red-hot rage. He can't talk to my mother that way. Maybe when I was a kid, he could get away with it. But not anymore.

Except he's still bigger than me. I've got to even things out.

I need a weapon.

Most things in this house that could serve as a weapon are in the kitchen, and he is in there. I look around the living room, and my eyes fall on the fire poker leaning against the fireplace. The end of that poker is sharp enough to tear through skin. I imagine sinking it deep into my father's chest.

Yes, that will do.

I march into the kitchen, gripping the fire poker in my right hand. My mother is curled up on the floor, clutching her face as she sobs into her hands, and my father is standing over her, reeking of whiskey. I arrive just in time for him to hurl a ceramic mug at her head, which shatters about an inch away from her face as she screams again.

"Hey," I growl at him. "Leave her alone."

Even though I spoke, it takes my father a moment to realize I'm in the room. And when he sees me, he smirks at my underwear. "Go to bed, kid," he says.

He never calls me by my name. It's always "kid" or "boy." Well, tonight he's going to find out that I'm not a kid anymore.

"Leave her alone." I raise the fire poker threateningly. "Or else."

My father looks me up and down. He stares at the sharp end of the fire poker in my right hand, and after a few seconds, he bursts out laughing. He looks over at my mother, "You believe this kid of yours, Luann? Threatening me with a *fire poker*."

My mom raises her face from her hands. I can't tell if her eyes are swollen from crying or because he hit her. "Tommy, please don't get involved. Go back to your room."

"Listen to your mother, boy," he says. "Get back to your room, and mind your own goddamn business."

"No. I'm not going."

My eyes meet his. I look a lot more like my mother— I've got her nose and chin and build—but he and I have the same eyes. Very, very dark and laser-beam focused on what we want.

In two quick strides, my father crosses the kitchen. For a moment, he's close enough for me to strike. I could shove the sharp point of the fire poker through his beer belly, and it would all be over. He would never hurt my mother again.

But I hesitate. He's my father after all. Could I really do that?

That hesitation is all it takes. He reaches out and snatches the poker right out of my hands before I can stop him.

"So, Tom." His dark eyes stay trained on mine. "What were you saying?"

I can't believe it. How did I let this get turned around on me? My mother, previously cowering on the floor, scrambles to her feet and dashes across the kitchen. "Don't you dare hurt him, Bill!"

He easily shoves her out of the way, like she's a rag doll. Her body crashes back to the floor, and her head hits the side of the stove with a sickening thud. The blow is not enough to knock her out, but it's taken all the fight out of her.

And now it's just me and my father, the fire poker gripped in his right hand.

"Listen to me, kid." His voice is low and menacing. "What happens between me and your mom—that's none of your business. You get me?"

I don't answer him. He lifts the fire poker and jabs the tip into my belly. It's not enough to break the skin, but it tears my undershirt, and I gasp with pain.

"Bill!" my mother sobs from the floor. "Please stop! Please!"

He whips his head around. "Shut *up*, Luann. Or else, I swear to God, I will shove this poker right through his gut."

He would do it. He's drunk enough and he's mean enough, and there's no way I could wrestle that poker back out of his hands. One good jab and the point will pass through my skin and impale my intestines. It will be a terrible way to die.

"You gonna leave us alone from now on, boy?" my father growls.

When I don't answer, he jabs me harder. The sharp point slices through my skin, and the white of my torn undershirt rapidly turns red with my blood. The pain is intense enough to make my knees wobble. My mother is sobbing and pleading for him not to hurt me, but she doesn't move. She knows she can't help me.

Part of me wants him to do it. Let him kill me, then spend the rest of his life in jail so my mother is safe. But a much larger part of me doesn't want to die. There's too much I want to do with my life. I want to become a surgeon. I want to lose my virginity to Daisy Driscoll, and someday, I want to marry her. I'm not sure if all that is possible for me, but I know what I *don't* want. I don't want to die in the kitchen of this crappy, run-down house at my father's hands.

"Fine," I croak. I hold up my hands. "Whatever you say."

He sniffs loudly. "And what are you going to do if you hear any sound in the middle of the night? You going to mind your own business?"

"Yes," I say through my teeth.

"What? I didn't hear that too good."

"*Yes.*"

Satisfied, my father lowers the fire poker. The sharp pain vanishes, replaced with a dull ache. The bottom half of my undershirt is damp with my blood. I've got to get this cleaned up before I go back to bed. I don't want to get blood all over the sheets.

"Get out of here, boy," my father snaps at me.

I really, really don't want to leave my mother alone, but she's pleading with me with her eyes, so I do like he tells me. But this isn't over. One of these days, he's going to go too far and kill her. I'm not going to let that happen.

CHAPTER 17

SYDNEY

Bonnie's funeral is today.

It's being held at a church in Brooklyn, which is where her parents live. It's ironic, because I'm fairly sure that in the time I knew Bonnie, she never once set foot in a church. It's not that she wasn't religious exactly, but... Well, she wasn't religious. But she wasn't *anti*-religion. She wouldn't be offended by the fact that her funeral was being held in a church, especially if that's what her parents wanted.

The part that might be more offensive to her is that she requires a funeral at thirty-three years old.

Gretchen, Randy, and I are stuffed into a yellow cab, riding out to Bensonhurst, the smell of hot leather seats heavy in the air. Randy wanted to take the D train instead of a taxi, but I didn't feel like dealing with the subway in my fancy funeral attire. And what if something happened and we didn't get there on time? Bonnie was such a stickler for promptness. She would have haunted us for at least the next year if we were late.

"Did you bring tissues?" I ask Gretchen, who is squeezed into the back seat between me and Randy.

"Loads," she confirms.

"Why do you need so many tissues?" Randy speaks up. "Is there going to be food?"

Randy is wearing a navy-blue suit that can vaguely pass for black. He looks like he made some attempt to comb his usually unruly dark-brown hair, but since he has had the window cracked open for the entire cab ride, all his hard work has been undone by the wind.

"We are going to a funeral," I remind him. When he looks at me blankly, I add, "It's *sad.*"

"Right, but…" He frowns. "I mean, you guys were just friends. It's not like she was your sister or your mother."

I can only stare at Randy in astonishment. He's not even trying to be a jerk. He is legitimately confused as to why we would be sad over Bonnie's death. Thankfully, before I can say anything I regret, Gretchen elbows him in the ribs. "You're an idiot," she says.

Well said.

The church is a gigantic structure that seems to take up half the city block. My gaze sweeps over the steeple, which has a cross mounted on top. The taxi pulls up in front of what looks like an endless staircase to enter the church.

Before I can reach for my purse, Randy hands a wad of bills over to the driver. "It's on me," he tells us. "It's your friend's funeral, and you guys are sad."

I feel a little guilty because I don't think Randy makes that much money as the super, but I've learned to be gracious when people offer to pay. I climb out of the taxi, and Gretchen is a step behind me. She is tugging on the black skirt that shows off her skinny yet shapely legs.

"Ugh," she says. "Do you think this skirt is inappropriately short for a funeral?"

"It's fine," I say, even though I secretly think it's a little too short. But what is she supposed to do? She can't exactly go home and change.

I'm about to follow Randy and Gretchen up the tower of stairs to the front door when I see a man leaning against the side of the church. My stomach flips slightly at the sight of Detective Jake Sousa. I tell my friends to go on ahead and save me a seat, and then I approach Jake, my purse clutched protectively to my chest.

Jake saw me a second after I noticed him. He offers me a grim smile. "My condolences," he says.

I don't want his condolences. I only care about one thing. "Have you arrested anyone yet?"

He hangs his head. "Unfortunately, no."

I can't believe this. It's been a week since Bonnie's murder, and with every passing day, it's less and less likely that they will ever arrest anyone. "Did you ever find her boyfriend?"

He shakes his head. "That's why I'm here. I'm kind of hoping he might show up."

"You think he's that dumb?"

"Murderers often visit the funerals of their victims. Several have been caught under those circumstances."

"Wow." I sneer. "You must be super desperate."

Jake drops his eyes. "Look, I'm sorry. I wish I had better news for you. You don't know how many hours I have put in trying to find this bastard. We don't even know if the boyfriend is the one who killed her. Maybe it's somebody completely different."

Frustration is written all over his face. When we were

dating, Jake had an amazing success rate in solving homicides. If I were murdered, he would be the detective I would want on the case. And I truly believe that if he can't find the person who killed Bonnie, nobody can.

But maybe nobody can. Which is a very depressing thought.

And a terrifying one.

"You're still dead-bolting your door at night, right?" Jake asks me.

"Yes," I confirm. "But don't worry. I'm not dating anyone."

He looks like he isn't sure what to make of that statement. Jake is this big, muscular detective who never seems to lose his cool, and it always used to amuse me to make him squirm just a little bit.

I can't help but think of Jake's profile on Cynch. He may have acted like he was too busy for a significant other, but he is still looking. He's still hoping to find his other half, even if he can't give her what she wants.

"If you see anything suspicious at the funeral," he says, "will you let me know?"

"I will."

He frowns at me, his lips pressed together. "Be careful, Syd."

Yeah, as if I'm not terrified enough without him saying that.

When I get inside the church, I notice a woman in her sixties standing in the back, wearing a black blazer and skirt, her eyes puffy and the whites almost painfully bloodshot. I recognize her as Bonnie's mother. I get a pang just looking at her. As awful as this is for me, it's got to be a million times worse for her.

She is in a conversation with someone else, but then our eyes lock. She murmurs, "Excuse me," to the person she's talking to and hurries over to me. I instinctively flinch. It's not that I don't want to talk to Mrs. Griffin, but just looking at her makes me horribly sad.

"Is it Sydney?" she asks.

"Yes." I nod. "I…I'm so sorry, Mrs. Griffin."

"Thank you." Tears flow from her already-moist eyes. "I miss her so much, it hurts my soul."

"I'm so sorry," I say again because I really just don't know what else to say.

"You were a good friend to her though, Sydney. I really appreciate that."

"Thank you. She was a good friend to me too. I'll miss her so much."

She dabs her eyes with a tissue that has seen better days. She didn't even bother with mascara, which was a wise choice. "The police told me she was seeing a man regularly. Do you have any idea who it was?"

"She did tell me she was seeing someone, but that's all I know."

"She…she didn't mention his name? Show you a photo?"

"I'm sorry, no."

"But how could that be?" she bursts out. "You girls talk all the time! And you all are constantly taking photos of every little stupid thing. Bonnie once sent me five pictures of a piece of sushi! How is it possible that there was not one photograph on her phone of this man that she was dating?"

I take a step back. "I…I don't know."

"You must know something!" The tears are flowing

freely now. "Please, Sydney! You've got to remember something about this man! You can't just let him get away with killing my baby!"

"I…"

"If it had been you," she snaps at me, "Bonnie would have done everything she could to find out who did this to you! She wouldn't just shrug her shoulders and tell your mother that she's sorry!"

Mrs. Griffin is practically hysterical now. Thankfully, one of her friends or relatives comes over, puts an arm around her shoulder, and leads her away from me. Although by this point, I am shaking like a leaf.

The worst part is she's right. I still remember the way Bonnie threatened Real Kevin to get him away from me. If our situations were reversed, she would not give up so easily. I've done nothing to help catch the monster who did this to her.

If only I could go back in time, I would ask her more questions about the guy. What was his name? Can I see a photograph? Where does he work? Of course, the answers may have been lies anyway. But at least it would have been something.

My legs can barely support me as I make my way to where Gretchen and Randy have found seats near the front of the church. I have to squeeze down the aisle to sit next to them, and Gretchen has started crying again.

"I saw Bonnie's mother shouting at you," Gretchen says. "Are you okay?"

"Yes," I lie. "She's just devastated. That's all."

"Of course she's devastated!" Gretchen sniffles. "It's all so awful!"

For a moment, I imagine my mother in the church at

my funeral, sobbing hysterically like she did when my dad died. The murder of your child is the kind of thing you never recover from. Gretchen and I will eventually move on, but Mrs. Griffin won't. Not ever.

Randy reaches out and laces his fingers through Gretchen's. She flashes him a grateful smile, which makes me feel even more sad that I don't have anyone to hold hands with. And maybe I never will. After all, my dates recently have been bad and worse, and now I'm terrified to even use Cynch.

I look behind me at the back of the church to see if Jake has entered. At least he's a comforting presence, even if things didn't work out between the two of us. But instead of Jake, I see something that completely shocks me.

It's Kevin.

Kevin is at Bonnie's funeral.

CHAPTER 18

What is Real Kevin doing at Bonnie's funeral?

Jake told me to be on the lookout for something suspicious, and Bonnie's mother practically accosted me for details about her murder. I have to say, seeing the man Bonnie threatened sitting in the back of the church is the most suspicious thing I have seen since discovering Bonnie's body.

Except…is that really him?

I'm not entirely certain. He's all the way across the nave, and the church is surprisingly dark. So it's possible I could be wrong. Entirely possible.

I crane my neck, trying to get a better look, but I'm interrupted by the doors of the church opening. It's the pallbearers, carrying Bonnie's casket.

There's no way I can keep from staring at the oak coffin making its way to the front of the church. Considering that only a couple of weeks ago, Bonnie and I were doing tree pose and enjoying chai lattes together, it seems impossible that she is now in that box for all eternity. I recognize one of the pallbearers as her brother, and he is just barely keeping it together.

They lay the coffin in its resting spot, although she will later be buried in a local cemetery. It's a closed casket, because of what was done to Bonnie, but she wouldn't have minded. She once told me she thought it was creepy when people had open caskets. Who wants to look at a dead person?

I would have liked to see her one more time though. I would have liked to confirm she will be wearing her favorite pair of black pumps. And that whoever dressed her made sure to put a scrunchie in her hair. That is what she would have wanted.

As the priest addresses us, I can't stop staring at the coffin. I can't believe Bonnie is dead and that her body is in that box. How is that possible? How could she be *dead*? She was so young, and there was so much that she wanted to do with her life. She used to talk about taking time off from work to take a trip to Latin America and just spend a year there, bouncing from country to country. She imagined saving up enough money to buy a house on the beach. She had never learned to play an instrument, and she said that one of these days, she was definitely going to learn to play the guitar. *When my life isn't so busy.*

But one thing that was really important to her was finding her other half. She didn't enjoy going on dates every single night. She did it because she was searching for love. She wanted someone to spend her life with.

Now none of that will ever happen. She will never fall in love. She will never play the guitar. She will never have a house on the beach. Instead, she's going to spend the rest of eternity buried in the ground.

The thought of it makes me feel like I'm going to start hyperventilating. I clutch my knees, trying to suck in deep breaths. This is okay. I'm going to be okay. I'm not going to end up dead in my early thirties like Bonnie.

Gretchen notices me freaking out, and she rubs her hand against my back. "You okay?" she whispers.

"Uh-huh," I manage.

Gretchen rubs circles on my back while I struggle to get my breathing under control. But it's hard. I just keep thinking about Bonnie in that coffin. Dead—forever. Rotting in the ground.

That won't be me. I won't let it be.

Never.

CHAPTER 19

BEFORE

TOM

When I get to school, there are two police cars parked right in front.

I almost do an about-face and go home. The presence of multiple police cars can't possibly mean anything good. I rub my abdomen, which has healed up for the most part since my father nearly impaled me with the fire poker.

Slug is leaning against the school, hastily stubbing out a cigarette with his sneaker at the sight of the police chief. Although they look like they couldn't care less about a couple of teenagers with cigarettes.

"Hey, Slug." I jog over to my best friend, knowing he will for sure know exactly what's going on. He always does. "What's up with the cop cars?"

A grin spreads across Slug's face. He has an angry-looking pimple right at the corner of his lips. "You didn't hear? They found Brandi Healey."

"Oh? You mean she came back home?"

"No, they found her *body*." He laughs at the look on my face. "Guess she didn't run away after all."

I feel like I'm going to choke. They found Brandi. That means...

"She was buried out in the woods only about half an hour from here," he says. "Because of all the snow during the winter, nobody found her. Apparently, some lady was walking her dog, and the dog dug up the body."

I lean against the wall of the school, wishing for once that I smoked like Slug, because a cigarette really seems like it would be great right now. "That's...terrible."

Slug nods. "And I overheard that they think whoever did this to her tortured her before they killed her. Like, they really made her suffer."

"Jesus."

"Some people are really sick," Slug says, although his voice is almost gleeful. "Hey, you knew her pretty well, didn't you, Tom?"

I take a big gulp of air. "Not really."

"Yeah, you did. You tutored her, didn't you?"

"Barely. She didn't even show up half the time."

"Man." Slug shakes his head. "If I had been tutoring that girl, I wouldn't have been able to keep my hands off her. She was *hot*, you know?" He laughs. "Not so much anymore though."

My hands ball into fists—I don't like the way he's talking about Brandi. "Don't talk about her that way."

He looks at me in surprise. "What's your problem, Tom?"

I shake my head. I don't want to talk about Brandi at all anymore, although I have a bad feeling that's all anybody is going to be talking about today. And if anybody finds out that I—

"Tom!"

It's Daisy's voice. She is running toward me, her face streaked with tears. Before I know what's happening, she hurls herself into my arms, clinging to me. I push all the dark thoughts from my head and focus on comforting Daisy.

"It's so awful," Daisy murmurs, "what they did to Brandi."

Naturally, Alison is following close behind. While I've got Daisy in my arms and I'm stroking her golden hair, Alison is staring at me. It's hard to read her expression exactly, but her narrow lips are a straight line. The other day, at the health fair, she brought up the fact that I used to tutor Brandi. But that's no secret. And it's not a big deal.

"My father said he's going to find out who did this to her," Daisy sniffles into my T-shirt.

"Do they have any suspects?" Slug asks.

Alison won't quit staring at me, and it's making my skin crawl. "Daisy, didn't you say your father told you he's pretty sure the killer was a student at the school?"

"That's what he said," Daisy confirms. "That's why the police are going to be asking everyone if they know anything."

The thought of being interrogated by a police officer makes me want to throw up. And if he doesn't like what I have to say...

"Will you walk me home today, Tom?" Daisy asks softly. "I know you're tutoring, but—"

"I'll cancel it."

"Really?"

I nod. The kid I'm tutoring today would just as soon

skip out on it anyway—his mom is the one who pays me. And who knows? By the time the last bell rings, I could very well be getting marched out of the school in handcuffs.

CHAPTER 20

BEFORE

TOM

Apparently, I am pretty low down on the list of people who knew Brandi Healey.

I spend the entire morning at school listening to names called out over the loudspeaker. The first twenty names or so are Brandi's friends. She sure had a lot of them. And then some of the guys in our class who were spotted in a lip-lock with Brandi at one time or another.

By the time I hear the name Thomas Brewer called over the loudspeaker, it's late morning, and I've worked myself into a complete panic. I'm so freaked out that I can barely manage to get out of my seat, and I nearly trip over my own two feet on the way to the door.

"Are you okay, Tom?" Mrs. Anthony, our English teacher, asks me.

Before I can answer, a kid in the back of the room blurts out, "He's just scared Daisy will think he was dating Brandi on the side."

And then a bunch of assholes next to him start

laughing. If they think it's funny to joke about it, that means nobody thinks I was dating her. So maybe I'm working myself up over nothing.

Between the door of my third-floor English classroom and the principal's office on the first floor, I almost manage to convince myself that I have nothing to be worried about. I practice a confident, easy smile that I plan to use when I talk to the police officer. This is not a big deal. They've already talked to at least two dozen kids. I'm just one of many.

But then when I see Chief Driscoll sitting in the principal's office, his large body stuffed into the wooden chair, all my confidence flies out the window. I had no idea *Daisy's father* was going to be the one questioning me. As much as I'm intimidated by my father, I'm much more terrified of the police chief. Being interrogated by Chief Driscoll is my worst nightmare.

No, he's not *interrogating* me. He's just going to ask a few questions. I need to calm down.

Calm down, for Christ's sake, Tom!

Chief Driscoll smiles when he sees me in the doorway. Instinctively, I freeze, and he waves a large hand to usher me into the room. He points at the small wooden chair in front of the principal's desk. "Hi, Tom," he booms. "Have a seat."

I don't so much sit in the chair as I collapse into it, my legs unable to hold me up.

"Hello, sir," I say, keeping my voice slow and respectful.

"Now, Tom." The smile vanishes from his face, and his expression turns grim. "Do you know why we called you in here?"

"I…I heard about Brandi."

He nods. "Terrible stuff. Truly terrible. And we need to catch the monster who did this to her."

"Right. Of course."

"So…" He rubs his big, thick hands together. My own hands are covered in sweat. "I hear you used to tutor Brandi in math?"

"Yes, just for a few months. And honestly, she skipped a lot of the sessions."

That's not entirely true. Brandi never skipped our sessions. *I don't want to miss out on seeing you, Tom.*

"How well did you know her?" the chief asks.

"Not very well."

"Uh-huh." He rubs at the slight stubble on his chin, even though I suspect he shaved this morning. "Do you know if she had a boyfriend?"

"A boyfriend?"

One corner of his lips quirks up. "She told some of her close friends that she had a crush on a boy in your class, but she didn't say who it was. It sounded like he liked her too. And according to a couple of her friends, she and the boy had plans to meet the night she disappeared. But like I said, we don't know who it was."

I fight to keep my voice even. "I have no idea, sir. I was just the dorky kid tutoring her in math. It's not like she would have confided in me."

"Right. I guess not." He sighs and leans back in his chair, which lets out a scary-sounding groan. "Such a terrible thing about Brandi. Makes me want to keep Daisy under lock and key."

I nod, trying to look sympathetic.

"Of course, I trust *you*, Tom." He manages a smile. "I said to Helen last night, 'Thank God Daisy is with Tom and not one of those other wild boys. He's one of the good ones.'"

I try to swallow, but it feels like my throat has closed off. "Thank you, sir."

"When are you coming over for dinner, by the way?" he asks. "My wife keeps asking me."

The dinner invitation calms me down. If he suspected me of anything, he wouldn't be inviting me to his house for dinner. Or would he? I don't know for sure, but he *definitely* wouldn't be okay with me hanging out with his only daughter.

I'm safe. For now. But if he finds out…

"Let me ask my mother if it's okay," I say. "But, um, yeah. That would be great."

I will never, ever come to his house for dinner.

CHAPTER 21

SYDNEY

By the end of Bonnie's funeral, Gretchen and I have used up all the tissues we brought. But on the plus side, I feel so emotionally drained that my panic attack has subsided.

People start filtering out of the church, and it's only then that I remember spotting Real Kevin in the back. I got so emotional when that casket came out, I forgot all about it. I swivel my head, thinking I can get a better look now, but…

Wait, where is he?

He was sitting in the back row. I saw him there. Right at the end of the row. Except I don't see him anymore. In the place where he was sitting, there's now an elderly man.

"What are you looking at?" Gretchen asks me.

"Um…" I don't know quite how to explain this to her. "Do you remember that guy who I went on that horrible date with? The one who attacked me?"

"Yes."

"Well, he was here. At the funeral."

"Really?" Her eyes widen. "Where?"

"He *was* here," I correct myself. "But…I don't see him anymore. I guess he left."

"What should we do?" She grabs my arm. "Should we call the police?"

Jake might still be here, but I feel stupid telling him about this. The more I think about it, the less certain I feel that it really was Kevin. I'm still so freaked out about our encounters that I may have let my imagination run wild. It's not like I'm thinking straight right now.

Anyway, I'm not even sure I know Kevin's real name. I have no extra useful information. No, I already told Jake about Kevin, and I'll leave it to him to investigate.

"Never mind," I mutter.

"Are you sure?"

I nod. "Yeah, I…I probably got it wrong."

But even after I convince myself that it wasn't Real Kevin at the funeral, I can't shake my sense of uneasiness. But I can't let this get to me. I need to take Jake's advice. I will keep locking my dead bolt every night and stay off Cynch, and hopefully he'll catch the monster who did this to Bonnie.

And then life will go on.

CHAPTER 22

TWO MONTHS LATER

SYDNEY

I am having the best freaking date ever.

For the month after Bonnie died, I was afraid of my own shadow, definitely too scared to jump back into the dating pool. Especially since Jake and the rest of the NYPD never made an arrest for her murder. That part infuriated me more than anything. At first, I was calling him every few days, asking for updates, and I berated him when there never were any. I vowed that I would not go on another date until they found out who did that to Bonnie.

But then one day, I was eating dinner on my sofa in front of the TV, wearing my usual uniform of a T-shirt and sweatpants, and it hit me that in exactly six months, I was going to be thirty-five years old. My life was slipping away, and after nearly two straight months of feeling sad about Bonnie, I decided it was enough. It was time to move on.

I reactivated my Cynch profile the next day.

And I'm glad I did, because I am having a great time

on this date. His name is Travis, and he looks exactly like his photo. He has reddish-brown hair, a square jaw, and tight muscles in his forearms, and he's a perfect six inches taller than I am.

And even better, he seems *nice*. We have things in common. We like the same movies (not *Rocky*), we have the same sense of humor, and best of all, he hasn't made me FaceTime his mother once in the entire time we've been having coffee together.

"I have to tell you, Sydney," he says as he sips on his cup of coffee, "this is the best date I've had in a long time."

"Me too," I agree.

We are having a coffee date at this pretentious little coffee shop that is packed because it recently got written up in the *New York Times*. I suggested coffee so I wouldn't be stuck with him if we didn't connect, but we have now ordered two blueberry muffins, one white chocolate and raspberry scone, and also something called a cronut—it's not quite a croissant and not quite a donut, but it definitely has a million calories. We have completely spoiled our dinners, because we just don't want to leave.

"Honestly," he says, "I was ready to give up. I have been on some doozies lately."

"Tell me about it," I giggle. "I could tell you stories that would blow your mind."

"I bet I could top you."

"I'm not so sure."

He grins at me, and I grin back. I don't want to get carried away, but I think this is going somewhere. I really think there's going to be a second date, then a third, and maybe a lot more after that.

And then, out of the corner of my eye, the door to the

coffee shop swings open. A man walks in, and I almost do a double take when I recognize who it is.

It's Mystery Man. After all this time.

Even though I'm having a great time with Travis, I can't help but stare at the handsome man with black hair settling down at one of the round wooden tables. Travis is amazing, but there was no electric jolt when I laid eyes on him. I haven't felt that once since the night I met Mystery Man what feels like an eternity ago. But even though I remember him quite well, he either doesn't see me or he doesn't remember me, because he doesn't even glance in my direction.

Just as well. Travis is great, and I don't need any distractions from a sexy guy who clearly isn't interested in me.

"Hey," Travis says, his smoldering blue eyes locking on mine. "I'm on, like, my third cup of coffee, and I'm never going to be able to sleep, but I kind of want to keep this going. What do you think about heading somewhere else for dinner?"

I smile to myself because I had been contemplating the same thing. "I would love dinner."

"Yeah?" His whole face lights up. "That is awesome."

Travis looks so thrilled that I forget all about Mystery Man entirely. I can't wait to have dinner with this guy. We can compare bad-date notes and share a bottle of wine. I'm really glad I didn't give up on dating. Bonnie was right—it really is a numbers game. Even though she was wrong about Dr. McHottie.

But then the smile on Travis's face fades away. Suddenly, he is staring at me with a look of horror on his face. His skin turns the same color as the cream on the table.

"Sydney," he gasps.

I can't figure out why he looks so horrified. Then I look down at the bloodstains on my shirt.

"Oh my God!" I clasp a hand over my nose. "I'm so sorry, I…"

This is just great. I haven't had one of my infamous, epic nosebleeds in over a year, and *of course* it would happen during the best date I've had in years.

I snatch a few tissues from the dispenser on the table, trying to sop up the blood on my face. "Let me just go to the bathroom and—"

And then something really awful happens.

Before I can even get out my sentence, Travis's eyes roll up in his head. And then he slides out of his seat and collapses to the floor, his head hitting the tiles with a loud clunk.

Wonderful. The best date I have had in years, and I made him *faint* from my stupid bloody nose.

The entire coffee shop goes silent, staring at me with my horror show of a bloody nose and my date lying unconscious on the floor. One woman screams, which I honestly feel is a little unnecessary.

"It's okay," I manage, a tissue still pressed to my nose. "Everything's fine. I just…"

That's when I notice that Mystery Man has stood up and is maneuvering between tables, coming toward me. Wow, he got to see my epic nosebleed too. This is just getting better and better.

Mystery Man crouches next to Travis on the floor, who is starting to come to, groaning and rubbing his head. Mystery Man frowns down at him.

"Are you okay, sir?" he asks.

"Yeah." Travis's eyelids flutter, and he rubs his head again. He's trying to sit up. "What happened?"

"Looks like you had a vasovagal episode and fainted," Mystery Man says. "I'm a physician, and I just wanted to make sure you're okay. We can call an ambulance if you'd like."

"A vaso…what?" Travis rubs his head. "No, I…I'm okay." He looks over at me and flinches. "Sorry, I…I'm just not a fan of blood, you know?"

Mystery Man glances back at me, and for a split second, he rolls his eyes. But then he turns back to Travis and starts asking him a bunch of questions about how his head and neck feel and if he can move his arms and legs. Travis seems fine, although embarrassed. He's not looking at me the way he was before. Actually, he seems like he's avoiding looking at me entirely.

"I'm okay," Travis tells Mystery Man. "Honestly. You should help *her*."

"I'm fine," I assure him, even though I've now gone through about five tissues in my attempt to sop up all the blood. My blouse is definitely ruined—at least for now. I've got some good tricks for getting out bloodstains that I've picked up over the years.

"You don't look fine," Travis points out. He is still avoiding looking at me, and his face is a few shades too pale. Sweat is beaded along his hairline.

"It's nothing to worry about," I say. "This happens to me sometimes."

If there was anything I could have said to make it *less* likely Travis would ever want to see me again, I have definitely hit on it.

"Listen, Sydney." Travis clears his throat. "You look

like you need some time to recover from…all this. So why don't we do dinner some other time?"

"Sure," I say. "How about on Friday?"

"Uh, maybe." Travis yanks his jacket off the back of his chair, his hands shaking slightly. "I'll text you through the app. Or something." He stuffs his arms into the sleeves of his jacket. "Anyway, bye."

It would not be an exaggeration to say that Travis ran out of the coffee shop as fast as he possibly could. He didn't even pay for his share of the coffee.

And now I am left with my bloody nose, a check for about six coffees and multiple muffins and danishes, a bunch of crumpled-up tissues covered in dried blood, and Mystery Man staring at me.

"I don't think we're having dinner on Friday," I finally say.

Mystery Man bursts out laughing. "I got that sense, yeah."

"It's not funny." Although, against my will, I find my lips twitching slightly. "Believe it or not, until my nose started gushing blood, that was the first good date I'd been on in a long time."

"With *that* guy?" Mystery Man looks in the direction of the door where Travis vanished, never to be seen again. "I find that hard to believe. You're much better off without him. I mean, what *grown man* faints at the sight of a bloody nose? Sort of pathetic, don't you think?"

"Well…"

"Really," he says, "you don't want to have kids with a guy like that. What's he going to do when your kid gets bopped in the nose with a soccer ball? You dodged a bullet."

"Maybe."

"Also, he stuck you with the check. What a jerk." Mystery Man reaches into his back pocket and pulls out his wallet. He grabs enough bills to more than cover our coffees and pastries, then tosses them on the table. "How hard is that?"

The twitching in my lips blossoms into a tiny smile. "Thank you."

I pull the tissue away from my nose. It looks like the blood is finally stopping. Why not? It already did its damage.

"There's a souvenir shop next door," Mystery Man tells me. "Let me get you a new shirt so you don't have to walk home with blood all over you."

"Seriously? Those places are a rip-off. You're going to pay a fortune."

He shrugs. "Better than being covered in blood, right?" When he sees the hesitation on my face, he adds, "I insist."

I can't help but smile. "Okay then."

"And then," he says, "if you're feeling up to it, I'd love to take you to dinner."

I stare at him, stunned. Is he seriously asking me out on a date after witnessing a volcano of blood literally erupting from my nostrils? But he doesn't look like he's kidding. His nice brown eyes are focused on mine, and there's a suggestive smile playing on his lips.

"Well," I say, "okay."

Mystery Man's smile widens to show off his straight white teeth, and once again, I get that jolt of electricity. Travis seemed great, but I didn't have that same electrical attraction with him. That's the sort of thing you don't get to experience very often. And it seems like Mystery Man feels the same way about me after all.

Maybe that stupid nosebleed was the best thing that ever happened to me.

"I'm Sydney," I say.

"Nice to meet you, Sydney," he says. "I'm Tom. Tom Brown."

CHAPTER 23

TOM

It's been a week, and apparently "no arrests have been made in the murder of Brandi Healey."

Chief Driscoll came back to the high school a second time and called several students back down to the principal's office, but I didn't make the cut this time. They're still looking for Brandi's mysterious boyfriend, without much luck.

Most of the people they call down are Brandi's close friends. The only person I know well on the list is Slug. I can't even imagine why the police want to talk to *him* about Brandi. He barely knew her.

Not only has the chief not questioned me again, but he asked me personally if I would escort his daughter home from school every day until he catches the monster who killed Brandi. I still have to tutor, but Daisy waits around—she doesn't seem to mind. She sits in the school library, quietly reading one of her thick paperbacks. Whenever she is concentrating on something, she sticks her tongue out slightly. It's adorable.

Walking Daisy home every day is something I can look forward to. Although today I'm looking forward to something else. In our biology lab today, we're dissecting a fetal pig. I have been waiting for this particular dissection lab for months, and it will only be slightly ruined by the fact that Alison is my lab partner.

I didn't know it was possible, but Alison has been even colder to me since Brandi's body was found. She can barely even look at me anymore, and when she does, there is venom in her eyes. This is our first biology lab since it all happened, and I'm half expecting to find out she's asked the teacher to switch partners. That would be okay with me. More than okay, even. But no such luck. When I get to the lab, Alison is already in her seat.

"Hi, Alison," I say in my most friendly voice.

She stares at me, as if astonished I would have the audacity to say hello to her. "Let's get this over with," she grumbles.

I already read the textbook the night before to prepare for the lab, so when the teacher sets down the tray with the tiny pig lying on it, its eyes squeezed shut, its facial features nearly perfectly formed, I know exactly what to do. But I'm trying to make nice with Alison, so I slide the scalpel in her direction.

"You can do the honors," I say.

"No, thanks." She pushes it back to me. "You can go ahead and do it."

"You sure?"

"Absolutely." And then she mumbles under her breath, "You always do."

I'm not going to say it doesn't bother me that Alison is sitting next to me, silently judging me while I'm doing nothing more than the work required to get an A in biology lab. She should feel lucky I'm her lab partner—I'm carrying her. She doesn't seem interested in the dissections at all. She doesn't seem to even want to *look* when I unravel the fetal pig's intestines. If it weren't for me, she wouldn't even pass the class.

And yes, I enjoy these labs. So what? Is there anything so wrong about that?

The hour passes by quickly, and near the end, Mrs. Shipley comes by to check our work. She sees the organs laid out carefully and flashes me an approving look. "Good job, Tom, Alison."

"Tom did all the work," Alison speaks up. "I mostly just sat here."

Mrs. Shipley doesn't seem to know what to make of this admission. "Did he?"

"Yes," Alison confirms. "He enjoys it so much, you see. I wouldn't want to take that away from him."

Mrs. Shipley's forehead wrinkles. "Well, you should both try to share the work equally. It's only fair."

With those words of wisdom, she wanders off to the next table. Alison is looking down at her nails, which are clipped very short. She's been making snide comments about my expertise in lab the whole time we've been partners, and I'm getting sick of it.

"What the hell is wrong with you?" I snap at her.

She looks up at me, her eyelashes fluttering. "There's nothing wrong with *me*."

The way she says it makes my whole body go cold. She's never liked me, but somehow it's gotten to a whole other level recently. Especially in the last week.

But I can't let Alison bother me. The school day is

almost over, and then I'll get to see Daisy and walk her home. Alison is *not* going to take that away from me.

She at least helps me get cleaned up, and after we wipe down our workstation, the bell rings. Dismissal. I can finally get out of here. I won't have to deal with Alison for a whole week, until our next lab.

I grab my backpack from under the table, ready to go meet Daisy by our lockers. But before I can get going, a hand reaches out to grab my arm. When I turn around, Alison is behind me. She's got her straight brown hair tucked behind her ears, and she's staring at me with her muddy eyes through her thick glasses.

"Tom," she says, "we need to talk. *Now.*"

CHAPTER 24

TOM

W e need to talk. *Now*."

Alison's face is dead serious as she says the words to me. There are bags under her eyes, and I get a quick glimpse of what she might look like when she's much older. Alison seems like the kind of person who was born middle-aged.

"I can't talk," I mumble. "I've got to meet Daisy."

It's not entirely a lie. I *do* have to meet Daisy. But that's not the reason I don't want to talk to Alison.

"It's important." She tilts her head to look up at me, and I suddenly realize how short Alison is—even smaller than Daisy. There's something about her that makes her look taller, especially since most of the time during lab, we're sitting down, but standing up, she barely comes above my shoulders. "It won't take long."

Some quality in her voice makes me feel like I don't have a choice in the matter. One way or another, Alison and I are going to have a talk. I may as well get it over with. "Fine."

The bell has already rung, and the kids are filtering out of the school. Daisy is waiting for me by her locker, so I tap out a quick text message to let her know I'm going to be late. I need to concoct a fake story to explain why, but I'll worry about that later.

A few doors down from the biology lab is a classroom that looks empty. Alison grabs me by the arm and pulls me inside. I only start to get really nervous when she closes the door behind us. What is this all about? What does she want to say to me that she doesn't want anyone else to hear?

"What is it?" My voice is filled with irritation to cover up my anxiety. "What is so important?"

Alison looks up at me. The lights are out in the classroom, and even though the windows are providing some natural light, the shadows on her face look ominous. "I want you to stay away from Daisy."

"*What?*"

"You heard me."

"Daisy is my girlfriend." Despite everything, whenever I say those words, I get a surge of happiness. *Daisy is my girlfriend.* I'm the luckiest guy in the world to be able to say those words. "I can't stay away from her."

"Right," she says, "so you need to break up with her."

What? "You're out of your mind, Alison." I shift my backpack on my shoulder. "I'm not going to have this conversation with you. I'm leaving."

I start in the direction of the door. My hand is almost on the doorknob when Alison blurts out, "I saw you kissing Brandi Healey."

Okay, she's got my attention.

I turn around, letting my backpack drop to the floor

with a resounding thump. "I don't know what you're talking about."

"Don't lie about it, Tom." Her voice is seething with hatred—she *despises* me. "I saw you. Outside the back of the school, just a few days before she disappeared. And it wasn't just a peck on the cheek. You were making out with her."

I'm going to be sick. I didn't think anyone saw that. I didn't think anyone knew except for me and Brandi, and then just me. Now, apparently, Alison knows too.

This is a problem.

"You're the boyfriend," she continues. "The mysterious boyfriend who was meeting up with Brandi the night she was killed."

That is not untrue.

"You're the one the police are trying to find," she says, "except Brandi didn't tell anyone it was you. But I *saw* you."

I lean against one of the desks, trying to get my thudding heart under control. I drop my eyes, unable to look at her. "I wasn't her boyfriend. It was just that one kiss. It didn't mean anything."

"So why were you meeting with her secretly late at night?"

I don't know what to say to that. I'm not going to lie—Brandi and I shared a very intense kiss. I'm also not going to lie and say I didn't enjoy it. But I finally decided that was as far as it could go. Even though I hadn't worked up the nerve to tell her my feelings yet, I was in love with Daisy. I didn't want Brandi, even though she seemed to want me very badly.

The night I was supposed to meet up with Brandi, I planned to tell her exactly that. But then she never showed.

"Did you tell anyone?" I ask.

"No," she says, "and I'm not going to, as long as you leave Daisy alone from now on."

"She's not going to be happy about that."

"She'll get over it. I'm not going to let you hurt her."

"I would *never* hurt Daisy."

"Frankly," she says, "I don't know what you're capable of. Everyone thinks Slug is the creep and you're the nice one, because you're polite and smart and good looking. But you're just as bad as he is. No, actually, you're much worse. Because you hide it. He's a creep, but you're *dangerous*."

"That's not true," I croak.

"Bullshit." Her eyes flash. "I've worked with you side by side the whole year in biology lab. I see the way you are. How are you so good at the dissections? Nobody is that comfortable just from reading the textbook. You're so...*into* it. What—did you kill animals when you were a kid and take them apart? Isn't that what psychopaths do?"

Each word she speaks feels like a punch in the gut. I lean forward, resting my palms on my thighs for support as I gasp for air. "Please stop talking."

"Stay away from Daisy."

Even with everything she's saying, even with all the threats, I shake my head. "Don't ask me to do that. I love Daisy. I would never hurt her."

"If you truly love Daisy," she says, "then you know I'm right. You know she's better off without you. As long as you're dating her, her life is in danger, and I'm not going to stand by and let it happen. I love Daisy too."

Her words hit home. I do love Daisy. But I have dreams about her every night that are like something out of a low-budget horror movie. I don't want anything to happen to her, and there is a tiny part of me that doesn't trust myself. I sometimes worry my relationship with Daisy could very well put her life in danger.

"Why didn't you go to the police about me and Brandi?" I ask. "Why come to me first?"

She shrugs, unwilling to answer the question. But I can see the truth in her eyes. Alison is afraid of me. She knows I've covered my tracks very well, and the chief is my biggest fan right now. She's afraid that whatever she tells the police won't be enough to send me to jail, and then she'll have played all her cards. She'll have made a dangerous enemy out of me, and she doesn't want that.

She is that scared of me.

"I'll give you a few days to think it over," she says. "Then I'm going to talk to Chief Driscoll."

If she tells Daisy's father that I was Brandi's secret boyfriend, there's a chance he might not believe it, but there's a bigger chance he'll never let me near Daisy again. That alone will end our relationship. Alison has created an impossible situation for me. I love Daisy, but every path I choose will lead to the end of us.

I don't know what to do.

Daisy is waiting for me by her locker as promised. When she sees me, her whole face lights up. I recognize the expression, because it's exactly how I feel right now. Every time I look at her, I find myself grinning like an idiot.

"Tom!" She picks up her heavy backpack from the floor—I'm ashamed to admit I haven't offered to carry it again since that first day. "Is everything okay?"

"Sure. Everything is fine. It just took a little longer to clean up after lab."

Everything is fine, except we might have to break up because your best friend caught me kissing that girl who was murdered and she's going to tell the police chief, who happens to be your dad. Other than that, everything is great!

"You look…" She cocks her head to the side. "Are you sure you're okay?"

"Uh-huh." I force a very crooked smile. "Let's go."

I follow Daisy outside, and we start on the path to her house without any detours, as I promised her father we would. The weather has gotten considerably warmer. All the snow that had stuck around during the winter is long gone. Usually I'm not a big fan of snow, but now I wish it had stayed around even longer. So I could have had more time before they discovered Brandi's body, even though it was inevitable.

"I'm sorry my father is making you walk me home every day," she says. "I know it's kind of silly. It's not like some guy is going to jump out of the bushes and kill me right in broad daylight."

I reach out for her hand. "I don't mind walking you home."

"Are you sure?"

"It's the best part of my day," I answer truthfully.

Daisy beams at me. "Mine too."

I love you, Daisy. I have loved you since the moment I first saw you. I'd do anything to keep from having to give you up. But I don't know if there's another way…

"My father is trying to convince me not to go away to college." She rolls her eyes. "As if I would stick around here after I graduate."

"Where do you think you're applying?"

She flashes me a shy smile. "I'm not sure yet. Where do you think *you're* applying?"

"I'm not sure either."

"Well, when it comes time," she says, "we should compare lists. Don't you think so?"

A couple of weeks ago, a comment like that would have floored me. Other guys might want to play the field in college, but that's not what I want. All I want is to spend the rest of my life with Daisy. And now, because of Alison, that's going to be impossible.

Although to be fair, it was pretty much impossible before. I was deluding myself if I ever thought otherwise.

"I love you, Daisy," I blurt out.

She stops walking, taken aback. Her pale eyelashes flutter as she absorbs my declaration. I don't know why I felt the need to say that. Maybe because I sensed that if I didn't say it now, I would never have another opportunity. Because there is a really good chance that in the next week or two, she's not going to feel the same way about me. In a week or two, she might not be speaking to me anymore.

She might even be afraid of me.

So I had to tell her how I really feel while there is still a chance she might appreciate it. Although looking at her face now, I'm not sure if it was a good idea.

"I..." she says.

Oh Christ, I made a mistake. I should never have said that. Stupid, stupid. "Never mind."

"Never mind?"

"No, I mean..." I pull my hand away from hers because it's gone clammy. "I just... I was being dumb. I shouldn't have said that."

"Yes, you should." She reaches for my hand again,

taking it in hers. Her hands are always so soft. How does she get them so freaking soft? She must use a special lotion. "Because I feel the same way. I…I love you too, Tom."

And as Daisy kisses me, I realize that I will never be as happy again as I am at this moment. I try to remember it and savor it, because very soon, things are going to get really bad.

CHAPTER 25

SYDNEY

I look like the victim in some kind of slasher film.

I have locked myself in the bathroom at the coffee shop, waiting for Mystery Man, a.k.a. Tom, to return with a clean shirt for me. I have managed to clean off all the blood on my face, but I stupidly chose to wear a pale pink color. It looks bad. If I had to walk home this way, I would definitely get some stares. There is a nonzero chance somebody might call the police.

On top of that, I don't exactly look my best. It's hard to look like a movie star after you've just lost half the blood in your body out through your nose. Part of me wishes that Tom would ask to reschedule our dinner for another night, but another part of me feels like if we do that, I'll never hear from him again.

There's a knock at the bathroom door, and when I pull it open, Tom is standing there with a white shirt crumpled in his hand. He thrusts it in my direction. "Small, right?"

I accept the shirt and hold it out in front of me. Oh no.

"I am not wearing a shirt that says 'I Love New York'!"

He smirks at me. "Why not? Don't you love New York?"

"I'm going to look like a freaking tourist!"

"At least you won't look like a murder victim."

I can't deny that he has a point. I reluctantly keep the shirt and lock myself back in the bathroom. I remove the dirty blouse and slide on my new, embarrassingly touristy T-shirt.

Well, it could be worse. At least it doesn't have a picture of an apple on it. And I do have a jacket I can hide it with.

I smooth out my hair and apply a fresh layer of lipstick. After another minute, I feel almost presentable again. I attempt to squeeze the blouse into my purse, but it's a lost cause—my little delicate purse fits my wallet and not much else. I guess I'll have to throw it out or else hold it in my hand for the rest of the date, which is not an appealing option.

I pull open the bathroom door, and Tom is waiting there, wearing a light Thinsulate jacket, his arms folded across his chest. Once again, I am struck by how handsome he is.

He flashes me a thumbs-up. "Looks great. I only wish I'd gotten you the Statue of Liberty snow globe to go with it."

"What do I owe you for the T-shirt?" This awful thing probably cost, like, fifty bucks.

"Don't be silly. It's my treat."

"Well, thanks." I hold up my bloody blouse. "Not to be gross, but I'm not sure what to do with this. It doesn't fit in my purse."

He pats his jacket. "This thing has huge pockets. Give it here."

I'm impressed that he's not so grossed out by my blood-soaked shirt that he's unwilling to touch it and that he'll even risk staining his pockets. Then again, he *is* a doctor.

"You ready?" Tom asks. "If we walk over to Sixth Street, we'll have our choice of a bunch of great Indian places. As long as you like Indian food?"

"Love it," I say.

He grins at me. "Look at that. We've got something in common."

We head through the coffee shop, and Tom holds the door for me. I've been on a lot of dates, but it's actually rare for a man to hold the door. On top of everything else, he's a gentleman too.

"By the way," I say, "I don't want you to think I get horrible nosebleeds like that all the time."

"Good to know." He cocks his head thoughtfully. "That was an impressive spontaneous epistaxis though. I mean, it wasn't *that* dry in the coffee shop. I hope you weren't picking it."

Even though he's teasing me, my face flushes scarlet. "*No.*"

"I remember that first time we met, you had…" He touches his forehead, where I had been attractively gushing blood on our first meeting. "You know…"

I may as well be honest. He's got to suspect something, and it's better he knows the truth than thinks I'm a picker. "Actually, I have a mild bleeding disorder."

"Oh yeah?" His black eyebrows shoot up. "Von Willebrand disease? Factor X deficiency? Factor II?"

"Von Willebrand disease," I confirm before he can keep guessing. I'm slightly impressed—even my primary care doctor didn't seem to know much about it. He had to google it right in front of me.

"It's the most common inherited bleeding disorder." He grins sheepishly. "Sorry, I'm kind of a nerd when it comes to this stuff. In med school, I was always the kid who knew way more than I needed to for the test. But it does sometimes come in handy at work."

Tom doesn't seem like any kind of nerd. He actually seems pretty much perfect, to the point where it's annoying. He's gorgeous, clearly very smart, charming, and he's a *doctor*. Of course, I've had a bit of an aversion to the idea of dating a doctor ever since what happened to Bonnie, although I'm now convinced that guy was lying about his profession as well as everything else. In any case, most women don't have *any* aversion to dating doctors.

But he's in his midthirties and still single. So there must be *something* wrong with him. Probably serious commitment issues, like half the other single guys in their thirties.

We arrive at the Indian restaurant, and again, Tom holds the door open for me. I am inspecting everything he does, watching for the usual red flags. He doesn't refuse to sit at the first place we are brought to because he must be sitting, like, due north or something, he doesn't inspect all the silverware for imperfections, and when we are seated, he doesn't declare that there's a weird smell in the restaurant and we have to leave immediately. He, in fact, pulls out my chair for me, which is refreshingly sweet.

"You have very good manners," I tell him.

He looks pleased by the compliment. "My mother taught me."

Oh—a mama's boy. I wait for some extended soliloquy about his sainted mother and about how no woman will ever live up to her. But it doesn't come. He is still frustratingly perfect.

"Are you close with your mother?" I ask.

He lifts a shoulder. "Somewhat. My dad died of a heart attack when I was in high school, so it's just been me and her since then."

"Oh." I clasp a hand over my mouth. "I'm so sorry. My father died of a heart attack a few years ago, and it was so sudden and devastating. It must've been even harder at such a young age."

"Yeah," he says, although his jaw tightens. It's clear he's not eager to talk about his father's death on our first date, and I can't say I blame him. Time to change the subject.

"So," I say, "where do you work?"

"I'm at NYU."

Nice—not far from my apartment. "And what kind of doctor are you?"

He hesitates, like he's not sure he wants to tell me. "I'm a pathologist."

"A *pathologist*? Isn't that the kind of doctor who cuts up dead bodies all day?"

He frowns as he makes a little tear in the napkin in front of him. "That's not all a pathologist does, you know. If you have a tumor and your doctor takes a biopsy, a pathologist is the one who looks at it under the microscope and tells you if you have cancer or not."

"Oh." My cheeks burn. "I'm sorry. So…is that what you do? Look at tumor samples under the microscope?"

"Well, no," he admits. "I'm a medical examiner. So I mostly do autopsies."

"So you cut up dead bodies all day."

He makes a face at me.

"And you enjoy that?"

"Well, it's my *job*. I find it intellectually stimulating, if that's what you're asking."

Okay, so the guy cuts up dead bodies for a living. That's…interesting. Maybe there's a good reason why he is still single.

"What do you do?" he asks, clearly eager to change the subject.

"I'm an accountant."

His face relaxes. "Oh, that's great. Very practical."

"Thank you. I was considering becoming a fortune teller, but then I was like, no, not practical. Accountant would be better."

He laughs. "I can see why somebody might get stuck between those two career choices."

"Anyway," I say, "I enjoy it well enough." I clear my throat. "That is to say, I don't hate it."

"I might have some questions about my 401(k) to ask you."

"Get in line."

He laughs again, his eyes crinkling in a way that I find undeniably sexy. I love the way he's looking at me. Part of me feels like he is way out of my league, but he's not looking at me that way. He's looking at me like he wants to throw me on the table and make love to me right now but is too polite to do so.

The waitress brings us glasses of water and offers to take our order. I've barely had time to glance at the menu, so I just get my favorite: chicken tikka masala. I appreciate the fact that Tom lets me order first and doesn't pass any sort of judgment on my food choices or pressure me to order something I don't want. He also doesn't stare at the waitress's rather large breasts.

"You know," he says after the waitress leaves, "I wanted to ask you for your number the first time I met you."

"Why didn't you?"

"Are you kidding?" He sips from his glass of water. "You just got attacked by your date. What kind of asshole do you think I am? And also"—he pauses—"I was sort of at the tail end of a relationship then."

"Oh." I raise my eyebrows. "A serious relationship?"

"Not exactly." He shifts in his chair, obviously not excited to talk about it. "Anyway, it's over now. Definitely over."

My eyes fall on his left hand, verifying once again that his ring finger is bare. And he doesn't have any wedding-band tan lines either. "Have you ever been married?"

"No, never." He grimaces slightly when he says it, as if it upsets him that he has never been married. "You?"

"No, never. But I'd like to get married." Oh my God, why did I say that? You never, ever say that on a first date—it's a cardinal rule. There's something about this guy that makes me let my guard down. "I mean, *someday*."

"Well then." Tom raises his water glass. "Here's to someday."

And as we clink our glasses together, I wonder if it's possible that Tom could be my someday.

CHAPTER 26

BEFORE

TOM

My uncle Dave—my mother's sister's husband—had a heart attack a couple of days ago.

My aunt and uncle live in Seattle, and my mother is flying out to see them. When I was little, I used to go with her whenever she went for a visit, but I've got school now, so I have to stay behind. With my father.

I'm not thrilled about it being just him and me in the house, but on the other hand, he'll probably just ignore me. He's got work and I've got school. There's a chance we might not even see each other at all the whole time my mother is gone.

"Be good for your dad, Tommy," my mother tells me before taking off in her Chevy for the airport.

Yeah, like *I'm* the one who gets drunk and starts throwing things in our household. "Okay."

She wrings her hands together. "Just leave him alone, okay?"

"Okay."

She kisses me goodbye and promises to call as soon as her plane lands. Like I'm going to be sitting around worrying that my mom's plane crashed. I've got much more important things to worry about.

For example, it's been two days since Alison's ultimatum, and Daisy is still very much my girlfriend. Alison keeps shooting me warning looks, but I still haven't made a move to end the relationship. I keep hoping something will happen and I won't have to do it, even though that's impossible.

I can't let Alison go to the police. Daisy told me in confidence that the police aren't having any luck finding out who killed Brandi, and they're pinning all their hopes on finding Brandi's secret boyfriend. I can't let them know I'm the guy they've been looking for.

If Daisy's father weren't so nervous about her safety, I would've liked to take her out for dinner tonight, but instead, I cook myself the skirt steak my mother had in the fridge, and I'm eating a late dinner at the kitchen table when a text pops up on my phone from Daisy:

Bored. What R U doing?
Dinner.
What's 4 dinner?
Steak. Made it myself.
Yum! Will U make it 4 me sometime?

I'd be happy to let Daisy come over for steak if only her dad would let her. I'd make her a whole feast. I'd attend culinary school just to make her happy. I'd do anything for her. *Anything*.

I can't break up with her. I just can't. There's got to be another way.

The front door slams, and I shove my phone into my pocket. My father must be home from his job at the hardware store. He always complains that he's doing menial labor, but he's lucky to have the job, considering he shows up for work drunk half the time and hungover the other half.

Sure enough, when he stumbles into the kitchen, his eyes are slightly bloodshot and he stinks of whiskey. He must've stopped by the local bar, O'Toole's, on the way home, which is what he does most nights.

"Where's Luann?" he demands to know.

I'm sure my mother told him a hundred times where she was going, but it doesn't surprise me he's forgotten. "Mom went to see Uncle Dave."

"It's always something with her," my father grumbles under his breath.

I don't know what to say. It's rare that my mother isn't home for dinner. She only goes to see Aunt Gloria twice a year.

"So where's dinner?" he barks at me. "I'm starving."

I look down at my own plate. I only cooked one steak, and I've almost finished it. "I don't know."

He glowers at me. "So you make yourself dinner, and you don't bother to make anything for your old man, even though I'm the one who puts the roof over your head and pays for all the food?"

"I didn't know you'd be home."

"Unbelievable," he mutters. "You'd think you weren't raised to have any manners."

He stumbles into the kitchen, but instead of going for the refrigerator, he goes for the liquor cabinet, which is filled with bottles that are all nearly empty. Liquor doesn't last long in our house. He rattles the bottles. "What the hell, boy? Where is all my whiskey?"

"You drank it?"

He slams the liquor cabinet shut, hard enough that the entire kitchen seems to shake. "Don't lie to me. I know you're sneaking drinks from my stash."

I'm not sneaking drinks—not even close. I've never even tasted alcohol. I won't touch the stuff after seeing what it does to my father.

But I know him, and once he gets an idea into his head, it's hard to dislodge it. If he thinks I'm swiping his liquor, he's never going to let it go.

"You know," he says, taking a step toward me, "you're not too big for a beating."

As he says the words, he reaches for his belt buckle. When I was younger, my father beat me with his belt buckle a handful of times. Just enough for me to learn to stay out of his way. My mother was always the one who took the brunt of his abuse.

"I'm going up to my room," I say. "There's plenty of food for you in the kitchen."

He snorts, although his hand leaves his buckle. "What are you going to do up there? Talk to your girlfriend, the police chief's daughter?"

I stiffen. I had no idea he knew about Daisy and me. The thought makes me uneasy.

My father is amused by the look on my face. "You think I didn't know? Your mom told me all about it. That girl is much too good for you, you know."

He's not entirely wrong. "Yeah," I mumble.

"Feel free to invite her over here." He winks at me. "That Daisy Driscoll is a pretty one. I wouldn't mind

159

having a shot at her. Be nice to have a break from your mom's saggy tits."

Nothing my father said before now had really bothered me. His threatening me with the belt buckle isn't anything new. Accusing me of stealing his crap is par for the course. But I don't like the way he's talking about Daisy.

I really, really don't like it.

He can see that his needling finally got to me, and a grin spreads across his ruddy face. "I saw her walking down the street the other day," he goes on. "She was looking good. Don't the Driscolls live on Peach Street? And isn't her bedroom the one in the back…on the second floor?"

My hand balls into a fist at the thought of my father getting anywhere near Daisy.

"I bet she'd like that." He licks his lips. "Not like anything *you* could do would satisfy her."

"Leave her alone," I say through my teeth.

"I'd make her real happy." The alcohol fumes coming out of his mouth are enough to make my eyes water. And there's another stale odor—one I can't identify. "Whether she likes it or not. But I think she'll like it a lot."

I don't even quite realize that I've grabbed the knife I'd been using on my steak until it's in my hand and I'm aiming it at my father's chest. "Don't even think about going near Daisy."

He looks down at the knife and up at my face. It takes him a second to burst out laughing. "You kidding me, boy? Didn't we try this once before and it didn't go so good for you?"

We did do it once before. But this time, he's not

getting the knife away from me. My grip is ironclad. "Stay away from Daisy."

It's hard not to appreciate the irony of the fact that those are the same words Alison said to me a couple of days ago.

"I don't think I will." Blatantly disregarding the knife, my father reaches into the liquor cabinet and selects a bottle of whiskey, even though it's nearly empty. He finishes off the last dregs. "In fact, maybe right after this, I'll go over and say hello to your sweet little Daisy." He looks down at the knife. "Why don't you put that thing away before you get hurt?"

I have watched my father beat my mother with his bare hands. I have felt him smack me across my backside with a belt. But I have never hated him quite as much as I do when I plunge the blade of the knife deep into his gut.

The knife is sharp. I sharpened it only about a week ago on the edge of one of the ceramic mugs, just like my mother taught me. The blade slides cleanly into his belly, and then, when it's inside, I twist it once for good measure. It's only after I pull it out again that I hazard a look at my father's face.

His face is frozen in a look of utter shock. His mouth is hanging open, and his usually ruddy skin has turned ashen. "Tom," he gasps as he clings to the kitchen counter.

And then he collapses to the floor.

He's bleeding badly. There's a puddle of blood forming below him on the floor, but it's not five pints. It's not enough to kill him, not even enough for him to lose consciousness. He is still alive, and he's trying to get back on his feet. He manages to get on his hands and knees, but that's the best he can do.

"Tom." He coughs, and his spittle is red when it lands on the linoleum. "I…I didn't know you had it in you…"

Maybe he didn't know. But I knew.

"Tommy…" His speech is slurred, and I'm not sure if it's from the alcohol anymore. "You gotta call an ambulance, kid. You gotta help your dad…"

When he looks up, his brown eyes—the same color as my own—meet mine. And that's when he knows I'm not calling an ambulance. That I'm going to let him bleed to death on the kitchen floor.

He feels around in his pocket for his phone. It's not there. He's always leaving it behind at the bar or maybe at work, so I'm guessing that's where it is right now. We've got a landline next to the sofa, but considering he can't even make it to his feet, it may as well be across the ocean.

Still, he tries for it. I stand frozen in the kitchen as he crawls across the kitchen floor, leaving behind a trail of smeared blood. He manages to make it onto my mother's favorite shag carpet and almost collapses, but he doesn't. The bastard is stronger than I thought he was. He might actually get to the phone. Either way, he's not dying anytime soon.

And that's when I realize I've got two options:

1. Get my father to a hospital so they can save his life.

2. Finish him off.

It's not a hard decision. I've done it in my dreams a million times before.

I stride across the kitchen, careful not to slip on my father's blood. I'm tracking bloody footprints all over the place, but I'm not sure it matters at this point. I step in my father's path, blocking him from moving forward. He reaches out for my ankle, smearing blood all over the leg of my jeans.

"Tommy," he rasps. "Please. Your old dad is hurt real bad. You gotta help me out."

I get down on my knees beside him. I look into his bloodshot eyes, which are a reflection of my own.

"You will never hurt her again," I say.

Those are the last words he hears before I cut his throat.

CHAPTER 27

SYDNEY

Tom and I have a great time at dinner.

It's every bit as good as my coffee with Travis. Even better, because I didn't have this kind of electric chemistry with Travis. On top of that, Tom is an excellent conversationalist and seems able to talk intelligently about any topic. And I love the way, when the check arrives, he scoops it up without even giving me a chance to try to pay.

"We can split it," I offer.

"You've *got* to be kidding me. I didn't spend the evening holding doors and chairs for you just to make you give me money for dinner."

Okay, it's a tiny bit old-fashioned, but I find it incredibly charming. Yes, I can afford to split dinner. But it's sweet that he won't let me. And I love how he helps me with my jacket after I stand up, which I button to my throat so that nobody knows that I love New York.

After we leave the restaurant, we linger in front of the

entrance. It's gotten nippier, and I hug my jacket around my chest as I stare up at Tom's face.

"Can I take you home?" he asks.

I have found that it is a good general rule for first dates not to let the guy know where I live, especially when he's a random guy I met at a coffee shop (albeit one who came to my rescue previously). Also, I am very worried that if Tom walked me home, I wouldn't be able to keep myself from inviting him upstairs, and once he was upstairs, I wouldn't be able to keep from ending up in the bedroom.

Which wouldn't be absolutely terrible, except that I didn't shave my legs. So…

"I'm going to grab a cab, actually," I say. "I'll be fine."

"Okay. Could I have your number then?"

His dark chocolate eyes never leave my face. "Yes, absolutely," I breathe.

I read off the digits of my phone number, and he types it into his phone. He genuinely seems like he's going to call me, but you never know. There have been plenty of times when I have been 100 percent sure I was going to get a call and didn't.

"I haven't been on a first date in a while," he says, "so you have to remind me of the etiquette. If I call tomorrow, is that completely uncool? Will you think I'm a loser?"

My lips twitch. "Well, I already think you're a loser, so you may as well call me tomorrow."

He seems to like that answer. "Also," he adds, "what do the kids do these days on dates? Is kissing on a first date allowed or…"

I suck in a breath. The thought of kissing this man is almost more than I can bear. "Yes. It's allowed."

His eyes twinkle. "Good."

And then he does it. He kisses me right in front of the Indian restaurant, and it's like every kiss I've had in my lifetime was just practice, working up to this. *This* is a kiss. It's the kind of kiss where every part of my body melts simultaneously, and I'm worried that when we stop kissing, I might fall to the floor in a pile of goo. It's that kind of kiss.

Although kissing Jake was quite nice too. I don't want to keep him from getting credit where it's due.

When Tom pulls away, the dazed look on his face mirrors my own. I'm glad we're not in my apartment, because we would definitely be pulling our clothes off right now.

"I'm calling you tomorrow," he promises.

"You better."

And then he kisses me again. It's just as good as the first time, and all I can think is, *How did I get this lucky?*

It's only after I get home that I realize Tom never gave me back my bloody shirt.

CHAPTER 28

Tonight I have another date with Tom.

It's our third date, if you count the one after my epic nosebleed. Thankfully, we got through a second date during which no part of me started spurting blood, and I felt like it was a major win. Tonight I'm considering inviting him over to my apartment, and it's honestly all I can think about during our four-o'clock yoga class.

"What are you smiling about?" Gretchen asks me as she rolls up her mat. After Bonnie's murder, we didn't go to yoga anymore for an entire month because it felt like it would be weird without her. But then Gretchen said her back was hurting without the class, and I was starting to get tense without it, so here we are. And honestly, it isn't that different with just the two of us.

"I have a date tonight," I admit.

"Ooh." Gretchen's eyes sparkle with excitement. "Is it with Dr. Perfect?"

That is Gretchen's nickname for Tom. It is weirdly

apt. So far, I haven't found anything wrong with the guy. Well, aside from the fact that he cuts up dead bodies for a living. "Yes, it is."

"Wow, you really like him, don't you?"

"I really do."

I'm falling for Tom faster and harder than I expected. We've only had two dates, and I'm already fantasizing about the place settings at our wedding and the house we would buy in the suburbs. Of course, I realize how stupid that is. Again, we are only on date three. There is plenty of time to discover that Tom is a total jerk.

And yet he doesn't seem like one. He seems like a genuinely nice guy.

"Do you think he could be the One?" she asks teasingly.

"It's too soon to know."

"Liar. You think he's the One. It's all over your face."

I can't quite meet her gaze, because she's absolutely right.

On the way out of the yoga class, Arlene has put out a plate of chocolate samples. See, this is why I love yoga. We get to spend an hour stretching as we listen to relaxing music, meditate, and then at the end, we get *chocolate*. Gretchen and I both grab a little square of chocolate.

"Enjoy!" Arlene says. "The chocolate is actually made by my friend's company. It's all natural, shade grown, and ethically traded. And it's over 90 percent cocoa."

"Sounds delicious," Gretchen says.

"Also," she says, "I'm so glad to see the two of you back in class again. I wanted to say how sorry I was to hear about Bonnie."

"Thank you," I murmur.

"If it helps," she says as she strokes the beads she always wears around her neck, "I have been feeling Bonnie's spirit in the studio when you're here. I think she is still joining you in class."

I want to say that doesn't help even a little bit, but Gretchen clutches her chest and tells her thank you so much. Despite what Arlene and Gretchen might believe, Bonnie's spirit is *not* lingering in the yoga studio. My friend is dead and buried in the ground, and nobody even knows who did it to her. And I'm beginning to worry we never will.

As Gretchen and I are walking down the steps to the exit, the two of us pop our squares of chocolate into our mouths. We exchange looks, and Gretchen spits the chocolate back into her hand. "Oh my God!" she cries. "It's like eating a square of dirt!"

I can't quite bring myself to spit the chocolate out, so I suffer silently until I manage to swallow it. Wow, that was some disgusting chocolate. (Note to self: never take chocolate offered during yoga class ever again.)

While I'm looking at the glass door of the building that houses the yoga studio, my heart skips a beat. There's a man standing near the door with a ponytail. Is that…Real Kevin?

I've been seeing him more than I should just based on pure coincidence. At least half a dozen times since our date, including that questionable sighting at Bonnie's funeral that I've become increasingly sure really *was* him. A few days ago, I was buying a bagel at a deli, and he got in line behind me. He acted surprised to see me, but I wasn't falling for it. I got out of the line and locked myself in the bathroom until I was pretty sure he'd given up and left. Before that, he came up behind me a few weeks ago when I was buying some gum at a newsstand. He tried to make conversation before I dashed into a subway station. It feels like he could pop up at any minute, and it's freaking me out.

Is that Real Kevin outside the yoga studio?

"Syd?" Gretchen frowns. "You okay?"

The guy comes a little closer, and his features come into focus. And oh my God, it's him. It's *Kevin*. Standing outside the glass door of the yoga studio, peering inside at me.

Our eyes make contact before I have a chance to pretend not to notice him. He feigns surprise and waves at me. I do not wave back.

"Who is that?" Gretchen asks me.

I turn away, hoping he'll get the message that I'm not going to come out and have a conversation with him. "It's that jerk I went out with months ago—you know, the one who tried to kiss me and I kneed him in the groin? I think he may be following me around."

"You mean the one who you thought you saw at Bonnie's funeral?"

I nod.

Gretchen rotates her head to try to get a look at him, and I grab her arm. "Don't look!"

"Sorry—I'm sorry." She pulls me off into the main studio, out of view of the glass door. "This is horrible, Syd! You need to do something about it."

"I don't even know his full name." Frankly, I'm not even sure Kevin *is* his first name. "I reported him to Cynch. And I told the detective investigating Bonnie's murder. So what else can I do? And he hasn't done anything, you know, *threatening* exactly."

"Ugh, why are guys such idiots?"

It's a question for the ages. "It's fine. I'm sure he'll get tired of me eventually."

Gretchen seems willing to accept this assessment of the situation. Bonnie wouldn't have let me drop it this way—she'd probably have marched me down to the police station to find out about a restraining order. But she's dead.

"Speaking of guys who are *not* jerks," Gretchen says, "I've got some exciting news."

I hate myself for bracing for the worst. "Oh?"

"Randy and I are moving in together!"

I instantly forget all about the Kevin sighting outside. "Gretchen, that's amazing!"

She looks so happy, and I can't help but throw my arms around her, even though I'm not entirely thrilled. Gretchen could do a lot better than Randy. I might not think he is as creepy as Bonnie did, but there's something about him that makes me uneasy.

Still, how am I supposed to say that to my friend? I have no choice but to be happy for her.

"It will take me all of five minutes to move my stuff to his apartment," she says. "I'm basically leaving everything behind. And guess what? This means you and I will be neighbors!"

"Yay!" I say, managing to muster up an appropriate amount of enthusiasm.

"Anyway," she says, "I'm heading down to my apartment now to grab some stuff. Do you feel like taking a subway ride?"

I shake my head. "Not particularly."

"Oh, right. You have your date with Dr. Perfect." She

171

winks at me. "Well, have fun! I'm assuming you don't need a rescue call."

"Definitely not."

Thankfully, Arlene is able to direct me to an alternate exit to the studio, through the back, so I can avoid Kevin. Gretchen walks off in the direction of the subway while I head back to my apartment building. My date with Tom isn't for a couple of hours, but I need to shower, and I'm probably going to obsessively try on everything in my closet between now and then.

While I'm crossing Eighth Avenue, my phone starts ringing in my purse. I pull it out just in time for a cab driver to whizz past me, splashing dirty rain water on my sneakers—all rain instantly turns black the second it hits the New York pavement. Jake's number flashes on the screen.

Oh my God, did they figure out who killed Bonnie?

The light for the crosswalk is flashing red, counting down the seconds until I get to the other side. They never give you enough time to cross avenue streets—it's like whoever put the timers in these lights thinks we're Olympic sprinters. But even so, I take the call. "Jake?"

"Hey, Syd." He pauses. "Where are you? It sounds really loud."

"I'm outdoors. Outdoors is loud."

"Right, right." He heaves a sigh on the other end of the line. "Do you have a minute to talk?"

I grip the phone tighter. "Did you find the killer?"

"No."

Disappointment surges through me. "You promised you would. It's been two months, Jake."

"I know, but—"

I step back onto the sidewalk, having successfully crossed Eighth Avenue without getting mowed down by a yellow taxi, which is never a given. "So why the hell are you calling then?"

"I'm just worried about you. I wanted to make sure you're okay."

"I don't understand. Why are you so worried?"

He's quiet for a moment on the other line. "Look, there's something you should know."

"Something I should know?" This doesn't sound good. "What should I know?"

"We found another victim."

"*What?*"

"You heard me." He sounds like he's gritting his teeth. "There was another hit in the database from about three years ago. Similar MO to the other two—the missing hair cut close to the scalp. Traces of DNA were found that match what we found in Bonnie's apartment."

I stop short in the middle of the sidewalk, suddenly feeling like I can't breathe. "Are you serious? So this is a serial killer?"

"Yes."

"But I didn't see anything about that in the paper."

"We're doing our best to keep it out of the paper. We don't want people to panic."

"You mean like the way *I'm* panicking right now?"

"Look." Jake sounds far too calm given the gravity of what he just told me. "We are going to find this guy. But in the meantime, keep doing what you're doing. Lock your doors. You're staying off Cynch, right?"

"Are you worried about my safety, or do you just want me to die single and alone?"

"Sydney…"

"Forget it. I'm kidding."

I'm still frozen on the sidewalk. Pedestrians are filtering around me on both sides, several of them shooting me dirty looks, but I can't seem to make my feet move again.

"Listen, Syd." Jake clears his throat. "If you're…I mean, if you're not doing anything, I could come over tonight to keep you company. I'll bring Chinese food. We don't have to talk about the case at all. We can watch a movie or something."

My mouth drops open slightly. "Are you asking me on a *date*?"

"No! I'm just saying, if you want some company tonight… You were saying you don't want to be alone, so I thought…"

"Well, you don't need to worry about me. I actually have a date tonight."

"You do?" I try not to feel offended by how astonished Jake sounds. "With who?"

A man in a puffy coat actually *gives me the finger* for my audacity to be standing still for five seconds on a New York City sidewalk, which buoys me to start walking again before someone cuts my throat. "With none of your business."

"I'm not trying to be nosy, Sydney," he says. "I'm just worried about you."

"Well, no need to worry. He's a really good guy. And…I like him a lot."

"Oh." Jake's voice drops a few notches. "Well, that's great. I'm happy for you. You deserve a great guy. And… you trust him?"

"Jake!"

"All right, all right." He sighs. "I'm just saying, please be careful. And if you have any concerns about the guy at all, if you want a background check or whatever, just give me a call. Anytime."

I have to admit, Jake has a way of making me feel safe. He is so tall and strong and serious. Back when we were dating, it was like I had a bodyguard looking after me at all times. It's comforting to know that even though we're not together anymore, he is still looking out for me.

But I don't need him to look out for me. I've got Tom after all.

CHAPTER 29

BEFORE

TOM

I know exactly how to cut my father's throat. I have to say thanks to all those surgical textbooks I bought and read cover to cover. Soon enough, there are five pints of his blood all over my mother's rug. And then some.

My father dies right in front of me. All I can think as I watch the light go out of his eyes is that he deserves this. He will never beat my mother again. He will never terrorize our family ever again.

But a few seconds later, the relief that he is finally gone morphs into panic. I killed my father. I killed my father *right in my living room*. I sliced his jugular with a kitchen knife. There's no way I can argue this was an accident or even self-defense.

I'm going to spend the rest of my life in prison.

Unless…

I scramble to my feet, my hands shaking. There's blood all over my jeans and my sneakers and my hands. There's so much on my hands. You don't realize how much five pints of blood is until it's all over your kitchen floor. I can't deal with this alone. It's too much.

And there's only one person I can call. There is one person who might help me out of this impossible situation.

I run my hands under hot water, trying to wash off the blood. The bar of soap turns pink as I scrub my hands with it, but after a lot of hot water, the soap turns back to white and my hands look normal again. It's more than I can say for my jeans and sneakers. Everything I'm wearing will have to be burned. But for now, I just need my hands clean enough to use my phone.

I select the first name from my list of contacts—the person I call the most. I stand in the kitchen, my head throbbing as the phone rings repeatedly on the other end of the line.

Pick up. Come on, buddy. I need you.

"Hello?" a familiar voice says.

"Slug," I choke out. "I need your help."

My best friend doesn't hesitate. "Sure. What do you need?"

"I…" I look over at my father's motionless body lying on the living room rug. "I did something really bad. Like, *really* bad."

A pause. "Okay. What's going on?"

"I can't tell you on the phone."

"I can't help you unless you tell me what's going on."

Can I actually trust Slug? My gut tells me I can. But what if he shows up here and freaks out? Still, I don't have any alternative. I can't deal with this situation by myself. "Could you borrow your parents' car and come over?"

"Sure. They already went to bed. They won't even know I'm gone."

He says it so cavalierly. Slug's parents are in their sixties—he was a not-so-happy accident—and they don't have the energy to deal with him. So he does pretty much whatever he wants and they don't care.

It's perfect.

Fifteen minutes later, Slug's parents' Oldsmobile pulls into our driveway. I watch from the window as he steps out, stretching his long legs for a moment before walking over to the front door. I yank open the door before he can hit the doorbell. Slug looks surprised, his skeletal wrist frozen in midair.

"Get inside," I tell him.

"Jesus, Tom." He stumbles into the foyer before I can slam the door closed practically on his foot. He looks like he's going to say something more, but then he notices all the blood staining my T-shirt. His mouth falls open. "Tom…"

"I didn't have a choice," I say tightly, even though that's not true.

My heart is pounding as Slug pushes past me into the living room. It takes him all of half a second to notice my father lying dead on the rug. He inhales sharply, and I hold my own breath, waiting to see what he says. I've known Slug most of my life, and I trust him, but it's safe to say this falls out of the realm of the usual favors that a guy can ask of his best friend.

"So," Slug says slowly, "you finally killed that son of a bitch."

"It was an accident," I say lamely.

"Yeah, some accident. His throat is sliced open."

I run a shaking hand through my hair, which I now realize *also* has blood in it. Jesus Christ, there is blood *everywhere*. That's something you don't learn in the anatomy textbooks, that's for sure. I've spent the last fifteen minutes cleaning blood from the kitchen floor, and I've done a decent job, but I don't know what we're going to do about my mom's rug. We'll need some sort of extra-strength carpet cleaner, and I'm sure even then, there will be traces left behind.

"You can't save the rug," Slug says as if reading my mind. "We can wrap him in it."

"Wrap him?"

"When we get rid of the body." Slug flashes me an exasperated look. "Isn't that what you called me to help you with?"

I look at my best friend. His face is really greasy, like the surface of a pizza, and his forehead is suffering from a particularly severe acne attack. But the craziest thing is how eerily calm he seems. I'm about to jump out of my skin, but Slug is cool as a cucumber.

"We'll wrap him up in the rug and put him in my trunk," Slug says. "Do you have any garbage bags I can line the trunk with?"

"Uh, sure."

When I don't budge, Slug lifts an eyebrow. "What are you waiting for? It's not like we've got forever to take care of this."

"Okay. How many do we need?"

"Six should do it."

How does he know the exact number of garbage bags he'll need to line the trunk of his car for a dead body? Or maybe I don't want to know the answer to that question.

After I bring him the garbage bags, I head upstairs to change my clothes. I don't know what exactly to do with my bloody T-shirt and jeans, but I'm not leaving the house wearing my father's blood.

I take a second to look in the bathroom mirror while I'm upstairs. Good thing I do, because there's a lot more blood on my face and hair than I would've guessed. Fortunately, the color of my hair is so dark you can't see it. I'll have to take a long shower after we're done dealing with this.

The skin of my face is extremely pale—like I'm half-dead—and there are dark purple rings under my eyes that look like bruises. I look like I've been awake since last week.

I put my phone on the dresser while I change clothes, and it buzzes while I'm in the bathroom. A text message. I hurry back to flip open the screen, and a message pops up from Daisy:

U need 2 watch this video!

I don't click on the video, which looks like it's something about a cat playing the piano. I'm not in the mood for cute animals right now. I'm not sure if I ever was, but definitely not now. I'm so far from being interested in cute animals, it's not even funny. I hate to ignore a text message from Daisy, but I can't bring myself to reply.

When I get back downstairs, Slug has managed to roll the carpet around my father's body. It's almost exactly the right length to cover him. Lucky.

Slug straightens up when he sees me, wiping his hands on his own pair of jeans. His jeans are too short—hand-me-downs from one of his older brothers. Slug is the only one of his siblings who is freakishly tall.

"I got my trunk covered with the garbage bags," he reports. "And I turned the car around so that the trunk is up against the garage door, but I couldn't back in because your dad's car is already in there. Anyway, we can just throw him right in there. Nobody will see."

"Right." It's hard not to be bothered by the fact that Slug is so *good* at this. And Slug isn't good at *anything*. Well, besides eating bugs.

"You okay, Tom?" He squints at me. "You're not going to start freaking out, are you?"

"I'm okay," I manage.

"Good." Slug eyes the large lump of carpet on the floor. "Because I can't lift him on my own. This is a two-person job."

Even for two of us, it's a struggle. Slug lifts one end and I lift the other, but my father was a big guy, and we're both grunting and trying our best not to drop him. Fortunately, Slug already has the trunk and the garage door open, so we make a beeline. As we get closer, I start to panic that the body isn't going to fit, but Slug doesn't seem worried, and sure enough, we manage to get it stuffed inside. As we slam the trunk closed, I fight a wave of nausea. I don't even know how we're going to get rid of this body. We have a long night ahead of us.

But suddenly, none of that matters anymore. Because when I look up from the trunk, I realize someone has been watching us. There is a figure standing on the sidewalk, and they have seen our every move.

Oh Jesus, it's Alison.

CHAPTER 30

TOM

Alison saw us stuffing my father's dead body into the trunk.

She had to have seen. It's dark out, but not *that* dark. And our porch lights are on, providing extra light. I don't know why I didn't turn the damn porch lights off. What's wrong with me? That's, like, Murder 101—turn out the stupid lights before going outside to stuff a dead body in the trunk.

But then again, maybe she didn't see. She's got her dog with her—a mutt who seems a lot friendlier than she is—and maybe she's too focused on picking up the dog's poop or whatever dog owners do during walks. There's no guarantee she knows what we were doing. I mean, even if she saw everything, all she knows is that we were stuffing a carpet into the trunk. Maybe we're having the house reupholstered.

Of course, if she hears my father has gone missing, she'll be able to put two and two together pretty easily.

"Hi, Alison," I croak.

Slug looks up sharply at the sound of her name. He stiffens but doesn't say a word. Under other circumstances, he would be nudging me and talking about how hot she is.

"Hello," Alison says tonelessly.

I sprint halfway across my yard to talk to her. It's too dark to see her face, which means I can't tell what she's thinking. Did she see us? *Did she?*

"Walking your dog?" I ask.

She looks down at the leash in her hand. "Uh, *yeah*."

"Kind of late for that, isn't it?"

She lifts a shoulder. "Rufus will protect me."

As if on cue, the mutt starts growling at me. Great. The dog is going to maul me now. Just what I need.

"Shush, Rufus," Alison hisses at her dog.

The dog won't stop growling. He's really worked up, and now he's straining at the leash, hard enough to jerk Alison forward.

Except he's not going for me. He's trying to run past me.

"Sorry," Alison grunts. "I don't know what's gotten into him."

I don't either until Rufus dashes over to the Oldsmobile. Slug looks panicked for a moment, backing away from the car with his hands up, but the dog comes to an abrupt halt at the trunk of the car. And then he starts barking like a wild animal, all his energy directed at the trunk.

"You got any raw meat in there?" Alison asks us. "He only acts this way around raw meat."

I don't even know how to begin to answer that, because I am frozen in absolute horror, but then Slug speaks up, "Yeah, I was just grabbing some hamburger meat and hot dogs from Tom for a barbecue my family is having tomorrow."

"Well, that would do it." Alison tugs on the leash, trying to pull away a very reluctant Rufus. "By the way, Tom, have you had a chance to talk to Daisy?"

Please, not this—not now. "Not yet."

"But soon?" She peers at me through her thick glasses. "Right?"

"Right," I say tightly.

Satisfied with my answer, Alison manages to pull Rufus away from the trunk of the Oldsmobile, and once they're back on the sidewalk, the dog reluctantly continues on his way. Slug and I watch Alison walk away, both of us practically afraid to breathe.

"She saw," he says when she is for sure out of earshot. "She had to have seen."

I look over at Slug, who is staring off into the distance, where Alison is only a tiny dot. "I don't think she did. It's pretty dark."

"She knows we were doing *something*," he points out. "And that damn dog wouldn't stop barking at the trunk. Once she finds out your dad is missing, she's going to put it all together."

"Maybe not."

"Come on. Are you really that stupid, Tom?"

I rub my face with the palms of my hands. "So what are we supposed to do about it?"

Slug is quiet. "I don't know. But it's a big loose thread."

I can't deal with this. I've already got enough to deal with. We still have a body in the trunk we have to get rid of. I can't even begin to think about Alison right now. "What are we going to do about the body?"

"I was going to say maybe we should throw him in the river. Make it seem like he got mugged and then tossed." Slug fingers the trunk of his car. "But now that Alison saw us, I'm thinking we should bury him. So they don't find him for a while."

Bury him. Like Brandi Healey was buried.

"Fine," I say. "Should I grab a shovel?"

Slug shakes his head. "I already got a couple in the back seat."

Of course he does.

CHAPTER 31

BEFORE

TOM

Four hours later, we're driving back into town, the trunk of the Oldsmobile empty.

My father's body is buried in the ground in what looked like an abandoned hiking trail about ninety minutes away from here. Slug knew exactly where to go. He said something about his brother taking him there to camp when he was little, and I didn't question it. I have to assume he's telling the truth, because the alternative is too terrible.

Slug has the radio on in the car, and he's singing along to a Dr. Dre song. He doesn't look like a guy who just buried a dead body, even though his fingernails still have dirt ground into them.

"You sure your parents won't be pissed you were gone all night?" I ask.

"Nah." He taps out a beat on the steering wheel. "My dad sleeps like a rock, and my mom pops Ambien like candy. They won't even know I left the house."

"Oh. Okay."

"But I need to get some sleep." He lets out a yawn. "So you're on your own getting your house cleaned up."

I don't mind that part. Sleep seems all but impossible, so I may as well spend the night scrubbing the kitchen floor with bleach.

"Get all your bloody clothes into the washing machine," he tells me. "Lots of steaming hot water, detergent, bleach—the works."

Why is Slug so damn knowledgeable about this stuff? "Okay."

"When is your mom getting back home?"

"She's gone another day." I squirm in my seat. There's dirt on the seat of my pants, and it's making me uncomfortable. "But they might notice when he doesn't show up for work tomorrow. Of course, that's not too unusual for him."

"What are you going to tell your mom?"

"I'll just say he took off on a bender."

He's done it before. One time, he was gone for over a week. She'll be worried, but she won't call the cops right away, because she'll know that'd end up being more trouble for him. We might have three or four days before she starts to get concerned. Of course, the fact that his car is still in our garage is a red flag, but it's too risky to get rid of the car.

"Also," Slug adds, "we have to figure out what to do about Alison."

I look up sharply. "What to do?"

"She *saw* us, Tom."

"I know, but…" I rub at the knees of my jeans, which are caked with dirt and blood in equal parts. "She didn't really see anything. I don't think she did anyway."

"Yeah? You want to bet your freedom on that?"

"So what are we supposed to do?"

Slug is quiet as gangster rap music plays in the background. His eyes stay pinned on the dark road ahead of us, illuminated by the headlights.

"Slug?"

"I'm just saying, Tom—it's a problem. A big problem."

I shake my head. "I thought you *liked* Alison. You're always talking about how great she is. How she's like a sexy librarian."

"She is." He shrugs. "But she saw us tonight, and if we don't do anything about it, it could be a problem. Do you really want to take that risk?"

"Yes," I say firmly. "I want to take the risk."

Slug doesn't say anything. He just keeps driving. I'm hoping that's the end of it. Alison didn't see anything. I know she didn't. If she had, she definitely would have said something.

CHAPTER 32

PRESENT DAY

SYDNEY

Date number three is just as amazing as date number one and date number two.

This time, Tom and I get poke bowls. I've never been that into poke, but Tom was going on and on about it during our last date, and he told me he knew a great place, which turned out to be not far from my apartment building. So we got our poke bowls, and as always, he grabbed the check before I could even try to pay.

And now we are walking back to my apartment.

And I have shaved my legs.

"So guess what?" I say. "I was passing by a liquor store, and I bought a bottle of tequila."

"Tequila." Tom nods in approval. "I haven't had tequila in years. Brings back memories of college."

"I even bought limes to go with it," I say. "You have to, right?"

"I'm fairly sure it's illegal to drink tequila without a lime."

"That's true," I say. "My ex is a cop, and I think he's arrested people for that."

Tom stiffens at my mention of Jake. I curse under my breath. I shouldn't have talked about an old boyfriend in front of a potential new boyfriend. Or maybe Tom is my actual boyfriend now rather than a potential boyfriend. Either way, I'm sure he doesn't want to hear about Jake.

"So," he says, "you have an ex who's a cop?"

"Uh, yeah. But it was a while ago."

"Are you still in touch?"

"Not at all." At least not until very recently. But he doesn't need to know that part. "Sorry, I didn't mean to bring up an ex. That was dumb."

"No worries. Everybody has a past, right?"

Tom mentioned before that he had been at the tail end of a relationship when we first met, but he has scrupulously avoided talking about it again. Aside from that one statement, he acts like I am the first girl he's ever dated. It's nice, actually. The last thing you want is a guy who is hung up on his ex.

And yet I'm curious. I'm curious about the kind of girls he dated before me. He is objectively a very good catch, and I have to believe he has dated some beautiful women. But what I want to know even more than that is why those relationships ended.

I suppose if we're together long enough, I'll find out.

It always comes out.

When we're about three blocks from my apartment building, Tom stops short. When I try to keep walking, he gives me a curious look. "Where are you going?" he asks.

"To my apartment," I say.

He frowns. He looks up at the building we're standing

in front of. It hits me now that this is where he rescued me from Real Kevin. "I thought you lived here."

"Oh, no." I shake my head. "I was pretending to live here so that guy wouldn't show up at my front door."

"Oh." He laughs. "Smart thinking. Okay then, lead the way." He licks his lips and gives me a meaningful look. "I can't wait for that tequila."

Me either.

As we walk the remaining three blocks, he laces his fingers through mine, which I find oddly sweet. But when we reach my block, he suddenly yanks his hand away from mine. And then, when we come to a halt in front of my building, all the color drains from his face.

"You live *here*?" he gasps.

"It's not as fancy as it looks," I say teasingly.

I start up the steps to my front door, but Tom hasn't budged. I don't know what is going on with him. He's holding on to the banister, and he looks like he's about to be sick.

"Tom?" I say. "Are you okay?"

He rubs his gut. "I, uh…I'm not sure. I don't feel so hot. Maybe it was the poke."

I would tell him to go home, but he doesn't even look like he can make it there. Also I've cleaned my apartment top to bottom and made my legs as smooth as a baby's bottom. After all that, it would be *so* disappointing if he didn't come upstairs. So I grab him by the hand and give him a tug. "Just come up for a minute, okay?"

Tom reluctantly lets me pull him up the stairs and into my building, although he looks like he's being led to the electric chair. While we're in the elevator, his eyes are darting all over the place. "How long have you lived here?" he asks me.

191

"About two years."

He mouths the words "two years" as he runs a hand through his black hair. "And...do you know a lot of people in the building?"

Okay, that's a strange question to ask. "Not really."

"Not really?"

"It's New York. Everyone keeps to themselves, right?"

"Right," he mumbles, but he doesn't look entirely satisfied by my answer.

"I did have one close friend in the building," I finally admit, "but she actually...she was murdered a few months ago."

He gawks at me. He opens his mouth, but no sound comes out.

"The building is safe though," I quickly add. "You don't have to worry about me. They think this guy she was dating was the one who killed her, but nobody can find him. He was apparently using a burner phone to contact her the whole time, if you can believe that."

"Jesus," he says. "That's... Wow. They've no idea who he was, huh?"

"If they did, he'd be in jail, wouldn't he?"

By the time we get to my apartment, I'm beginning to wonder if this is a mistake. Tom seems really antsy, and I don't understand why. I would think he was freaked out about what I told him about Bonnie's murder, but he was already panicked before I said a word. What does he have against my building? Did he hear a rumor that it's haunted by an evil spirit? Is there an *odor* I'm not aware of?

Not that I love this building so much. Ever since one of my closest friends was killed here, it's like there's a dark presence. And I still think about her all the time. I might have moved on enough to start dating again, but I'm not going to forget Bonnie. Never.

I hope Jake finds the monster who killed her. I won't be able to completely relax until he has.

When we get into my apartment, I head straight to the kitchen to grab the bottle of tequila. I feel like this is the kind of thing that alcohol might fix. Tom follows me into the kitchen, his brow deeply furrowed.

"Sydney," he says.

I grab one of the limes from the refrigerator. I take a knife and start cutting it into slices. "I'll have our drinks ready in two minutes."

"I…I think I'm going to pass." He rests a hand on the kitchen counter, his fingers obsessively drumming against the marble. "I just remembered I have an early meeting tomorrow morning."

"A meeting with the dead bodies?"

He shoots me a look. "No, it's a staff meeting."

He is so full of it. A staff meeting? Really? How come an hour ago, there was no staff meeting? Anyway, I've never met a guy who wasn't willing to trade sleep for sex. No, he wants out of here.

Except why? Why is he so freaked out all of a sudden? What did I do wrong?

Either way, I have a feeling that when Tom leaves this apartment, I'll never see him again.

I'm so aggravated that the knife slips. The blade nicks my left index finger, which is holding the lime in place, and because I'm me, there is instantly a pool of blood below my finger.

"Shit!" I cry. Great. This night is just getting better and better.

"Jesus," Tom gasps. "You really cut yourself badly."

It occurs to me now that on three of the four occasions that I have encountered Tom, I have been bleeding significantly. If he weren't eager to leave before, this should definitely do the trick.

Good job, Syd.

But when I look up at him, some of the color has returned to his cheeks. He doesn't look at all disturbed that I am once again bleeding profusely. But I suppose he *is* a doctor. He even knew what von Willebrand factor was before I told him.

"Where is your first aid kit?" he asks me.

"It's on the top shelf in the bathroom."

Tom dashes off to my bathroom, and a few seconds later, he returns with the kit. Meanwhile, I'm using paper towels to try to stanch the flow of blood. It is surprisingly ineffective. This is the kind of cut that would bleed a lot even in a normal person, so in someone like me, it's a slightly terrifying amount of blood. It's cheap-horror-movie amounts of blood.

"Wow." Tom gazes down into my first aid kit. "You are really well stocked."

"Um, thanks."

"This is a premium kit." He sifts through the contents with growing excitement. "Tweezers, scissors, a cold compress. You've even got a tourniquet in here!"

"Do you think I need a *tourniquet*?"

"No." He grins at me, his shoulders finally relaxed again. "I'm just saying, this is really a primo kit. Now let me get this cleaned up for you."

My personal experience is that most people are at least a little squeamish when it comes to the amount of blood

I manage to squirt out. I once cut my finger in front of Gretchen, and she ran out of the room clutching her hand to her mouth. But Tom isn't squeamish. At *all*. He uses some gauze to hold pressure on my wound, and when it seems slightly under control, he constructs what is actually a very effective bandage on my left index finger. Usually I need to change my first bandage about five minutes after putting it on, but this one might make it till the next morning.

"Thank you," I say as I admire his handiwork. "It's useful dating a doctor."

Too bad we will never see each other again. That meeting excuse was such bullshit.

But weirdly, Tom seems to have forgotten all about his meeting, and helping me with the cut on my finger seems to have calmed him down. He stands next to me in the kitchen, leaning against the counter, a smile playing on his lips. "Happy to be of service."

I look up into his brown eyes, and once again, they are filled with desire, after I thought it had vanished on the street outside my building. He holds my gaze, and then he drops his lips onto mine.

After a kiss that practically melts my bones, Tom murmurs in my ear, "You want to take this to the bedroom?"

"What about your meeting?"

"Sleep is overrated."

"What about our tequilas?"

"All I want," he whispers in my ear, "is you."

Okay then.

CHAPTER 33

BEFORE

TOM

The next morning, it feels like it was all an awful dream. It doesn't help that I only slept about two hours, which were broken up by dreams in which my father burst through our front door, covered in dirt, a gaping hole in his neck. Maybe it really was all a dream. After all, how could I have killed my own father and buried his body out in the woods?

I drag myself out of bed and splash water on my face until I feel a little more awake. My mother doesn't usually let me drink coffee, but I could use a cup this morning like nobody's business. The whites of my eyes are laced with red, and my black hair won't quit sticking up, no matter how hard I try to smooth it down with water.

When I get out of the bathroom, I pass my parents' bedroom. Part of me is hoping that my father will be lying in bed, snoring loud enough to wake the dead, and that the whole thing really was an extremely vivid dream. But of course, he's not there.

He never will be again.

I throw on my clothes in a haze and stumble down the stairs, clinging to the banister to keep from tumbling to my death. It isn't until I get downstairs to find the rug still missing from the living room that it hits home.

I killed my father last night. I slashed his throat. I wrapped his body in the rug and buried him in the woods.

I stand in the spot where the rug used to be, struggling to feel any kind of emotion for the man who called himself my father. I didn't love him—I don't know if I ever did. And I'm not sorry he's dead. He deserved to die. He deserved even worse than what happened to him.

But even so, I shouldn't have killed him. Murder is wrong, and I know that. But when I had that knife in my hand, I couldn't stop myself. The urge to plunge the knife into his soft belly was almost overwhelming.

And the truth is I enjoyed watching him die. It was one of the best moments of my life.

There's something very wrong with me. My mother and Daisy might not see it, but Alison sees it, and so does Slug. I don't know what to do about it. But Alison was right about one thing: I'm dangerous.

I stumble to the kitchen and start up the coffee machine. I usually make myself a cup whenever my mother isn't around to tell me not to. Tomorrow, she's coming home from Seattle. And the first thing she's going to ask when she comes through the door is, "Where is your father?"

I'll just tell her I haven't seen him. Better to play dumb. Bill Brewer is notoriously unreliable, and it wasn't my job to babysit him while she was gone.

While I'm waiting for the coffee to brew, my phone

rings in my pocket. Sure enough, it's my mother. Probably trying to catch me before school. I consider letting it go to voicemail, but if she can't track down either of us, she might really call the police. Better to take the call.

"Hi, Mom," I say into the phone. I'm trying to sound like a guy who hasn't spent most of the night awake.

"You sound exhausted, Tommy!" Oh well, I guess that didn't work. "Is everything okay?"

"Yeah, sure. How is Uncle Dave?"

"He's doing well. They put a stent in his heart. Did you know they could do that?"

"Yes." Even though it's a long way away, I've considered becoming a cardiac surgeon. I love the idea of cutting through a person's chest and getting to see their heart within. I would love to hold an actual heart in my hand—a human one, not the cow's heart that we dissected in biology a few months ago.

Of course, if I were a surgeon and looking into a living person's chest, would I be able to stop myself from doing something stupid? When I close my eyes, I can still see my hand plunging the knife into my father's belly.

"Listen, Tom." My mother's voice jogs me out of my thoughts. "Your father isn't answering his cell phone. Is he around?" Before I can answer, she adds, "If he's sleeping, don't wake him up."

Of course. She doesn't want to get screamed at by my father for disturbing his precious slumber—or risk his taking out his anger on me. "I think he's at work."

"This early?"

"I guess so."

She's silent on the other line. "But you did see him come home last night, right?"

"Right." Technically, it's true.

"Okay… Well, maybe I'll try him at the hardware store then."

"Are you sure it's a good idea to bother him? He didn't seem to be in a good mood."

"So you *did* see him this morning then?"

Damn. It feels like my mother is determined to catch me in a lie, and she doesn't even have any idea what I've done. "I mean, he just seems like he's in a bad mood lately. Like always, you know? That's all."

"Okay." She's quiet again on the other end of the line, thinking this over. Finally she says, "I won't bother him, but can you text me when he gets home tonight?"

"Sure."

"Thank you, Tommy. I love you so much, sweetheart."

"Uh-huh. Bye, Mom."

I put down the phone, my brain running a mile a minute. What am I going to do tonight? Do I pretend my father came home? That seems like a bad idea. I don't want to get caught in a lie.

I gulp down the cup of coffee, grab my backpack off the floor in the foyer where I dropped it last night, and head out in the direction of school. The weather is nice—brisk and breezy, with the promise of hitting the sixties this afternoon. It's hard to enjoy it though. I can't stop thinking about last night. And about what I'm going to do when my mother gets home.

And about the Alison problem.

I have this feeling it's all going to work out though. I'm not sure how I know it, but it's like a little voice in my ear whispering, *It's going to be okay, Tom. It's all going to get taken care of.*

I don't know if it's the fresh air or what, but by the time I get to school, I'm feeling pretty good. Yes, I did something unthinkable last night. But I did a good job covering my tracks. Slug will keep my secret, and I'm certain Alison didn't see a thing. Nobody is going to find out. It's all going to work out for me.

And then I see the police cars parked in front of the school.

There are two of them again. There's been one parked there intermittently since Brandi's body was found, but this is the only time since that first day that *two* cars are parked in front of the school. And then, just when I'm starting to panic, a third police car pulls up.

Oh no.

Could this have to do with my father? Did they already figure out what I did and now the police are here to arrest me and Slug?

No, that's impossible.

Except the police are here for a reason. *Three* cars. Something terrible must've happened.

There are a few clusters of students in front of the school, and everyone is talking in hushed tones. What the hell *happened*? I'm going to lose my mind if I don't figure it out very soon.

Before I can approach one of the students, a voice calls out my name: "Tom! *Tom!*"

I turn around just in time to see Daisy hurling herself at me. She was upset when Brandi's body was found, but that was nothing compared to now. She clings to me, her body shaking with sobs. I stroke her golden hair, trying to comfort her even though I don't know what's happened.

"Daisy," I murmur. "Calm down. Everything is going to be okay."

Daisy raises a tear-streaked face. "What are you talking about? How can anything possibly be okay? Alison is *missing*."

Alison is missing?

Jesus Christ, I think I'm going to be sick.

CHAPTER 34

PRESENT DAY

SYDNEY

That was…

"Unbelievable" would be the only word to describe it. Although it doesn't seem strong enough. It feels like a new word needs to be created to encompass the last two hours spent in my bedroom. Like, I don't know… mind-blowingly…unbecredifabulous.

Except it still doesn't seem like enough.

Tom put on quite the performance. If this whole doctor thing doesn't work out for him, he has other career options, that's all I'm saying.

"Wow," he says as I snuggle in the crook of his arm. "That was incredible."

Unbecredifabulous, actually. Except I don't understand why he is acting like *I'm* the one who made it incredible. The best I could say is maybe it was both of us. Maybe we have some sort of incredible chemistry.

How is he still single? I really can't wrap my head around it.

Tom tightens his grip around my shoulders, making me feel all warm and cozy. I'm not sure if his meeting was fictional or not, but he doesn't seem like he wants to leave anymore. I almost feel like if I asked him to move in, he would eagerly agree.

"That really was amazing," I say. "I feel like I need a cigarette or something, even though I don't actually smoke."

He laughs. "I know what you mean. Honestly, the first time I saw you, I got this feeling about you. And I just knew we would be great together. You know?"

"I know. I felt the exact same way."

My phone buzzes on the nightstand, which is over on his side of the bed. A text message. Tom shifts slightly, and as he turns his head to glance down at my phone, his body tenses. Uh-oh.

"*Jake* wants to know if you got home safely from your date," he says. "So...what would you like to tell him?"

Wow. Thanks, Jake, for spoiling our postcoital bliss.

I reach for my phone, groaning at Jake's message on the screen. It's even worse than I expected:

Please let me know you got home safely tonight. And if you need me to do a background check on this guy, I'll do it. Don't trust anyone.

"That was an interesting thing to say," Tom says tonelessly. "Mind if I ask who Jake is?"

I grimace. "Remember how I said I have an ex-boyfriend who is a cop? Well, that's him."

"I thought you said you didn't talk to him anymore. And yet for some reason, you have to tell him you're safe when you get back from dates?"

"I know, I know." I sit up next to Tom in bed. He doesn't seem interested in cuddling anymore, and there is an extremely wary expression on his face. "Look, we reconnected because he's been investigating some local cases lately, and he's gotten a little paranoid. I shouldn't humor him though."

"Uh-huh."

"I'm putting a stop to it. I promise."

I tilt my phone in Tom's direction so that he can see the words I am typing on the screen:

I'm sorry, but my social life is none of your business. I don't need you to do a background check on anyone.

I send the message and then look back over at Tom. "Okay? Are we good?"

"I guess so." But his tone is still guarded. "How serious were things with that guy?"

I tuck a loose strand of hair behind my ear. "I'm not going to tell you it wasn't serious. We did live together. But it ended years ago. Like I said, I just happened to run into him recently, that's all."

"Okay…"

"Look, it's not like we're kids. I'm sure you've lived with women in the past."

He hesitates, and I'm not even sure what I want his answer to be. I don't want to hear about some super-serious relationship he had and why it went wrong. But at the same time, if he's never lived with a woman by his age, that's also a red flag.

"No," he finally says. "I haven't."

Okay. He is in his midthirties. How is it possible

he has never had a relationship serious enough for attempted cohabitation? Definitely commitment issues. "Oh."

"My career has taken a lot of time," he says somewhat defensively. "I mean, between medical school and residency, and I take calls at the hospital... I've been very focused on that."

Of course, nobody is as absorbed in his career as Jake, and still he managed to get married once, and we lived together. And it's not like Tom is an antisocial weirdo. There's something he isn't telling me. I'm sure of it.

"Have you ever been in love?" I blurt out.

He seems shocked by the question. He stares at me, his bare chest rising and falling. Finally, he says, "Yes. Once. But it was a long time ago."

"A long time ago?"

"High school." He rubs his face with his palms. "I knew her since we were kids, but we didn't start dating until high school. She was the most amazing person I had ever known. And...I genuinely thought we would get married. We were only sixteen, so in retrospect it sounds really dumb, but that's what I thought. That's what I wanted more than anything."

"So...what happened?"

"She..." He squeezes his eyes shut. "She died."

I clasp a hand over my mouth. "Oh my God. I'm so sorry."

"Yeah." He turns away. "Honestly, I really don't want to talk about it."

"It's okay," I say gently. "We don't have to talk about it."

Even though this must have happened twenty years ago, the pain on his face is raw. He obviously really loved this girl. I wonder what happened to her. An accident? Cancer? What claims the life of a sixteen-year-old girl?

At least I finally have an answer as to why Tom is still single after all these years. He's in love with a dead girl.

CHAPTER 35

BEFORE

TOM

Alison Danzinger is missing.

Daisy fills me in on most of the facts, although she's too upset to make much sense at first. Apparently, when Alison never came to breakfast this morning, her mother went upstairs to make sure she was awake, and her bed was empty.

That was about an hour ago. There's an AMBER Alert for Alison, and the police are hoping she just ran away. They say she had a minor argument with her parents last night.

"There's no way Alison would ever run away," Daisy confides in me. "She sometimes fought with her parents, but she would never want to worry them. She's not like that. She is such a sweet and good person."

"Uh-huh," I say, even though I disagree. I wonder how Daisy would feel about her best friend if she knew Alison was blackmailing me into breaking up with her.

Daisy wipes her puffy, swollen eyes. "I have this terrible feeling something really bad has happened to her."

I feel the exact same way, but I'm not going to tell her that. I'm not that sadistic. "I bet she's fine. Maybe she just went out for an early walk and her parents overreacted."

"No." Daisy shakes her head. "Alison would never go on a walk without Rufus. He goes nuts if she goes out without him. He starts barking up a storm."

You should see him around dead bodies. "I bet she'll turn up. Don't worry."

They're going to be questioning all the students again. Because it worked *so* well before. Daisy explains this to me while I try to ignore my growing uneasiness. Alison didn't run away. This isn't some kind of misunderstanding.

I part ways with Daisy after entering the school. Even though it's at the other side of the building, I head straight for Slug's locker. I manage to catch him there, tossing a couple of his books inside, looking like he doesn't have a care in the world. When he sees me, he waves. "Hey, Tom."

How does he do that? After the night we had last night, how can he pretend like nothing even happened? He doesn't even look *tired*. His acne even looks a little better.

"Hey." I clear my throat. "Did you hear that Alison is missing?"

"I did hear about that. I guess someone took care of our little problem for us, huh?"

And then he *winks* at me. I nearly choke.

"Slug," I whisper, "you didn't… I mean, last night…"

"Relax, Tom." He slams his locker closed and snaps the padlock back into place. "I didn't do anything to Alison. And neither did you, right? Sometimes things just work out in your favor. Call it luck."

Luck is when you're playing poker and you get a full

house. Luck isn't a teenage girl disappearing because she knows something about you that you'd rather she didn't know. But it's clear Slug doesn't see it the same way. And at that moment, I realize something very important.

I might be dangerous.

But Slug is something far worse.

CHAPTER 36

BEFORE

TOM

Just like after they found Brandi's body, the police call students into the principal's office one by one, searching for information that will help them locate Alison.

I am much higher up on the list this time.

When I get to the principal's office, Chief Driscoll is waiting for me there, just like last time. He's wearing a starched white dress shirt and a tie checked with several shades of brown. He has a grim expression on his broad face, and there's a deep crevice between his eyebrows. He is the chief of police in this town, and the fact that something bad happened to two girls in a short period of time doesn't look good for him. He wants to find Alison in one piece and return her to her family.

Unfortunately, that's not going to happen.

"Hello, Tom." He regards me without the slightest hint of a smile. "Please have a seat."

Like last time, I settle into one of the plastic chairs in front of the desk. Before my talk with him about Brandi,

I had never even been in the principal's office. I'm not the kind of kid who gets in trouble like that.

"I'm sure you know what this is about," he says.

"I hear Alison is…missing."

"Yes." He scratches at the stubble on his chin. "Her parents saw her go to bed last night, and then she wasn't in her bed this morning."

"So…someone broke into the house?"

He shakes his head. "No signs of that. So it looks like she opened her door for somebody she knew, or else she left the house on her own."

I can read the message between the lines. He thinks one of the students is responsible, possibly the very same one who was supposed to meet Brandi the night she was killed.

"Is there any reason you know of that Alison might have left her house in the middle of the night last night?"

I hesitate for only a split second. "No."

"Are you sure, Tom?"

Damn, why did I hesitate? I bet Slug won't hesitate when Chief Driscoll asks him the same thing. "I'm sure."

"Because I'm very worried about Alison. I'd like to find her and bring her home as soon as we can. And anything you know, no matter how unimportant you might think it is, could be the thing that helps us find her."

I spread my arms apart. "I'm sorry. I don't know anything. I didn't know Alison that well."

"Tom." The chief's shrewd eyes zero in on me. "Why are you talking about her in the past tense?"

My heart sinks into my stomach. "Oh. I, uh…I mean, I *don't* know her that well." My face feels like it's on fire. "Sorry."

"She's your lab partner. And she's Daisy's best friend."

Damn, he's done his homework. "Yeah. I mean, I knew her—*know* her. But it's not like we were friends." Oh Christ, what's wrong with me? "*Are* friends, I mean."

I am definitely not impressing him. He looks at me for a long time, then finally he laces his fingers together and leans forward. "Why aren't you friends?"

Because she hated me. Because she was threatening me and blackmailing me. "I don't know. We're different people. Different interests."

"I see." He leans back again, but there's a curious expression on his face. "So you and Alison don't get along."

"I didn't say that. I just said that we weren't friends— *aren't* friends." Against my will, the volume of my voice is going up. I clear my throat, trying to get it back to normal. "We get along just fine."

Please, please let this be over soon.

"That's not what Alison's friends told me," he says.

My heart sinks. "Oh?"

"They told me Alison hated you. That she was trying to convince Daisy to break up with you."

"I, uh…" The palms of my hands have become sweaty, and I rub them on my jeans. "I didn't know that."

"No?"

My mouth is too dry to get out any words, so I can only shake my head. Still, this isn't that big a deal, is it? Yes, Alison hated me. But that's not proof that I killed her.

"One more question," he says. "Where were you last night?"

He's asking for an alibi. That's not good. "I was home."

"The whole night?"

"Yes."

"With your parents?"

"My mom is in Seattle visiting my aunt and uncle," I say. "So it was just my dad."

"Okay," he says thoughtfully. "I'll have to give your father a call then."

"Sure." Good luck with that. "Anything else?"

"Yes," he says. "You don't need to walk Daisy home from school anymore. I'm going to be picking her up myself."

His message is loud and clear. He doesn't trust me around his daughter anymore. To be fair, I doubt he trusts anyone, but definitely not me.

CHAPTER 37

Tom and I are on date number six.

We are meeting in Chinatown, close to my absolute favorite dim sum restaurant, where I only got food poisoning one time. I've been dying to take him here, but he's proven himself to be a bit of a workaholic, so we've been scheduling our dates around his work shifts. But the dim sum restaurant stops bringing around carts at three, so he told me he'd take a taxi here right from work. When he said that, I got a little nervous, considering what he does for a living, but he promised he would shower before meeting me.

While I'm waiting on the corner, my stomach rumbling slightly at the aroma of stir-fried noodles that seems to permeate the street, my phone starts ringing. I fish it out of my purse. My mother's name is on the screen. I check the time—I have a few minutes until Tom is supposed to be here, so I take the call. Maybe it will distract my rumbling stomach.

"What's going on, Mom?" I ask.

"I just heard fantastic news," she says breathlessly.

"Oh?"

"Yes! My cousin's daughter Jackie just had twins at forty-two years old!"

My mother's good news is becoming increasingly insulting. "Wow. Great."

"At forty-two! Twins! That could be you, Sydney."

I shift my phone to my other ear, looking down the street to make sure Tom isn't coming toward me. "I'm not really worrying about that right now, Mom."

"Well, why not?" she huffs. "You're in your midthirties and you're single!"

Am I in my midthirties? I'm thirty-four. Doesn't that count as *early* thirties? I mean, I'm younger than thirty-five, so that's still early thirties, right?

"And you're not even seeing anyone," she continues.

I haven't told her about my five dates with Tom, mostly because I don't want her getting overly excited or pushing me for details. But it's almost worse when she's complaining about me being alone.

"Actually," I say, "I *am* sort of seeing someone."

"You are?" she gasps, as if I've told her something extremely shocking. "Who?"

"Nobody you know."

"Well, what's his name?"

"Tom."

"Tom short for Thomas?"

"I guess so."

"What's his last name?"

"Brown." Unsurprisingly, Tom was very difficult to google.

215

"And what does he do?"

Of course, that would be the first thing she would want to know after his name. "He's a doctor."

She doesn't need to know what kind of doctor he is. Sometimes I wish I didn't know.

"Oh wow!" She sounds delighted now. "That's great!"

I lift my eyes from my phone and discover that Tom is climbing out of a taxi midway down the block. He stops for a moment on his way over to me to hand a few dollar bills to a homeless man sitting on the street, which is something he does more than anyone else I have ever met. Our eyes meet, and he waves at me. "And also, he's coming this way, so I'm going to go."

"Can I say hello?"

"Absolutely *not*. Goodbye, Mom."

I manage to hang up just as Tom gets within earshot. He's changed out of whatever he was wearing to the hospital, and his hair looks damp, like he recently showered. Good. I definitely don't want to smell dead body on him.

Because we are now on date number six, he feels very comfortable leaning in for a kiss. And as always, it's enough to make my legs go weak. Eventually, I'm sure that giddiness will go away, but I'm enjoying it while it lasts.

"Hello there," he breathes in my ear. "I hope I'm not too late."

"Only a few minutes."

I lead him down the crowded block, and for a moment, I wonder if he'll take my hand. But he doesn't. Tom isn't a hand-holder, which is fine. Jake wasn't either.

We pass one of the fish markets that are present on nearly every block, then a store selling various tchotchkes and souvenirs. Tom must not have been to Chinatown in a while, because he seems intrigued by the items they're selling, even though I'm more focused on getting to dim sum before the cutoff.

"Hey," he says, "do you want me to buy you a decorative fan?"

"Thanks, but I'll pass."

"How about a miniature turtle?"

Sure enough, there's a tub filled with baby turtles no longer than my pinkie finger. They are actually pretty adorable. Do turtles make good pets? I have no idea, but I suspect a turtle purchased off the street is probably teeming with turtle bacteria. "No, thank you."

"How about some illegal fireworks? I bet they have some."

I roll my eyes at him. "Great. Just what I need, to blow a few fingers off."

"When I was an intern, I had a patient come in after a firecracker exploded in his hand," he says. "We had to amputate his first and second metacarpals. They let me scrub in. It was really cool."

His eyes are lit up the way they always are whenever he talks about anything medical. "Oh, please, tell me more," I say.

"Well, the burns were extensive, involving the entire palmar aspect of the—" He stops talking when he sees the look on my face. "You were being sarcastic."

"Obviously."

Despite all my experience with blood, the thought of a person getting their fingers chopped off turns my stomach, and I certainly don't want to hear about it when we're about to eat. But Tom looks so crestfallen that he can't tell me all about the hand ravaged by a firecracker. He's quiet the entire rest of the way down the block.

But by the time we get to the dim sum restaurant, he seems to have cheered up. When I show him the door, he jumps in front of me to open it first, holding it for me like he always does. That is definitely not an act on his part. He really is a gentleman. What can I say—he's perfect. Well, except for his job. "After you," he says.

As we're walking inside the restaurant, we pass two elderly women who are on their way out. One of them does a double take when she sees Tom. "Dr. Brewer?" she says.

He blinks at her. "Yes?"

"Dr. Brewer!" She's a small, round woman with close-cropped gray hair and comically oversize glasses. "I thought that was you! My name is Velma Stewart. I'm a patient of yours." Tom looks at her in astonishment, and she adds, "I mean, my husband was. He passed, and you did his autopsy a few months ago."

"Oh!" Recognition fills his eyes. "Yes. Yes, of course. How are you, Mrs. Stewart?"

"Better now." Her eyes become misty for a moment. "I just wanted to thank you for coming to talk to me. You told me that Harvey died quickly and in his sleep and that he didn't suffer. That gave me so much peace. And then you let me ramble on telling you stories about him for about an hour even though I'm sure you were extremely busy."

His cheeks color. "Oh, I didn't mind."

"You are such a good listener," she says. "You were so kind to me. It was one of the worst times of my life, and it really helped that you were there to listen. Bless you, Dr. Brewer."

Tom looks embarrassed, but he's smiling. "I'm glad I could help."

The old woman sets her gaze on me. "You have a good one there, young lady." She looks back over at Tom. "And he's so handsome too!"

Well, I knew that part.

The woman thanks Tom about five more times, then she ambles out of the restaurant, leaving the two of us to have our dim sum lunch together. I can tell he really enjoyed that interaction, and he's still smiling when we sit down in our booth.

"That was nice," he says. "I don't get to interact with patients too often. Obviously. Sometimes I really miss it."

"Did you always know you wanted to be a pathologist?"

"Actually, when I was younger, I wanted to become a surgeon."

I can imagine that. He's so smart and knowledgeable, and I have noticed he's very good with his hands. He would have been a great surgeon, I bet. "Why didn't you?"

"Uh…" He rakes a hand through his black hair. "I guess I just… I don't know. Turned out it wasn't for me."

I glance over my shoulder at the door—the old woman is long gone. "Why did she keep calling you Dr. Brewer? I wasn't sure if I should correct her."

Tom hesitates for a split second. "My last name is Brewer."

What? "You told me your last name is Brown!"

"No, it's Brewer."

"You definitely said Brown!"

I remember it well, mostly because I was thinking at the time that Tom Brown was an impossible name to google because there would be so many hits. And sure enough, my search turned up nothing, even when I added "MD," "New York," and "pathologist." Not that Tom Brewer would be much better.

Tom lifts a shoulder. "Sorry, you must've heard me wrong. I'm one hundred percent sure my last name is Brewer. I can show you my driver's license if you want."

I'm not sure what to make of this. I was certain he said Brown, but we were in a loud coffee shop, and my nose was gushing blood, so I admit it's possible I might not have heard him correctly.

He leans in close and smiles so I can see his white teeth. "Do you still like me even though I'm Tom Brewer, not Tom Brown?"

"I suppose."

"Good." He gets up from his seat, brushing his palms on his blue jeans. "And now I'm going to go wash my hands in the bathroom, because I was just in a taxi. Grab me some shrimp shumai if they come by with it."

Excellent. Now I have a chance to google him since I know his real name.

As soon as Tom disappears into the bathroom, I whip out my phone. I'm not messing around, so I punch into the screen "Thomas Brewer MD pathologist."

Right away, I get a hit. I click on it and…

Okay, that's interesting.

CHAPTER 38

The one hit for Thomas Brewer is on the website for Mount Sinai Hospital. When I click on it, there's a recent photo of him, followed by a small bio. He looks incredibly handsome in the photo, dressed in a crisp white coat, his dark eyes staring into the camera. His bio mentions an undergraduate education at Cornell University followed by medical school and a residency at the University of Pennsylvania. Impressive. But one thing stands out to me.

I'm fairly sure Tom told me he was working at NYU.

NYU and Mount Sinai are nowhere near each other. When he mentioned it to me, I remember thinking that his hospital was fairly close to my apartment. I would not have thought that if he'd said Mount Sinai.

What the hell?

I return to the search, scrolling to find other hits. There's nothing else. He doesn't have a Facebook profile. I don't see him on Instagram or Twitter, at least under his real name. And when I search on Cynch, I can't find an active or inactive profile.

By the time Tom gets back from the bathroom, I am thoroughly confused. He slides into the booth across from me and grabs the menu.

"Let's get some food," he says. "I'm starving."

At that moment, a waitress comes by with a cart teeming with plates of food. Tom—always an adventurous eater—grabs a plate of chicken feet. I stick with the pork dumplings. But while Tom eagerly digs into his food, I just stare at my dumplings, my appetite gone.

"Hey," I say as casually as I can, "what hospital did you say you worked at?"

This time, there's no hesitation. "Mount Sinai."

"I could have sworn you told me you worked at NYU."

He arches an eyebrow at me, an amused smile playing on his lips. "Were you looking me up on your phone while I was in the bathroom?"

Busted. Although part of me feels that he is more busted than I am. "So what if I was? You definitely told me you work at NYU."

"I used to work at NYU," he says. "I recently switched over. Maybe I was so enamored with you that I misspoke."

Is that possible? I suppose it is. But the whole thing, combined with the wrong name, leaves me feeling slightly uneasy. I could accept that one was a mistake, but both?

Then again, I can't forget that the only reason this is happening in the first place is because a woman came up to Tom to gush about how compassionate he was when she was suffering from the loss of her husband. And I believe it. I've dated a lot of guys, and I can tell that Tom is a nice guy. It's hard to believe that he really would have lied to me.

"How come you don't have a Cynch profile?" I ask.

A smile plays on his lips. "Is this a trick question? You and I are dating, right? Do you *want* me to have a Cynch profile?"

"No," I say. "I just mean most single people in the city are on that app."

"I'm just not into dating apps."

"Then how do you meet women?"

He grins at me. "Mostly I just look around for girls having nosebleeds and offer to buy them a new shirt. Usually works."

"Ha ha, very funny."

He arches an eyebrow. "But if it bothers you, I'm happy to put up a profile on all the dating apps."

Now he's being a smart-ass, which I suppose is fair given my line of questioning. "No, thank you."

"Or"—he reaches across the table for my hand—"maybe you can delete your profile too, and we can just see each other. How about that?"

I suck in a breath. Even though things have been getting more serious with Tom, I'm still surprised to hear him say that, especially given his relative lack of previous relationship experience. I'm surprised but not unhappy. Just the opposite, in fact. Maybe he's finally ready to forget that dead girl from high school.

"That sounds very nice," I say.

And just like that, I have a boyfriend.

CHAPTER 39

TWO MONTHS LATER

SYDNEY

Tom drinks his coffee with half a packet of sugar.

He always prepares it the same way. When the waitress brings him his coffee, he picks up the sugar packet, pinches it in the middle, and then empties exactly half of it into his coffee. If it's not enough, he will tip the packet to get a few more grains of sugar into the black liquid. It's practically scientific the way he always does it.

When you've been dating someone for two months, you start to notice these things about them. It's when the cracks start to show.

"What would happen if you accidentally drank a coffee with an *entire* pack of sugar?" I ask as I watch him go through his ritual. It's Sunday afternoon, and we're having a lazy brunch together at a diner.

"Well, I would die, obviously." Tom grins at me. "And what about you? What would happen if you didn't drown your coffee in, like, half a cup of cream?"

"Hey, it's not that much."

"It isn't? Look at your cup. You're basically drinking cream with just a tiny bit of coffee in it."

Okay, he isn't entirely wrong. So we both have our quirks. But in general, most of his quirks are very tolerable. He's been to my apartment many times, and he never leaves the toilet seat up or pisses on the seat or uses half the toilet paper in one shot, and he's just generally pretty good about the toilet, which is kind of where a lot of guys go wrong.

He's got plenty of other good qualities, besides his superior toilet habits. He's generous—he always pays for everything when we're together, and whenever they ask in a store if he wants to round up for charity, he always says yes. He likes the same kind of movies as I do, or at least he's pretending to. He can be laugh-out-loud funny sometimes. And if I end up with one of my epic bleeding episodes, whether from my nose or a finger or God knows what, he doesn't get freaked out, which is a bit of a miracle after other guys.

He's also spectacular in bed. I stand by my initial assessment of unbecredifabulous.

Not that it's all great. Like Jake, he is a workaholic. He's at the hospital a lot, including weekends. And the worst part is thinking about what he does when he's there. He's *cutting up dead bodies*. Sometimes he will come see me at my apartment me after work, and I can't help but think about it as he's kissing me. Even more disturbing is the fact that he *feels like* kissing me after what he's been doing all day.

But I guess he's been doing it so long it's become normal to him. It probably doesn't bother him at all.

While I'm finishing off the last of my French toast, a

little boy runs past our table, his parents close behind. The boy is maybe three years old and pretty darn adorable. He's wearing a set of overalls, and his hair is blond and curly. Tom watches the progress of the kid, a slightly tender expression on his face.

"Cute kid," I comment.

He nods, and for a moment, there is something sad in his expression. "Yeah," he finally says.

It's weird, because there are moments when Tom seems terrified of any sort of commitment, and yet there are other times when we come across a family being cute together—like now—and I can see the longing in his eyes.

I have gently broached the idea of children, just to see where he stands on it. I'm very clear that I am not expecting him to impregnate me in the near future, just trying to get his general thoughts on the idea of fatherhood. But he has been remarkably evasive.

Tom reaches for my hand across the table. He smiles at me, tracing the blue veins on the back of my hand with his thumb. It's something he does a lot. I wonder what he's thinking. He looks like he wants to say something but isn't sure if he should.

"Do you know why veins are blue?" he asks.

Okay, that definitely wasn't what I expected him to say. "Is it because the blood in veins doesn't have oxygen in them?"

"Common misconception." He presses his thumb into a vein running over the back of my hand until it compresses. "But untrue. Deoxygenated blood is still red, although darker. The reason veins are blue is because skin absorbs blue light. The subcutaneous fat will only allow blue light to penetrate to the veins, so this is what you see reflected back by your retina."

Tom is always full of "interesting" facts like that. On one of our dates, he gave me a spontaneous lecture about von Willebrand factor. He seemed a bit embarrassed after, but I thought it was sort of sweet that he bothered to learn about my disorder.

I mean, he must have read up about it. There's no way he could have known all that off the top of his head.

"So," I say, "any interest in seeing a movie this afternoon?"

"Actually, I can't."

"Working?"

He shakes his head. "My mother is driving in this morning, and I'm going to see her. She's coming over to my place, then we're going to have dinner."

Considering his father is out of the picture, he seems to have a healthy enough relationship with his mother. "Do you want me to come?"

He yanks his hand away from mine, no longer interested in my veins or why they look blue. He looks like he's about to spit out the coffee he just drank. "To dinner with *my mother*?"

Well, that answers that question, doesn't it? "You don't have to say it like I suggested you drink poison."

"We've only been dating for a few months, Sydney."

My cheeks burn. I have completely lost my appetite for the rest of the French toast. "Right. I get it."

"A few months isn't very long."

"I said *I get it*."

Tom toys with his napkin, obviously trying to figure out a way to make this right. It's not the first time I've gotten a reaction like this out of him. When I suggested a double date with Gretchen and Randy, he looked like he was about to pop an aneurysm. Granted, he's right—we've only been dating a few months. But at the same time, I wish he didn't look quite so horrified when I suggest things like this.

"Maybe next time," he mumbles.

Yeah, right. But what can I do? I can either dump the guy because he has commitment issues, or I can hope that things change and continue enjoying incredible sex.

"So what are you doing with your mom then?" I ask.

He rubs his chin. "I thought I might take her to that Middle Eastern restaurant you dragged me to a couple of weeks ago. That was really good. What was it called again?"

"Uh, let me check."

Tom takes another drink of his coffee while I scroll on my phone, trying to figure out the name of the place we went to. Gretchen recommended it, so I have to scroll through our text messages. While I'm doing this, our waitress comes over and flirts shamelessly with Tom. To his credit, he just smiles politely back. He's charming but not a flirt, which I appreciate.

Finally, I find the link to the restaurant's name and address. I copy the link and text it to Tom.

"I sent you the link," I tell him.

I look over at his phone, which he placed on the table at some point during the meal, waiting for it to buzz with a text. But it stays silent.

"That's weird," I say. "Did you get my text with the name of the restaurant?"

"Uh…" He looks down at the screen of his phone, which is black. "Yeah, I think so."

"How do you know that? You didn't even touch your phone, and the screen is black."

"Well, the phone is on silent."

"No, it's not. It just buzzed ten minutes ago."

"I don't know." Tom grabs his phone and shoves it in his pocket. "I'm sure I got your text. Anyway, do you really want me looking at my phone while we're eating together?"

"You're constantly looking at your phone while we're eating!"

"Well, I get texts from work. I have to see if they're important."

I don't know why Tom is being difficult right now. I'm not asking him to fly around the earth backward. I just want him to look down at his phone so that he can confirm he got my message. It would take all of half a second.

"Why are you being weird about this?" I narrow my eyes at him. "Why can't you tell me if you got my text or not."

"Jesus. Fine." He takes the phone out of his pocket and taps on the screen. "I got your text. Okay?"

"So what's the name of the restaurant?"

Tom looks down at the screen, then up at my face. He lets out a long sigh. "Fine. I didn't get the text message."

Okay, I am utterly confused. Why is he lying about this? It doesn't make any sense. "So should I send it again?"

His jaw tightens. "Send it later."

But I'm not listening to him. I send the text message a second time and look up at him. "Did you get it?"

"I…my phone is broken. Don't worry about it. My mom likes Italian food better anyway."

He is squirming in his seat. He looks so uncomfortable. What the hell is going on?

"Send me a text message," I say.

"What? Why?"

"Why *don't* you want to send me a text message?"

Tom finally puts down his phone on the table. "Look," he says, "this is my work phone. That's why I don't get your text messages on it."

"Your *work* phone?" I look down at his iPhone, which looks like the standard one that everybody I know owns. It seems to be the one he always carries. "So where is your personal phone?"

"I don't have it with me. It's at home."

"So you carry your work phone but not your personal phone?"

He shrugs. "I guess. Like I said, I need to make sure there are no emergencies at work."

"What kind of emergencies? Your patients are already dead!"

He shoves his phone back in his pocket. "Look, you asked me a question, and I gave you the answer. I don't know what you want from me."

What do I want? I want to know why the number I have for him is clearly not his main phone number. Because I don't believe that the phone he carries around all the time is not his personal phone. That was a bullshit excuse if I have ever heard one.

But there's no point in insisting on an answer. One thing is very clear—Tom is not willing to tell me the truth.

CHAPTER 40

BEFORE

TOM

Almost as soon as I get home from school, I get another call from my mother.

Again, I hesitate before picking it up. She's probably heard about Alison's disappearance, and she's not going to be thrilled to hear my father is nowhere to be found. She's not getting back till tomorrow, and I don't want her to panic.

Still, I have to answer the phone. Given everything that's going on, if I don't answer, she'll probably have the police at my door within the hour. I have to pretend like everything is completely fine. This will have to be an Academy Award–winning performance.

"Hi, Mom," I say, trying to sound as normal as I possibly can.

"Tommy!" Her voice crackles on the other line. "I've been so worried about you! I heard on the news about that missing girl. Isn't that Daisy's friend?"

"I guess," I say. "I didn't know her very well."

Why can't I stop talking about her in the past tense, for Christ's sake?

My mother doesn't seem to notice though. "It's so terrifying," she goes on. "Especially after that other girl turned up dead. Have you heard anything about what might have happened to her?"

"No," I say, even though I actually could give her a very informative answer.

"Anyway," she says, "are you okay?"

"Fine."

"Where's your father?"

I knew the question was coming, and yet I still don't have a great answer. "He went to work."

"Actually, I decided to call him at work after all, and they said he never showed up this morning." She pauses. "Is he asleep upstairs? You don't need to cover for him."

"I, um…" If I tell her he's asleep upstairs, she might ask me to wake him up. I can't risk it. "He just left. He said he was going to O'Toole's."

I know from experience that nobody ever picks up the phone at the bar. The lie feels safe.

"Okay."

My mother lets out a long breath. She sounds so worried, and I almost feel sorry for her, except I don't. Her life is going to change for the better because of what I did to that man. Both of our lives are going to change for the better.

Well, as long as I don't get caught.

"I'll be home tomorrow," she says. "Just…be careful, sweetheart."

"I will, Mom."

"It feels like there's something very evil out there.

232

Just stay home and don't let anybody in the house besides your father."

So…nobody then.

Tomorrow my mother will be home, and I'll have to try to convince her that we shouldn't call the police on my father. It won't be difficult. She hates calling the police about my father's antics, because it makes us look like trash. But it certainly wouldn't be the first time someone called the cops on my father. He has a reputation in our small town for being an asshole when he's drunk.

As for Alison though, that's a completely different problem. I just have to hope for the best.

CHAPTER 41

BEFORE

TOM

We didn't get any homework at school today because Alison's disappearance was such a distraction, so I've spent the majority of the afternoon and evening watching the local news. I tried watching a few sitcoms, but I couldn't focus and eventually went back to the news.

It's mostly the same story again and again. Seventeen-year-old Alison Danzinger was discovered to be missing from her home this morning. The police are searching for her and following up several promising leads. No persons of interest have yet been identified in her disappearance.

At some point, I force myself to eat dinner—a bag of Doritos washed down with a bottle of Sprite. Somewhere between opening the bag and scraping the bottom, I drift off on the sofa. I wouldn't have thought it was possible, but I spent most of the last thirty-six hours awake.

I am jarred back into consciousness by the sound of my cell phone ringing. I locate it in the folds of the sofa, and my heart leaps at Daisy's name on the screen. I haven't spoken to Daisy since she sobbed in my arms this morning.

"Tom…" She's crying when I answer the phone, as if she never stopped after this morning. "Oh, Tom."

"What? What's going on?" I'm half scared she's going to tell me that her father is on his way here to arrest me.

"They found Alison."

For a split second, this strikes me as a *good* thing. Alison just ran away, and now she's been found. And maybe my dad really is at the bar right now.

Except if it's a good thing, how come Daisy is crying so hard?

"They just pulled her body out of the river." Her sobs become almost hysterical. "Tom…"

The river. That's where Slug wanted to throw my father's body initially. It's his favorite spot.

Daisy is crying too hard to give me any more details. I haven't seen anything on the news, so I assume Daisy must've heard from her father.

I wonder what else he said to her.

"She was mutilated," Daisy manages. "I heard my father talking about it on the phone. He said she… It looks like she was *tortured*."

Like Brandi.

I get a terrible sinking feeling in my stomach as I remember how Slug's name got called when they were interviewing students for a second time about what happened to Brandi. I had thought he barely knew her, but obviously, I was wrong.

What did I unleash?

I hear loud voices in the background on the other end of the line, and Daisy's voice becomes hushed. "I better go. My father doesn't want me talking to you."

Even though I suspected it, that one is a jab in the chest. "He doesn't?"

"I'm sorry. It's not you. He just doesn't trust any kids at the high school right now."

It's a relief to hear that I'm not a primary suspect. Although why would I be? All he knows is that Alison and I didn't get along. Yes, I am the mystery "boyfriend" who was meeting Brandi the night she was killed, but as far as I know, the chief isn't aware of that. The only other person who knew is Alison, and she's gone.

Before I can say anything else, there's another loud voice in the background. "I have to go, Tom. I'll talk to you later."

"I love you, Daisy," I say into the phone, but she's already hung up.

CHAPTER 42

BEFORE

TOM

By the next morning, there's no shortage of news coverage about Alison Danzinger. I've seen the footage of the river where Alison's body was found no less than five million times. I keep watching it again and again and again.

School gets called off, so it's just me in the house, alone, obsessively watching the news. I want to give Slug a call or send him a text, but I'm scared someone is monitoring our phone lines or something like that. Anyway, the only person I *really* want to talk to is Daisy.

My mother walks in the door at about four o'clock, a large duffel bag hung on her shoulder. I jump off the couch to help her carry it inside, but she's much more interested in hugging me, so I drop the bag.

"Oh, Tommy." She squeezes me much too tightly. But unlike my father, my mother's much smaller than I am and couldn't hurt me even if she wanted to. "I was so worried about you!"

"I'm fine."

"But that girl…" My mother pulls away from me. "They found her dead, didn't they?"

"Yes. They did." And now I can talk about her in the past tense all I want.

She's quiet for a moment, pressing her lips together.

I take the opportunity to grab her bag again. "I'll take this upstairs for you."

Before she can protest, I hurry upstairs with the duffel bag on my shoulder. I bring it to my parents' bedroom and leave it on the bed. My father hasn't slept here for the last two nights, but he never bothers to make the bed, so the sheets are still in disarray from two days ago. It looks like he could have slept here last night. Nobody can prove otherwise.

When I get downstairs, my mother is standing in the living room, wringing her hands together. "Tom, where is your father?"

Great. She's barely stepped in the door and already she's started in about this. I thought maybe I'd have at least until dinner. "At work, I guess."

"I called the store. He didn't come in again today."

I lift a shoulder. "I don't know then."

"Did you see him this morning?"

"Yes."

She chews on her lower lip. "You know, his car is in the garage. I was going to pull mine in, but his is already there."

"I guess he walked wherever he went."

As if my father ever walked anywhere. He never passed up an opportunity to drive drunk. But he's got plenty of friends who could have driven him somewhere.

I knew the car would make my mother suspicious. But it would be worse to abandon it somewhere on the side of the road, where the police could easily discover it.

She frowns. "But you saw him this morning?"

"You asked me that. I told you I did."

She drops her eyes. She seems to be looking at something. I'm driven nuts trying to work out what when suddenly she blurts out, "What happened to my rug?"

Oh Christ, the missing rug. I forgot about that. "I spilled cranberry juice all over it, and it got stained, so I threw it out."

"You threw it out?" Her eyes widen. "Tom, you shouldn't have done that! I could have gotten it cleaned."

"I'm sorry. It was a really bad stain, and I figured there was nothing we could do."

"Is it still out by the curb then or…"

"Sorry, the garbageman took it to the dump. It's too late."

"Oh, Tom," she sighs. "I wish you hadn't done that. I really loved that rug. I know it was a little ragged and it snagged our feet, but I've had it for a long time, and I was attached to it."

Somehow, I imagine a similar conversation would take place between the two of us if I told her what really happened to my father.

"Anyway…" She looks down at her watch. "I'm going to lie down for an hour or so, then I'll get started on dinner. Do you think your father will be home in time to eat with us?"

"He said he probably wouldn't."

She doesn't look surprised. "Okay, just the two of us then."

She trudges up the stairs to the bedroom, her shoulders sagging. I watch her go all the way up, and I wait for the sound of the bedroom door closing before I turn on the television to watch the news one more time.

CHAPTER 43

PRESENT DAY

SYDNEY

Okay, I agree. That phone thing is super weird."

Since Tom blew me off to spend time with his mother without me, I went over to Gretchen and Randy's apartment. Randy is off running errands, but Gretchen was willing to listen to the entire story about Tom's phone not taking my calls. And she looks properly perplexed.

"What do you think it means?" Gretchen asks as she stuffs a handful of popcorn into her mouth. Gretchen is the kind of person who always feels like she needs to make a snack when I come over, which is kind of sweet.

I lift a shoulder. "I mean, it's not *good* that my boyfriend is apparently calling me and texting me from a secret phone."

"He could be telling you the truth. You said he's a workaholic, so it makes sense he wants his work phone with him. And he doesn't have a purse like we do to carry multiple phones."

"Yeah." I grab some popcorn, which Gretchen has

placed in a wooden bowl on the coffee table. "I wouldn't make that big a deal out of it, but he got so uncomfortable when I started asking him about it. It really seemed like he was hiding something."

"So what do you think he's hiding?" Her eyes widen. "Do you think he could be married?"

"I really, really don't think so. I've seen his apartment. There's no woman living there. Plus, he doesn't seem worried about being seen in public."

Although…

Whenever we go out to eat, we always go to a different restaurant. *Always*. Jake and I had a diner we went to nearly every weekend, but Tom seems very resistant to having a "regular" place.

"So…what then?"

I don't know what to think. I genuinely don't think there's another woman in the picture, but the fact that Tom only carries around his work phone is a decidedly bad sign. It means he's even more of a workaholic than I suspected. That's the kind of thing Jake would do. And we all know how wonderfully that worked out.

And I don't want things to fall apart with Tom the way they did with Jake. He's such a good guy. He's sweet, he's intelligent, he loves his mother, and also, he is *very* easy on the eyes.

Oh my God, I'm really falling for him.

"Let's have dinner together," Gretchen suggests. "I'm an excellent judge of character. I'll tell you in two seconds if he's two-timing you."

"Sorry, he won't do that."

"Why not?"

"You should have seen his face when I suggested

meeting my friends. I told you—he has commitment issues." I make a face. "He's still hung up on this girl he was in love with in high school."

"Oh my God!" Gretchen covers her mouth. "In high school? Seriously?"

"I know, but it sounds like he wanted to marry her, and then she died or something. He looked so sad when he was talking about her."

"Aw, that's sweet though."

I lean back against the cushions of the sofa, my head spinning. I don't know what to do. I really am starting to fall for Tom, but at the same time, the number of red flags has become almost unacceptable. I could deal with his unwillingness to meet my friends, but this phone thing is really bugging me.

Maybe I should have Jake do a background check on him.

Of course, that would be completely humiliating. I don't want to tell my old boyfriend that the guy I've replaced him with is so untrustworthy that he requires a background check if I'm to proceed with our relationship. I'd rather Jake think that I am dating an amazing guy and that he missed out because he couldn't make time for me.

Besides, Jake has his hands full. I haven't seen anything in the papers about an arrest for Bonnie's murder or for those other two women either. If they arrested anyone, I would definitely know about it.

"By the way," Gretchen says, "my exhibit at the museum is going to be closing soon. I want you to come by and see it before it's gone!"

I laugh. "I already saw it!"

"I know," she admits, "but I want my friends to be

there one more time before they take it all down! I worked so hard on it!"

"I know you did. That was all you could talk about for months." It used to really bother Bonnie how much Gretchen talked about it, but I don't mention that. There's no point in tainting Gretchen's memories of Bonnie by cluing her in that her friend sometimes found her very irritating.

"It consumed me," she admits. "Even the night before, I was at the museum half the night working on it!"

I frown. Something about Gretchen's statement tugs at me. But I can't quite put my finger on what it is, and before I can figure it out, a key turns in the lock to the front door, and Gretchen's eyes light up. "Randy is back! I wonder what he got."

"What was he getting, exactly?" I say.

"One of the tenants gave him a gift card for some extra work he did," Gretchen explains. "So he took it to a department store in Herald Square. He said he was going to buy something to christen the apartment now that I've moved in. Isn't that sweet?"

"Like a painting?"

"I have no idea. But Randy has such great taste, so I'm sure it's something good."

Randy has great taste? I glance around their bare-bones apartment, which looks only slightly different from the way it did when it was his bachelor pad. And the guy only wears jeans and T-shirts, sometimes a hoodie. What exactly is she basing her "great taste" assessment on? But whatever. Gretchen is in love, and she thinks Randy is perfect.

Randy bursts into the apartment, and he's holding something large—at least two feet wide—in his arms. I'm not entirely sure what it is though. It looks like…a glass structure filled with dirt. From Gretchen's expression, I can tell she is equally perplexed. She climbs to her feet, her hands on her hips.

"What *is* that?" she asks.

"It's an ant farm!" Randy says proudly.

"A *what*?"

It would be an understatement to say that Gretchen does not look thrilled. In fact, she looks like she wants to punch Randy in the face, except that he might drop the ant farm and break it open.

"It's an ant farm," Randy repeats. "I thought we could put it over there by the window. That way, we'll be able to see everything happening on the farm."

"Oh no!" Gretchen jumps in front of him, as if to block him from entering the room with his glass container filled with ants. "I don't want that thing in my apartment. No way."

"Why not?" His forehead scrunches up. "It's so cool."

"No, it's not!" she cries. "What if the ants get free?"

"The ants won't get free."

"The ants will *definitely* get free!" Gretchen throws up her arms and looks over at me. "Sydney, help me out here."

"An ant farm is pretty gross, Randy," I say.

He lowers the ant farm onto the floor, and Gretchen instinctively takes a few steps back. "Well, I don't know what you want me to do, Gretchen. I can't return it. Am I supposed to throw them away?"

"I don't care what you do with them!" she cries. "You can flush them down the toilet for all I care!"

Randy's face darkens. "I'm not doing that. That's *horrible*."

Gretchen is really freaked out about those ants. I don't blame her. I wouldn't want them in my house either. Her face has turned all pink, and now I feel like a bad argument is brewing.

"I better go, Gretchen," I say. "But…um…good luck."

As I hurry out of Gretchen and Randy's apartment, something is still tugging at me. Something Gretchen said. But I can't quite put my finger on what it is.

I'll figure it out eventually.

CHAPTER 44

I end up ordering in Chinese food for dinner.

I order way too much. I always get way too much when I order Chinese food, but it's not like I can get a delivery guy to come over here to bring me one measly container of chicken with broccoli. So I end up ordering three or four dishes, figuring I'll eat it eventually, and then it all sits in the refrigerator until it starts to smell bad and I have to throw it all away... And then a week later, I'm craving Chinese food and I go through the entire cycle again. I call it the Circle of Chinese Food.

While I am eating my beef chow fun, debating if I should take a Tums now or after the meal is over, I consider sending Tom a text message. We left things a bit frosty after he refused to let me meet his mother and got all evasive about his phone. Of course, if I do send him a text message, God knows where it will go.

No, let him have a night to stew and decide whether

he wants to tell me the truth. Anyway, I've got other things on my mind.

Namely, my conversation with Gretchen. I keep going over what we were talking about, and something keeps tugging at me. But what is it?

Even the night before, I was at the museum half the night working.

It's hard to forget the day Gretchen's exhibit opened. It was the same day that Randy and I found Bonnie mutilated in her bedroom. Bonnie and I had made plans to go together to see it. Naturally, that ended up not happening.

Even the night before, I was at the museum half the night working.

When I was talking to Jake about possible suspects, I mentioned Randy. I didn't want to incriminate him, but I felt compelled to point out the fact that he had a copy of the keys for the entire building and that Bonnie repeatedly complained that she thought he was creepy. It wasn't evidence that he was a murderer, but Jake told me he had been ruled out.

Mr. Muncy has an alibi for last night. His girlfriend was with him the entire time.

Except Gretchen, his girlfriend, was *not* with him the entire night. She was at the museum half the night working on her exhibit.

Holy crap.

I snatch up my phone and select Gretchen's number from my list of contacts. The phone rings a few times before she picks up. "What's up, Syd?"

"Gretchen," I say. "Where were you really on the night that Bonnie was murdered?"

There's a long pause on the other end of the line. "What?"

"When I was at your apartment earlier," I say, "you told me that the night before your exhibit opened, you were at the museum half the night working on it. But you told the police you were with Randy the whole night. Except you weren't."

Another extended silence. "Right. Well, I must've made a mistake. I was home the night before the exhibit opened. It was the night before *that* when I was at the museum half the night."

"Gretchen..."

"It's true!"

I grind my teeth. "Please stop. I know what you said. And I remember when the exhibit opened."

"Sydney..."

"*Tell me the truth.*"

Gretchen's voice breaks. "Fine. I was at the museum. I lied to the police. Is that what you want to hear?"

"Oh my God!" I exclaim. "You lied to the police? Seriously?"

"What was I supposed to do?" she whimpers. "Look, Randy didn't hurt Bonnie. He never could have done something like that. But if he didn't have an alibi, they would have been all over him! He's the super, and he has the keys and also..."

"And also what?"

Gretchen is silent.

"Gretchen, what is it? What's going on?"

"This is going to sound worse than it is," she says softly.

I frown. "What is?"

"A number of years ago," she says, "like *way* before

248

Randy and I even met, there was this girl who accused him of stalking her."

My mouth falls open. "*What?*"

"And then there was this assault charge too, but it was *so* unfair," she goes on. "He told me all about it, and seriously, he didn't do anything wrong! But with that in his record, we both thought it would be better if he had an alibi."

We both thought it would be better. "Gretchen," I say, "did Randy *ask* you to lie for him?"

"No!" she cries. "I mean, it was his suggestion, but I *completely* agreed. He didn't push me into anything!"

This is just great. "You have to go to the police and tell them the truth."

"*No.* Please don't make me, Syd." If she wasn't crying before, I have definitely pushed her over the edge. "Randy is not a murderer. He's *not.* You don't really think he could have done those terrible things to Bonnie, do you?"

"I don't know."

"He didn't!" she sobs. "I love him, Sydney. I've never felt this way about a man before. I want to spend the rest of my life with him."

My stomach turns slightly at the idea of Gretchen marrying Randy Muncy. I've known him for two years, and he might be a little quirky, but I am having trouble imagining him doing all those terrible things to Bonnie, and Gretchen clearly loves him with all her heart. Still, there is something about him that makes me uneasy.

I chew on my lower lip, trying to decide what to do. I've got Jake's number in my phone, and Bonnie's murder is still unsolved. I could call him and tell him about Gretchen's lie. But at the same time, if I genuinely don't think he killed her, what will I have accomplished? I'll have made my friend's life a lot worse, betrayed her trust, destroyed Randy's reputation, and possibly jeopardized his job...and for what? If it doesn't lead to justice for my friend, there's no point.

Besides, Jake told me they had unidentified, matching fingerprints at the two crime scenes. But if Randy's fingerprints are on file, it *couldn't* have been him.

Could it?

"Syd?" Gretchen sniffles. "Are...are you going to tell anyone?"

"I guess not."

"Oh, thank you!" I can imagine Gretchen's eyes filled with tears, her small nose bright pink. "Thank you so much, Syd! You are the best friend ever. If Randy and I get married someday, I'm going to make you the maid of honor at my wedding!"

Ugh. It would almost be worth it to turn Randy in just to avoid that dubious honor.

Gretchen spends the next several minutes tripping over herself to tell me how grateful she is and how lucky she is to have Randy. I soak it in, but the whole time, I can't help but wonder if I am making a terrible mistake.

CHAPTER 45

BEFORE

TOM

After eating nothing but junk food and soda for the last two days, it's nice to have my mother cooking dinner tonight. Slug, on the other hand, would happily eat nothing but junk food for every meal, and I think sometimes he does, which is part of why his skin is so bad.

While we eat a hot meal of chicken and rice at the kitchen table, my mother talks about Uncle Dave's procedure because she knows it's usually the sort of thing that would fascinate me, but I'm not in the mood right now. I pretend I'm listening though. I nod at all the right places, and I manage a smile when she tells me Uncle Dave made it home and is doing well. But in reality, it's all just background noise.

"How is Daisy doing?" my mother asks me when she finishes the story about Uncle Dave.

"Daisy?"

"Well, she and Alison were close, weren't they?"

"Sort of."

"She must be very upset."

I wouldn't know. I tried calling Daisy multiple times today, and each time, her phone went to voicemail. I don't want to tell my mother that Daisy's father won't let her talk to me, because then I'll have to tell her why.

"You know," my mother says thoughtfully, "I wonder—"

I have no idea what terrible thing my mother is wondering about, because at that moment, the doorbell rings.

She swivels her head in the direction of the front door. "Do you think your father forgot his key?"

I don't know who is at the door, but I know it's not my father searching for his house key. "Maybe."

Mom wipes her face with a napkin, then heads over to the front door. I rise from my own seat and quietly creep over to see who is there. I'm convinced it must be the police, but instead, I find my mother talking to a middle-aged man with a beer belly and a comb-over. He seems to be handing her something, then they talk for another minute in quiet voices.

Who is *that*?

My mother closes the door behind her, and she looks surprised to see me standing in the foyer. "Tom," she says. "I didn't see you there."

That's when I notice what's in her hand—the object the man handed to her. It's a phone.

"That was the bartender at O'Toole's," she says. "Your father left his phone there." She adds, "Two nights ago."

I don't know what to say to that. "Oh."

"Did he tell you he lost his phone?"

I shake my head slowly. "No, he didn't mention it."

She looks over her shoulder at the door, then back

at me. "And the bartender says he hasn't been back there since leaving his phone. And he hasn't been at work either. So where do you think he's been?"

My mouth is dry. I remind myself that even if she is suspicious that something happened to my father, it doesn't mean she knows *what* happened. Although she did see me threatening him with a fire poker once. Still…

She looks down at the floor, and I can almost see the gears turning in her brain. I wish they would stop. Can't she just stop thinking about it and let us enjoy our dinner?

"Tom," she says, "when did you put the rug out by the curb?"

That damn rug again. I should never have let him crawl out of the kitchen. I should've slit his throat right there, and then we wouldn't be having this discussion.

"Two days ago," I say.

"So Tuesday?"

"Yes."

She frowns. "But garbage pickup is on Monday. So how could they have already taken the rug away?"

I open my mouth, but nothing comes out. She has made an excellent point. I don't know how to explain why the rug is gone. It doesn't make sense that I would have driven it down to the dump myself. And I already told her that the garbageman took it. I can't tell her the truth, that's for sure.

My mother lifts her chin to look up at me. Over the last two years, I've surpassed her in height, which is still a little strange for me. As she studies my face, I can't help but notice her exposed carotid artery, and I can just barely make out its quickened pulsation in her neck.

"Tom?" she says softly.

She's waiting for me to say something, but there's nothing I can say. Thankfully, I am saved by the sound of the doorbell ringing yet again. My shoulders sag in relief. I don't know if the bartender has another question for my mother, but at least I've got a few minutes to plan out what I'm going to say next.

But my relief is short-lived when I see who is standing at our front door.

It's Chief Driscoll.

CHAPTER 46

The chief of police is at my front door.

It was hard enough when he questioned me at school. But showing up at my home is on another level. Why is he here? Is it about Alison?

"Sorry to bother you, Mrs. Brewer." Chief Driscoll is wearing the same checked tie and white dress shirt he had on this morning but this time paired with a blue blazer. "I just have a few questions for Tom."

Despite the fact that she was quizzing me herself a few moments ago, my mother steps between me and the police chief. "About what?"

He presses his lips together, obviously nonplussed that she won't step back and let him in. "About Alison Danzinger."

My mother considers this, but she doesn't move away from the door. "Why do you need to talk to Tom about her?"

"Alison was brutally murdered." Chief Driscoll's voice

is grave. "I'm talking to everyone who knew Alison well in hopes that we can find the monster who did this and bring them to justice."

I am almost hoping that my mother will continue to refuse to allow him into the house, but instead she steps aside. At the same time, I instinctively take a step back.

"You can talk in the living room, Jim," Mom tells him.

I follow my mother into the living room, giving myself a pep talk in my head. I already talked to the police chief. He doesn't know anything, or else he would be handcuffing me as we speak. He's just fishing.

I sit on the couch, and my mother sits next to me, her leg nearly touching mine. The chief sits on my father's armchair, across from us. He's wearing that same grim expression he had in the principal's office, except much worse. Because back then, they were hoping they might find Alison alive. Now they know what has happened to her.

There's no hope for Alison. All they can do is bring her killer to justice.

"Tom." He grimaces. "Daisy told me she spoke to you about how we found Alison."

"Yes." Although she didn't tell me anything that hasn't been all over the news for almost the last twenty-four hours.

"I've also heard from several students," he continues, "that you and Alison did not get along. She wasn't happy about you dating Daisy."

My mother stiffens beside me, and I have to struggle to keep my composure. "It wasn't a big deal."

He clears his throat. "And you told me you were home the night before last?"

"Right," I confirm. "All night."

"And your father was here with you?"

"Right."

The chief casts a look in the direction of the stairs. "Is your father here right now? Can I speak with him?"

"My husband isn't here at the moment," my mother speaks up. "But I'll have him call you as soon as he gets back."

"Where is he?"

"Still at work," my mother says without hesitation.

He nods, accepting my mother's lie. I don't know why she lied on my behalf. She knows he's not at work.

"Please have him call me as soon as possible," the chief says.

"Absolutely." My mother wrinkles her brow. "But honestly, Jim, I'm not sure how you think Tom could possibly be involved in this. You've known my son since he was a baby. Do you really think he would do anything to hurt Alison?"

I'm hoping he'll agree with her and say he's just doing his due diligence. But that same sober expression never leaves his face. "I have to tell you, Luann, after talking with several students in the class, I have some concerns about Tom."

What the hell does *that* mean? Who is talking to him about me? And what did they say? What *concerns*?

"What concerns are you referring to?" my mother snaps at him.

"Just some rumors." He rubs his hands over his knees. "About Tom and Alison. And about Tom and Brandi."

Oh no. Somebody told him about me and Brandi. Now he probably thinks I killed her.

"I'll tell you what," the chief says to my mother. "When your husband gets back, why don't the three of

257

you come down to the station. I'd like to discuss all this in more detail and get a formal statement."

Come down to the station? That sounds…terrifying.

"My husband will be tired when he gets back from work," my mother says stiffly.

"Tomorrow morning then."

"I just don't understand all this suspicion around my son, Jim," she says. "You know Tom is a good boy. You wouldn't have let him date your daughter otherwise."

"No," he agrees, "I wouldn't have."

It's at that moment I realize Chief Driscoll will never let me near Daisy ever again. Even if all this somehow blows over and I don't end up behind bars, what I had with Daisy is over. We're not going to the same college. We're not going to get married. It's *over*.

But right now, I can't even think about any of that. I just want the chief out of my house.

He stands up from the armchair, brushing off invisible dirt from the legs of his pants. He starts to turn to head for the door, but all of a sudden, he stops short.

"Hey," he says, "what's that?"

I follow his line of vision, which is directed at the side of the sofa. My throat constricts when I realize what he's looking at.

There is a spot of dried blood on the sofa.

I thought I cleaned off every bit of blood, but to be fair, it was *everywhere*. I wouldn't be surprised if there's more blood that I missed in some crack or crevice of the house. The sofa is not that close to where I slashed my father's throat, but arterial spray is very strong, and I'm sure I hit his carotid in addition to the jugular I was aiming for.

Of course, Chief Driscoll can't know for sure that's

what it is. It looks like a brownish red circle on the tan fabric. But when I look up, my mother's face is the color of a sheet of paper.

"We were painting," she says finally.

"Painting?" He lifts an eyebrow. "That's a strange color for paint."

"We were painting an art project." She looks over at me. "For Tom."

"I see." He nods slowly. "You mind if I get a sample of that...paint."

"Actually, I do mind." My mother lifts her chin. "Tom and I were in the middle of having dinner, and we've given you enough of our time already. I don't see the point of you taking a sample of some paint on our sofa."

"It'll just take a second, Luann. I got a kit in the trunk of my car."

She narrows her eyes at him. "Don't you need a *warrant* for something like that?"

Chief Driscoll takes a moment to absorb her words. Finally, he stuffs his hands into his pockets. "If you want me to get a warrant, I'll go ahead and do that then."

My mother practically shoves the police chief out our front door, and I can't breathe normally until she's turned the lock. As soon as the dead bolt has been turned, my mother leans against the door, her shoulders heaving slightly, her eyes downcast.

"Mom?" I say.

She is looking down at the floor, where the rug used to be. "Go to your room, Tom."

"But—"

"Go. Please. I..." She lifts her eyes to look at me. "I need to be alone right now."

I do what my mother tells me. I head up the stairs to my room and shut myself inside. And when I come out to use the bathroom half an hour later, my mother is crouched in the living room, scrubbing at the base of the sofa.

CHAPTER 47

PRESENT DAY

SYDNEY

The next morning, I have a Zoom call with a new client. It's still sort of offseason for me, but a lot of people want to get their finances in order before the end of the calendar year. The man I'm meeting with is named Orson Finley, and our meeting starts in a few minutes, but I'm dreading it. I had a lot of trouble sleeping last night. I can almost feel the purple circles under my eyes, and there's a dull throbbing in my left temple. The last thing I want to do is meet a new client, but it would be unprofessional to cancel.

I'm still not sure I'm doing the right thing by not going to the police about Randy's lack of an alibi. Do I genuinely think Randy is capable of murder? No, I don't. I really don't.

But on the other hand, it wouldn't be the most shocking thing in the world. It wouldn't be like finding out, I don't know, that my *mom* is a serial killer.

Ultimately, the reason I don't go to the police or even

Jake is because of Gretchen—I can't do it to her. If Randy has a criminal history, casting suspicion on him could be enough to wreck his life. Our landlord would almost certainly fire him if they thought there was even a tiny chance he could be responsible for Bonnie's murder. And it would take time and resources away from finding the real killer.

The alert goes off on my phone that it's time to log in to my call. I get on my computer, and before I connect, I give myself a once-over in the camera. I dabbed on some concealer that seems to be doing the trick, and I used some lipstick to brighten my face. My hair didn't want to behave this morning, so I pulled back my blond-streaked strands into a ponytail. I ended up using that scrunchie Gretchen gave me to remember Bonnie, and I try my best not to think of the clump of hair missing from her scalp.

I connect the Zoom call, and a second later, a face fills the screen. As the man's gaunt face and messy ponytail come into focus, recognition dawns on me, and the smile drops off my lips.

"Kevin," I gasp. "What the hell?"

The man on the screen is Kevin, a.k.a. Real Kevin, a.k.a. Orson Finley, I guess. At this point, I have no clue what his real name is. All I know for sure is that he has wasted a *lot* of my time.

"I'm really so sorry to do this, Sydney"—his words come out in a jumble—"but every time I manage to find you, you don't want to talk to me."

"Right. Most people would take a hint." I reach for my mouse to disconnect the call. "Goodbye, Kevin. Or Orson. Or whatever your name is."

"Please don't hang up!" He leans closer to the screen so that I can see the dark circles under his eyes. "Please,

Sydney! We had one of the best dates I have ever been on. I mean, do you think I introduce my mother to every girl I go out with?"

God, I hope not. "Kevin—"

"You have to give me another chance," he pleads with me. "Please—just hear me out. Give me sixty seconds."

"Kevin…"

"Sixty seconds. *Please.*"

Against my better judgment, I nod. I'll give him sixty seconds to get it all out of his system, and I hope he'll leave me alone for good after that.

"You need to know," he says, "that I'm ashamed of the way I treated you that night. I'm not an aggressive person, but I thought you felt the same way I did, and I took things too far. I'm ashamed, and my dear mother would be ashamed of me too if she knew. I own that, and I'm really sorry, Sydney."

The last thing I expected was an apology from this man (or any man, really). Despite everything, I am impressed. "I appreciate that."

"So what do you think?" he presses me. "Would you consider giving me a second chance?"

Even though I appreciate his apology, I'm dating someone else. And even if I weren't, there's no way I'd ever go on another date with a guy who attacked me. How could he think I would? "I don't think so, Kevin."

His brown eyes bulge from their sockets in front of the camera. "Please, Sydney. I'm begging you. I'd make you so happy."

"I'm sorry," I say, gently but firmly, "but the answer is still no."

"All I want is a chance to sit with you and look at you

face-to-face," he pleads with me. "It's not right that I only get to see you through a window."

Wait, *what*? "What did you say?"

"I said I want to see you face-to-face."

"No," I say through my teeth. "What did you say about the *window*?"

Kevin has a deer-in-headlights look. "Window?"

Shit.

Before Kevin has a chance to utter another word, I hit the red button to disconnect the call. As soon as the screen goes black, I jump out of my ergonomic chair and cross the room to the window. *It's not right that I only get to see you through a window.* Has that creep been *watching* me?

Horrified, I stare out my window down at the pedestrians and cars below. From the height of my apartment, the pedestrians look like ants and the cars like children's toys. Nobody could possibly see me up here…could they?

Then I lift my eyes to look at the buildings surrounding me. There are two buildings that have a very decent view of my own building. And within those buildings, there are literally hundreds of windows. Hundreds of opportunities for someone to be watching me.

A chill runs down my spine.

Maybe I should give Jake a call. Then again, he isn't one of those cops who's willing to use his badge to bend the rules and intimidate some jerk who won't leave me alone. He'll tell me I need to get a restraining order, and I just don't need to deal with that hassle right now on top of everything else.

Besides, if I call Jake, I'm not going to be able to keep from telling him about Randy's lack of an alibi.

I grab the string to lower the blinds, and I let out a

sigh as they drop down, cutting off my view of the outside world and anyone else's view of me. There—problem solved.

Just as I'm contemplating what to do next, the doorbell rings. I jump away from the window, my heart pounding. Who is ringing my doorbell at nine in the morning? I didn't buzz in any package-delivery people.

I look back at the computer screen. The Zoom call has ended, but what if Kevin wasn't at home during the call? His background was blurred, so he could have been anywhere.

What if he is right outside my door?

I grab my phone off my desk. Okay, there's no reason to panic. If Kevin is outside my door, I will call the police. The doors are pretty well made, and I doubt he could force his way in, especially with the dead bolt in place.

I locked the dead bolt, didn't I?

The doorbell rings a second time, the sound drawn out as if someone has jammed their finger into the button and left it there. Somebody badly wants to come inside.

My heart is jackhammering in my chest as I run over to the front door, still feeling eyes on the back of my neck even though the blinds are closed. Right away, I can see that I didn't lock the stupid dead bolt. Oh my God, how could I have been so *stupid*?

This is fine. I'll call the police. Then I'll call Gretchen and Randy. Actually, this will be a good thing. I've been struggling to find a way to report Kevin given I don't know anything about him, but if the police catch him here, then filing a restraining order will be a lot easier.

I check the peephole and...

Oh. It's Randy.

I unlock my one flimsy lock and throw open the door. Randy is standing in the hallway in his T-shirt and blue jeans, shifting between his dirty sneakers. He isn't much taller than Jake, but somehow he looks like a giant tree hovering over me.

"Hey, Syd," he says. "Can I talk to you?"

I hesitate. I can't help but remember that Randy doesn't have an alibi for the night of Bonnie's murder. There were no signs of forced entry, and he had a key. But I'm also having trouble imagining that Randy came to my apartment to kill me at nine in the morning. And if he did, as I mentioned, he has a key, so he wouldn't have to ask permission.

"Okay," I say. "Come in."

I step aside to allow Randy to enter my apartment. He looks incredibly nervous, which is making me nervous. What is he nervous about?

"So, listen," he says. "I need to show you something. But…you can't tell anyone. Okay?"

"Okay."

Randy reaches into the pocket of his blue jeans. I swear to God, if he pulls out a clump of Bonnie's hair from his pocket, I am going to faint dead away. His pockets are deep, and he fishes around for a few seconds until he pulls out what he wants to show me, and it feels like all the air has been sucked out of me.

Oh no. *No.*

CHAPTER 48

I feel sick when I see the object in Randy's palm. *Sick.*

"I bought it yesterday," Randy tells me, his eyes shining, "right before I got the ant farm."

With that preamble, Randy opens the blue velvet box in his hand. The ring inside is made of white gold and has a tiny diamond that sparkles in the overhead lights.

Sick.

"I can return it if I need to," he says quickly. "So if you don't think Gretchen would like it, I could get another one."

How about you return the ring and *not* get another one? How about you *don't* ask my best friend to marry you? "Um…"

His face falls. "Is the diamond too small?"

The diamond is really tiny, but I'm sure Gretchen will love it. The diamond isn't the problem. The problem is the guy giving her the diamond. I may not think Randy is a killer, but I still don't think he's good enough for

Gretchen. She could do so much better, but she's not even looking because she's stuck with him. "It's a bit small."

He stares critically at the tiny gem. "I know. Believe me, I wanted to get her an enormous diamond, because that's what she deserves. But they say three months' salary, and this cost me six months' salary. I can't do any bigger than this."

"If money is an issue, maybe now is the wrong time to propose? Maybe wait a few years."

He rubs the back of his neck. "But I *love* her. Gretchen is the best person I've ever met. I want to spend the rest of my life with her—making her happy."

His usually slightly beady eyes are open wide—he seems incredibly sincere. Randy might not be my favorite person in the whole world, but he loves Gretchen. And she's wild about him too. I would be an awful person to try to keep them apart.

Right?

"I think she'll love that ring," I say begrudgingly.

His face brightens. "You really think so?"

"Definitely."

"Thanks, Syd." He snaps the blue velvet box closed and shoves it back in his pocket. "I'm trying to figure out how I should ask her. Like, I should get down on one knee, right?"

I can't help but smile. "Yeah, you definitely should."

"Do you think it would be lame if I wrote down what I want to say on index cards?" he asks. "I really want to get it perfect."

"Honestly, I think she's going to say yes no matter what."

Randy grins at me. I don't know if I have ever seen

him smile that wide. I can't even imagine what he's going to look like when Gretchen agrees to marry him. And while I do believe she could do better, I can't deny that he clearly loves her. Gretchen's had her share of heartbreak, and she deserves a happy ending.

At that moment, I realize that I can never tell anyone that Randy doesn't have an alibi for the night of Bonnie's murder.

CHAPTER 49

Things have been a little tense between me and Tom.

He texted me a few times the day after he blew me off for his mother, but I decided not to answer. I was irritated enough to let him stew a bit and still wound up over the situation with Real Kevin.

But then he sent me a text message inviting me to his apartment for a homemade candlelight dinner. And I decided I had punished him enough.

Despite the fact that Tom must earn at least several times as much as I do, his building isn't any fancier than mine. Like me, he doesn't have a doorman. But even worse, he doesn't have an elevator. And he lives on the fifth floor. By the time I get up there, I am slightly out of breath. What can I say—yoga is not an aerobic workout. I have to check my armpits to make sure they're not sweaty.

Tom looks thrilled to see me when he opens the door. He grabs me and kisses me for, like, sixty seconds, which is a lot in kissing time.

"I missed you," he whispers in my ear.

"Well," I say, "I might come to your apartment more if you didn't live in a fifth-floor walk-up." I place a hand on my chest. "My heart is still pounding. I might be having a heart attack."

"You know, when you're exercising," he says in that excited voice he always uses when he's telling me some factoid about the human body, "the blood vessels supplying your muscles expand to bring more blood to them, so the heart has to pump more blood. Your heart beats faster to maintain your blood pressure."

"Wow, fascinating, Dr. Brewer."

He laughs. "Anyway, it would be impossible to get my furniture downstairs if I wanted to move. So I'm pretty much stuck here forever."

If Tom and I ever decided to live together, he could move into my building. Or else we could find a different place to start fresh.

But even as I'm thinking that, in my heart, I know that Tom will never ask me to live with him.

"Come on in." He takes me by the hand and tugs me into the living room, where he indeed has a candle burning on the table. He has set up two place settings, including bottles of water, because what comes out of his tap is slightly brown, and between them is a brown paper sack. "Let's eat before it gets cold."

"Hmm. I feel like I was promised a *homemade* dinner."

He nods soberly. "Yes, I realize that. But then I got stuck late at work and realized that while I'm an excellent cook, I'm also excellent at calling Luigi's to order a delicious dinner for two."

Fair enough. "Okay, let me grab utensils."

I walk into Tom's kitchen, and as I'm heading over to the drawer to get the silverware, I notice movement on the floor in the gap between the refrigerator and the cabinets. I crouch down to get a better look, and then…

"Tom!" I scream. "Oh my God, get in here!"

Tom comes running into the kitchen, just in time to find me cowering by the sink. He follows the direction of my gaze, where a small gray mouse seems to be stuck in the space next to the refrigerator. A freaking *mouse*.

"Oh!" he says. "That mouse has been terrorizing me for the last month. I guess the glue paper I bought worked."

I clasp my hand over my eyes. "I can't look! It's so gross."

"It's just a mouse." I peek through my fingers just enough to see him smirking at me. "Just go in the other room. I'll take care of it."

I am happy to oblige. I dash back into the living room, trying not to think about that wriggling vermin on the floor of the kitchen.

I wait at the dining table, holding my breath. I hear loud scuffling noises from the kitchen, and I try not to imagine Tom handling that mouse with his bare hands. I'm holding my breath when, all of a sudden, there's a loud bang. Then a second one. A few minutes later, Tom emerges from the kitchen holding a handful of silverware. (I hope he washed his hands.)

"All taken care of," he says casually.

I frown, wondering about the noise I heard. "What did you do to the mouse?"

"I put it in a bag and then smashed it with a hammer."

I gasp. Smashed it with a *hammer*? "For real?"

"Uh, yeah."

"How could you? That was a living creature."

His jaw drops. "Are you freaking serious? You were screaming and couldn't even look at it! I told you I was going to get rid of it, and I did. I didn't tell you that I was going to rehabilitate the mouse and make it my pet."

"Still. You didn't have to do *that*. That's…awful."

"Well, what would you have preferred?"

"You could have released it into the wild!"

He gapes at me. "It was stuck on a piece of glue paper. And we're up five flights of stairs. How did you want me to do that exactly?"

I wring my hands together. What he did is bad enough, but I'm even more unsettled by the fact that he barely seems bothered by having to smash a living creature to death with a hammer. "I don't know."

"I'll tell you what. Next time I have a mouse stuck in a trap, *you* can go ahead and release it into the wild." He raises his eyebrows. "Now can we eat this delicious meal I ordered?"

Fine. I suppose he has a point. But still, everybody knows that glue traps are inhumane. He could have gotten another type of trap that wouldn't have required him to kill the mouse. Maybe I'll buy him some more-humane traps.

I dig into the brown paper bag and discover that he has ordered chicken parmigiana for me and chicken piccata for himself. And lots of crusty rolls. As I slide into the seat across from him, the silverware glints in the overhead lighting. I notice the knife he placed on one side of the plate is larger than your standard steak knife.

"My God, what did you think I'd be cutting?" I say as I pick it up.

"Well, it's a slab of chicken. You need a knife, right?"

"Yes, but…" I turn it to the side. "Jesus, this is sharp. Most of my knives at home don't look sharp enough to cut through a piece of *bread*. Do you get these sharpened?"

"Christ no." He picks up his own knife to cut into his chicken. "I just don't use them much, so they stay sharp."

This knife is definitely making me wary. With my bleeding issues, I would probably lose a pint of blood if I cut myself with one of these. I'll have to be extra careful.

As we dig into our food, I tell Tom all about my encounter with Kevin on Zoom. I try to play it down and make it into something almost comical, but by the end of the story, his face is bright red—almost purple. He looks absolutely furious.

"The nerve of that jackass!" he growls. "I should have called the police on him the first time. I *knew* he was trouble." His hand balls into a fist, and if Kevin were standing in front of us, I have no doubt Tom would be throwing a punch right now. "You can't let him get away with this, Sydney."

"Unfortunately," I say, "I don't know much about him. All I got from the Cynch app was his first name and a phony photo."

"So? There are other ways to find a person. It's not like this guy is some sort of criminal mastermind."

"Like what?"

"Hire a private detective? Hell, I bet some high-school kid who is good at hacking could figure out where he lives based on your Zoom session."

"Maybe." I'm not convinced it will be that easy to find Kevin. In any case, it's not what I want to think about right now. Especially since it seems to be getting Tom so angry. "Hey, I found out some interesting news the other day."

"What?"

I carefully slice another piece of chicken, attempting not to sever my finger in the process. "Gretchen's boyfriend came to my apartment and showed me a ring he bought her. He's planning to ask her to marry him."

"Oh." Tom could not possibly look less enthusiastic. And why should he be excited? He has refused to meet Gretchen and Randy, so why would he care that they're getting married? "That's great."

I play with the spaghetti curled up in a pile on my plate. "I suppose you're going to refuse to be my date to the wedding."

"Wedding?" He raises his eyebrows. "Syd, the guy hasn't even popped the question yet. These engagements last forever. I bet they won't get married for two more years. Do you really need me to make plans for two years in the future?"

This is essentially the reaction I'd expected from him, but it still irritates me.

"I don't need you to save a date," I say through my teeth. "But it would be nice if you didn't look quite so panicked at the idea of going somewhere formal with me and actually meeting people that I know."

"I don't—"

"You do. You know you do, so please don't make it worse by lying about it."

Tom's brown eyes drop to his dinner. "Look, I'm not saying you're wrong, okay?"

"Okay…"

"But, there are things about me that you don't understand. That you could *never* understand."

"Try me."

He drags his fork across his plate. His shoulders rise and fall, and it almost looks like he's mumbling to himself. Except I'm not sure what he's saying.

"I like you, Sydney," he says. "I like you a *lot*. I really, really do."

"But?"

It's so quiet in his apartment, I can hear his neighbor's cat begging for dinner. Tom rakes a shaking hand through his black hair.

"Okay," he finally says.

"Okay?"

He raises his eyes, and a smile twitches at his lips. "Okay, I'll be your date for the wedding, whenever it is."

He's right—it probably won't end up being until some date in the far away future. But still, it's nice to know he's willing. Maybe there really is a future between the two of us. Maybe someday we'll be getting an apartment together. This could be something. He could be *the One*.

My eyes meet his across the table. God, he is *really* sexy.

And now he's giving me that look, which makes it hard to think straight. He's not hungry for dinner anymore. And neither am I.

CHAPTER 50

BEFORE

TOM

At some point, my mother's footsteps ascend the stairs, and then the door to her bedroom slams shut.

I can't imagine what she must be thinking about me right now. She knew that spot on the sofa was blood. She hasn't asked me again to explain where her rug went. And she recognizes at this point that my father is not coming home for the night.

Plus, I can't stop thinking about the way she looked at me before I went upstairs.

She must strongly suspect I did something to my father. Does she think I'm responsible for what happened to Alison too? To Brandi?

If she thinks that, I don't know why she's cleaning up the blood I left behind. She should be driving me to the police station herself.

At about ten o'clock, I sneak down to the living room, which is dark. I flick on one of the lights, then walk around the sofa to see what that spot looks like where my mother was scrubbing. The bloodstain is a lot lighter than it was earlier, but it's definitely still there. She wasn't able to get it out apparently. I'm sure there's enough there to analyze the fibers and figure out it's not paint. I'm sure they can figure out it's blood.

But at least it's not Alison's blood.

My stomach growls loudly. I only ate about half my dinner, but even though my body seems to want food, I don't feel like eating. It's like I've permanently lost my appetite.

All I can think about is Daisy.

She told me on the phone that she's not allowed to talk to me anymore, and I'm betting her father is monitoring her phone. It's clear what the police chief thinks of me. Yet I'm not quite ready to let her go. I've spent my whole life in love with Daisy Driscoll, and now, just when I managed to win her over, she's being taken from me. It doesn't seem fair.

I need to see her. Even without her father's blessing.

I cast a glance in the direction of my mother's bedroom upstairs. I'm sure she's in bed for the night. If I slip out, she'll never know.

Before I can overthink it, I grab a hoodie from the closet and throw it on. I shove my keys and my phone into my pocket, and I slip out the back door, leaving it unlocked.

Daisy's house is only a few blocks away from mine. I jog over there, the hood of my sweatshirt covering my hair. It's not much of a disguise, but it's better than nothing. If I'm lucky, her father will be out in the field or at the station.

Daisy's bedroom is all the way in the back of her house.

They don't have any cameras or security, because this isn't the sort of neighborhood where you need something like that, and it's not like anyone would break into a police officer's house. In any case, I'm able to go around the back without any trouble. I crane my neck to look up at the second-floor windows, and I locate the familiar one with plastic bubble letters spelling out DAISY in different colors. The light is still on.

Now I've got to get her attention.

I pick up a couple of pebbles from the ground. I've got to be careful, because I don't want to break her window, but I need to throw them hard enough to get her attention. I count to three, then I toss one of the smaller pebbles at the window. Bull's-eye.

I wait for a moment, but I don't see any movement from the window.

I pick out a second pebble and throw that one. Again, I hit my target. Finally, the shadows shift behind the glass. My breath catches when Daisy's pale face appears at the window.

"Daisy!" I stage-whisper. "I need to talk to you!"

She shakes her head no.

I lace my hands together, pleading with her. *Come on, Daisy. Please.*

Finally, her shoulders sag. She points to the back door, where she can slip out easily without anyone seeing her. I briefly entertain the thought that she might tell her parents I'm waiting for her so they can throw me out, but then, a minute later, the back door cracks open and there she is, alone, her blond hair gleaming in the moonlight, a sweater wrapped around her slim body.

"Daisy," I breathe.

I can't help myself—I dash over to her and wrap my

arms around her. But it quickly becomes obvious she doesn't want to be hugged. Her whole body has gone rigid. I pull away, frowning.

"Daisy…" I say.

When she looks up at me, there are tears glistening in her eyes. "I told you I'm not allowed to talk to you anymore, Tom."

"I know, but—"

"My father thinks you killed Alison." She blinks up at me, and a single tear falls from her right eye. "He thinks you killed Brandi too. You and Slug together."

I swallow hard. I knew the chief strongly suspected I was Brandi's secret boyfriend, and I guessed that I had become a chief suspect. But it's a blow to hear he shared those suspicions with Daisy.

"Slug was peeping at Brandi through her window," she adds. "She caught him doing it. Did you know that?"

"No."

"And she's not the first girl he's peeped at. A few others came forward too."

I didn't know any of that, although it explains why the chief was questioning Slug a second time. Christ, I can't believe Slug would do that. If I had known, I wouldn't have called him the other night when I was in trouble.

I really opened a can of worms. I knew Slug was weird, but I had no idea what he was really like. I had no idea he could be dangerous.

"Daisy," I whisper, "you can't possibly think that I would…"

"I don't know what to think!" She wipes her eyes with the back of her hand. I get a rush of sadness that I might never get to hold her hand again. "And that's not all."

It's not? What else could there be? How could it be any worse than her father, the chief of police, thinking that I'm a murderer? "What is it? Tell me."

She drops her voice an octave. "The night Alison disappeared? She called me."

Oh no.

"She told me she saw you and Slug together," she goes on. "She said you two were stuffing something into your trunk, and it was really suspicious. She was freaking out, telling me I had to break up with you."

Oh *no*.

"Look," I say, "Slug was at my house, and he was just borrowing some sports equipment and putting it in his trunk. It wasn't a big deal."

"She said there was blood on your hands."

Suddenly, I am very glad Alison is gone. Slug was right—she *was* a problem.

"Daisy." I take a deep breath. "We've known each other forever, and I would never lie to you. I love you. I would *never* hurt Alison. I swear on my life."

I study her face, watching to see if she buys it. She wants to believe it. She wants to believe me so badly.

"Daisy?" I say.

She blinks away another tear. "It doesn't matter if I believe it or not. My father still thinks you did it. Do you know how much trouble you're in?"

"Daisy—"

A light goes on upstairs in her house, and Daisy's body goes rigid. "I've got to get back upstairs. My parents will kill me if they see me with you."

No. This can't be the last time I see Daisy. It *can't*. I'll lose my freaking mind. "Will you meet me later tonight?"

I ask desperately. She starts to shake her head, and I add, "Please, Daisy?"

She hesitates. "Okay. I can sneak out when my mom goes to bed. Meet me at one in the morning behind the Dairy Queen off Maple Street. It's always deserted over there."

She's willing to meet me. That means she doesn't think I'm a killer.

Impulsively, I reach out and grab her. I press my lips against hers, and for a moment, she resists, but then she melts into me like she always does. There is nothing better than kissing Daisy Driscoll.

And then I feel the beating of her carotid artery under her jaw. I slide my finger against it, fascinated by the pulsations. I remember the way my father's blood spilled out from the gaping hole in his neck.

I wonder what Daisy's blood would look like spilling out of her throat.

As our lips separate, a voice in the back of my head tells me that maybe it isn't such a great idea to meet up alone with Daisy in a deserted parking lot. That maybe I can't trust myself with her. That maybe Alison was right about me and that if I really do care about her, I should let her go.

But it's too late to back out now.

Daisy hurries back into the house, and I watch the door swing shut, even though I need to get out of here while I still can. But kissing Daisy always makes my knees weak. I need a minute.

Finally, I scuttle out of the backyard, moving quickly and quietly. I had been so intent on watching Daisy, I didn't know that somebody was watching me.

Not until I come face-to-face with Slug.

CHAPTER 51

PRESENT DAY

SYDNEY

Tom and I ended up having a particularly sweaty session tonight, and although it's not his standard practice, as soon as we are spent, he informs me he's hitting the shower. "You made me work up a sweat, woman," he says, which makes me laugh. "Want to join me?"

"No, I'm still recovering," I tease him, which in turn makes *him* laugh.

I lie in Tom's queen-size bed while he hums classical music in the shower. It might be Beethoven, but I honestly have no idea. My body is still thrumming from what he did to me. Even if he never agreed to go to a wedding for the rest of our lives, I could never break up with him. I would miss this far too much.

My phone, over on his bedside table, starts to ring. I glance over at the screen—my mother. She's been a little calmer now that I'm dating someone regularly, although I have expressed to her in as gentle a way as possible that things might not be working out with Tom. She did *not* take it well. If I am not married by forty, someone might have to euthanize her.

I consider letting the call go to voicemail, but then I brace myself and pick it up. "Hi," I say. "I'm kind of busy right now."

"Oh." She doesn't seem to know what to make of that. "Are you with Tom?"

"Yes."

"And how is that going?"

"It's going...okay."

She can hear the strain in my voice. It's not going great. Maybe Tom and I aren't breaking up, but we're not getting married anytime in the near future. The best I can hope for is a wedding date.

"You know," she says, "I was in my Bible-studies class the other day, and I was reminded of a very interesting story. Did you know that Sarah and Abraham gave birth to Isaac when she was ninety years old?"

I stare at the phone, astonished. "Why are you telling me that?"

"I'm just saying, there's always hope."

I am really *not* in the mood for this conversation. "I have to go."

"Whatever happened to that tall, handsome police detective you were living with—Jake?"

I flinch. "Why are you asking me about that? We've been broken up for years."

"I was just thinking, Jake was so nice. And he really liked you, Sydney."

"Good*bye*, Mom."

I hang up on my mother. I'm so agitated by that irritating conversation that I don't quite manage to put the phone back on the bedside table, and it drops into the gap between the table and the bed.

Great.

I climb off the bed and crouch down next to the table. I reach my hand into the gap, feeling around for my phone. My fingers touch something that feels like the cold, smooth surface of the phone, but then there's also something else there. Something that feels like velvety fabric.

Hmm. What's that?

I grab both items and pull them out from the gap. Sure enough, the first item was indeed my phone. But the second one makes my heart drop into my stomach.

It's a black scrunchie.

What the hell is Tom doing with a scrunchie in his bedroom?

It's not like I found some general evidence that another woman has been in here. That would be fine—Tom isn't a monk, after all, and clearly you don't develop that level of expertise by sleeping alone. But a *scrunchie*? Who wears a scrunchie in this day and age?

Or should I say, who wears a scrunchie besides *Bonnie*?

I had thought it was far too big a coincidence for Tom to be Bonnie's mystery boyfriend. But as I look down at this scrunchie, I realize I have underestimated him. All the pieces fit together.

After all, *was* it such a coincidence? I met him three blocks away from our building, shortly after Bonnie had been escorted home by her beau. He's a doctor. And he had the strangest reaction when I started talking to him about Bonnie's murder. Not to mention that he might have given me a fake name when we first met.

Was the truth staring me smack in the face all along? Was I blinded by Tom's good looks and my urgency to get married and have a child before age ninety?

But no… It's impossible. Tom isn't a killer. I'm even more sure of that than I am of the fact that Randy isn't a killer. Tom is a *good guy*. The best.

Isn't he?

I stand in the middle of the bedroom, looking down at the phone in my hands. I bring up my list of favorite contacts, and Tom is right there in the middle. I don't entirely know why, but before I can stop myself, I click on his name.

I am rewarded with the sound of a phone ringing. But it's not coming from the phone on his dresser, which is lying silent. This sound is muffled, like the phone is in one of the drawers.

I allow it to continue ringing. As Tom belts out Mozart in the shower, I cross the room to his dresser and start yanking open drawers. The first one just has a bunch of folded shirts in it. The second has pants. The third looks like it contains boxer shorts, but when I open it up, the ringing becomes less muffled.

Bingo.

I dig around in the drawer. It takes me about ten seconds to find the phone hidden away at the bottom with a call flashing on the screen, identified as simply "S."

A second later, the call goes to voicemail. I gingerly remove the phone from the drawer so I can examine it more closely. This is *not* a personal phone that Tom uses to talk to friends and family. This is a burner phone.

Tom has been communicating with me on a burner phone.

I flip open the disposable phone and discover it does not require a password, so I'm able to scroll through the calls and text messages. Every single call and text message on the phone is from me. This phone is solely for interacting with me.

What the hell?

I look over at the bathroom. The shower is still running strong. Tom tends to take long showers. I've got at least another five minutes—maybe longer if he decides to brush his teeth. I'm going to need every second of that time.

I drop the burner phone back into the drawer and slam it shut. Wearing nothing but one of Tom's large T-shirts that he lets me wear when I spend the night, I dart into the living room. The dining table is still set up from our meal, although Tom blew out the candle before we headed to the bedroom. I look down at the utensils on the table, wondering if you could get a decent print off them. I'm not certain.

Then my gaze falls on Tom's water bottle.

Perfect.

I pick up the water bottle with my thumb and forefinger, trying my best to preserve any fingerprints he left on it. I left my purse on the coffee table in the living room, so I hurry over and gently drop the water bottle inside. It isn't until I've zipped my purse closed that I hear the voice from behind me.

"What do you think you're doing, Sydney?"

CHAPTER 52

I have made a terrible mistake.

I should never have tried to take that water bottle. I should've just picked up my purse and made a run for it, even if all I'm wearing is a T-shirt and underwear. I made the stupidest mistake that a woman can make—I didn't run when I had the chance.

And now Tom is standing a few feet away from me in the living room, wearing an undershirt and boxer shorts, his black hair still shiny and wet from the shower. His eyes are dark and impassive.

"What?" I ask.

"I said, what are you doing?"

"Oh." I look down at my purse and manage a smile. "I was just going to grab my phone."

"Your phone is in the bedroom."

He's right. I left my phone on top of his dresser. I really, really wish I hadn't done that. If I hadn't, I would be calling 911 right now.

Instead, I manage a laugh. It sort of sounds like I'm being strangled.

"I didn't see it, I guess," I say. "I'll go grab it then."

Tom's eyes narrow. "Are you okay?"

I can*not* let on that I suspect anything about him. Because if he realizes I've caught on... Well, we know what happened to Bonnie. Maybe this is why he finally killed her. "Of course. Why wouldn't I be okay?"

He doesn't answer. He just keeps staring at me.

"Actually," I say, "the truth is I'm not feeling so hot."

"What's wrong?"

I dredge up the excuse that makes most men overly eager to send me on my way. "I just got my period."

But Tom doesn't seem the least bit thrown by that revelation. I guess that shouldn't surprise me. "I've got some ibuprofen in my medicine cabinet if you need it."

"Yeah, um..." I rub the general area where I'm pretty sure my uterus is. "I would rather just head out. I'd rather be in my own space."

Tom is quiet. In a movie, this would be the moment when the bad guy realizes that I have caught on to him and that he can't let me leave—at least not alive. I watch the wheels turning in his brain. Tom is an extremely smart man. He's got to figure it out.

And then another terrible thought occurs to me:

Where did I leave the scrunchie?

If I left it on the dresser, next to my phone, the jig is up. He will recognize that I found a hair accessory belonging to a dead woman. And I will never leave this apartment.

Damn it, where did I leave that scrunchie?

"You should stay," he says. "It's late. You don't really want to go home in the middle of the night, do you?"

I rub my abdomen again. "I'd just feel better sleeping in my own bed."

"You can have my bed to yourself if you want. I'll sleep out on the couch."

"No, I…uh…" I clear my throat. "I would really rather just go home."

His gaze drops to my purse. If he checks inside, I'm done. I can't explain to him why I stuffed an empty water bottle into my purse. Although I'm sure I would manage to come up with some sort of lame excuse.

It's all about the scrunchie. If he saw it, I'm dead. If he didn't see it, I might get out of here alive.

My heart is beating so hard I'm astonished he can't hear it. But after a few seconds of contemplation, he steps aside.

"Okay," he says agreeably, "but at least let me call you an Uber."

I can't believe this. He's actually letting me leave.

I go back to the bedroom with Tom at my heels. I'm suddenly certain the scrunchie will be right smack in the middle of the bed and that when I turn back to look at Tom, he'll be holding a butcher knife, which he will then use to stab me to death. But the scrunchie isn't on the bed.

Where the hell is it?

It takes me a second to locate it—it's lying on the carpet, next to the nightstand. But since the carpet is dark, the black scrunchie is difficult to see. Although it's certainly not impossible. I imagine his gaze falling on the black fabric, his forehead furrowing as he tries to figure out what it is. The recognition dawning on his face.

I've got to get the hell out of here…

Tom sits on the edge of the bed while I put my clothes back on. I'm certain he's going to notice the scrunchie at any moment, and my heart is pounding so hard my chest hurts. But then, while I'm slipping my shoes on, Tom disappears into the bathroom. I take the opportunity to quickly kick the scrunchie back under the nightstand.

There. Now he'll never know that I know.

Tom returns to the bedroom with a couple of pills in his palm. He holds them out to me, and I eye them with barely concealed suspicion.

"What's that?" I ask.

"Ibuprofen."

Right. I am *not* taking random pills handed to me by this man. I'm not a *complete* idiot. "No, thanks. I'll be fine."

"Are you sure? You look pretty uncomfortable."

I smile as convincingly as I can. "Like I said, I just want to go home."

My heart continues to pound in my chest as Tom escorts me to his door. He blocks my way as he leans in to give me a kiss goodbye, and it almost makes my skin crawl. It's a far cry from the kiss we had when I first arrived.

"Well," I say, "goodbye!"

"Sure, I'll see you later." His eyes spend a moment probing my face until I start to squirm. "When you're feeling better."

Yeah, right. If he lets me out of this apartment, I am never, ever coming back.

"Do you want me to walk you downstairs?" he asks. He's still blocking the door, and all I want is for him to *move* so that I can get the hell out of here.

"No. *No.*" I laugh, trying to sound casual even though it's the most fake laugh I've ever heard. "I don't want you to have to go up and down five flights of stairs. I'll be fine. It's really not that late. And I'll call my own Uber."

"You sure?"

"Definitely."

"Because I don't mind."

Oh God, is he ever going to let me leave? "Really, I just want to be alone."

Finally—*finally!*—Tom turns to unlock his door, and I step outside. I'm convinced that at any moment, he's going to pull me back inside and wrap his fingers around my neck. Or smash my skull open with a hammer like he did to the mouse. But he doesn't do any of that. He simply closes the door behind me and locks it, and that's that.

I make it all the way to the stairwell before I start running.

CHAPTER 53

During the entire ride from Tom's apartment, I'm certain that when I get home, he's going to be waiting for me in front of my building with a butcher knife hidden under his coat, ready to slash my throat. But he isn't.

I get up the stairs as quickly as I can, then I lock the door to my apartment, as well as the dead bolt. And then I stuff a chair under the doorknob. I don't know if it will make any difference at all, but it makes me feel better at least. All the shades are already drawn, thanks to Real Kevin. Then I go to my bedroom, where I toss and turn for the next several hours.

I manage to wait until 6:30 in the morning before I shoot off a text message to Jake. I recall he was always an early riser, so I've got my fingers crossed he will get the message and I can talk to him before I lose my mind.

I need to talk to you in person as soon as possible. I can meet you wherever you want.

Almost instantly, a reply from Jake pops up on my screen:

I can be at your house in half an hour.

Twenty minutes later, the sound of my doorbell ringing nearly makes me jump out of my skin. Even though it's almost certainly Jake at the door, I grab a knife from the kitchen and bring it with me while I check the peephole. Sure enough, Jake is standing there in a crumpled white dress shirt and trench coat, the trademark stubble on his chin.

When I open the door, his tall, broad frame fills the doorway. He looks down at the knife in my right hand, and his eyes widen. "Syd? What's going on?"

I pull him inside by the arm and lock the door behind him. Then I hurry over to the coffee table and pick up the freezer bag lying on top of it. Inside is the water bottle I took from Tom's apartment.

"I need you to check this for fingerprints," I tell him.

"Okay. Why?"

I take a deep breath. "I want to see if it matches up with the unidentified prints found in Bonnie's apartment."

Jake takes the freezer bag out of my hand. He looks down at the water bottle inside. "Where did you get this?"

I have to tell him the whole story, but I really don't want to. It's humiliating to admit that the guy I've been dating could be a serial killer. Not that Jake is particularly judgmental, but he will judge me for that. I don't blame him.

So I don't want to deal with having to tell him unless it's true.

"Can you just…" I squeeze my fists together. "Can you just run the prints please?"

"*No.*" He shoots me a look. "Sydney, I want to help you. But you handing me a water bottle and expecting me to check for prints without even telling me why? That's not a reasonable thing to ask." He folds his muscular fore-arms across his chest. "I'm not leaving this apartment until you tell me what this is all about."

It's not an unfair request. The truth is I would have been stunned if he'd done it without that information. But now I have to tell him everything.

"The prints belong to a man named Thomas Brewer," I say.

"Okay, and why do you think Thomas Brewer killed Bonnie?"

I have to tell him. There's no way around it. "Because I've been dating him, and I found some of her belongings in his apartment."

Jake's face blanches. "Are you serious?"

I nod slowly.

"You're dating a guy you think is a serial killer? Is that what you're trying to tell me?"

My face burns. "Look, he seemed like a really nice guy. He's a doctor." Well, a pathologist who cuts dead people up for a living.

"Thomas Brewer…" He frowns. "Wait, that's not Dr. Brewer, the medical examiner?"

I nod again.

"Holy shit." He shakes his head. "I've *met* him before. He's a really smart guy—a hell of a medical examiner. He didn't seem like a creep. You really think he could have done this?"

"I…I do." I bite down on my lower lip. "Honestly, I barely got out of his apartment last night."

"Are you kidding me?"

"No. I was really scared he was going to…you know…"

Jake looks dazed as he pushes past me and drops down onto my sofa. He is still holding the freezer bag with the water bottle in it, and he stares down at it, his eyes glassy. "So you're saying you could have ended up like Bonnie."

"Well…" I sit down next to him. "I didn't. I got away."

"You should have called me right away."

"It's fine. I got out. I didn't want to bother you in the middle of the night."

"Are you joking?" His dark eyes are flashing. "Sydney, please bother me in the middle of the night, okay?"

"Okay, I just…"

"How could you put yourself in danger like that? He could have killed you, for Christ's sake!"

The outburst renders me temporarily silent. Jake doesn't yell much, but when he does, it's loud enough to make the whole room shake.

Jake drops the freezer bag on my coffee table and then buries his face in his palms. "Jesus, Syd."

"Jake…"

"If he had done anything to hurt you," he says in a low growl as he lifts his face from his hands, "I would have slit his throat."

I suck in a breath. Jake has always seemed utterly in control of his emotions, but I've never seen him like this—with his face bright red and a vein pulsating in his temple. He's the kind of cop who always does everything by the book and certainly not the kind of cop who would exact vigilante justice on a man who attacked a girl he used to date.

Maybe he's changed.

Jake has to take a few deep breaths to get his emotions under control. The color in his face finally returns to normal, and his shoulders relax.

"Okay," he says. "I'm going to run the water bottle for prints. And in the meantime, I'm going to have a patrol car sit outside your building."

"You don't have to do that."

"Don't you dare say no." The crease between his eyes deepens. "Syd, I'm not going to let anything happen to you. If that psychopath got to you, I…I would never be able to forgive myself. Especially since…" He drops his eyes. "Especially since if I hadn't been an idiot and had treated you right, you wouldn't be in this situation to begin with."

We sit there on my sofa for a moment staring at each other. I can't say he's wrong. "The past is the past. You can't change it."

"Sometimes you can make it right though."

I'm not sure what he means by that, and he doesn't elaborate. He picks up the freezer bag from the coffee table and promises that he'll let me know as soon as they have the results. I don't know how long it takes to run fingerprints, but I don't think it will be long.

CHAPTER 54

BEFORE

TOM

Slug has been watching me.

I don't know how long he's been standing there, but he definitely heard at least part of my conversation with Daisy. And he doesn't look happy.

"I can't believe you got Daisy to meet you," he says. "She must really be wild about you."

I look up at Slug. When we were little, we used to be the same height, but in the last couple of years, he shot up so that he's a lot taller than me. That said, in a fight, I might be able to take him. He's so skinny, it looks like a strong breeze could carry him away.

Of course, if he has a weapon, that changes everything.

But I don't want to fight Slug. In spite of everything, he's my best friend. When we were in grade school, nobody wanted to hang out with either one of us. Slug was more obviously weird and creepy, but I had trouble making friends too. For some reason, I couldn't relate to the other kids. Whenever I talked to them, I felt awkward.

I wasn't like that around Slug though. We were out-casts *together*. He never judged me about my alcoholic dad, and I never made fun of him for eating bugs or the fact that his parents were as old as most grandparents. Most years, when we had birthday parties, it was just him and me. Nobody else used to show up, even when we passed out invitations to the whole class.

I wonder if Slug and I will celebrate our next birthdays together.

Somehow, I don't think we will.

"Are you following me?" I ask him.

"What if I am?" he grunts.

"That's a shitty thing to do."

I push past him out of the Driscolls' backyard. Whatever else, I can't be caught back here. That wouldn't be good for either of us. Slug doesn't make any moves to stop me and in fact falls into step next to me.

"Alison talked to her," he points out.

Damn. He heard our conversation. I had been hoping he didn't. "It's fine. I explained it all to her."

"And you think she believed it?"

"Yes."

"You mean the way Alison believed it when we told her we had hamburger meat in the trunk?"

I don't have anything to say to that.

"Daisy is a problem," he says.

I shiver. It's the same thing he said about Alison, just hours before she was murdered.

"She's not a problem," I say. "I'm going to handle it."

"Right. The same way you handled Alison."

I don't like his sarcasm. He doesn't know for sure Alison would have turned us in, and the way he "handled" things made it all much, much worse. "Look, I'm going to talk to her. It'll be fine."

Slug's angular features look almost skeletal in the moonlight. "Right. Whatever you say."

"Slug," I say firmly, "I want you to stay away from Daisy, okay? Will you do that?"

His jaw tightens. "You're my best friend, Tom, but I'm not going to jail because you can't manage to do what needs to be done."

With those words, Slug stalks off, leaving me alone on the street.

CHAPTER 55

PRESENT DAY

SYDNEY

I take a quick shower after Jake leaves, but I can't focus on much. I really should be working, but that would be an impossible task. I mostly just pace across the living room.

A few hours after Jake left, my phone starts ringing. His name appears on the screen, and I snatch it up.

"Well?" I say.

"It's a match."

For a second, it feels like the walls are closing in around me. I just barely make it over to my sofa, where I sit down just before my legs give out under me. "What did he match with?"

"His prints matched with some unidentified ones that we found at Bonnie's apartment and also at the apartment of the other girl who was killed before her. He was definitely in both of their apartments."

"I can't believe it."

"You can't? You're the one who brought me the water bottle."

He's right. I was the one who was suspicious of Tom. But in my heart, I was thinking it was nothing but paranoia. After all, how could my boyfriend have killed all those girls?

And if I hadn't discovered that scrunchie, would I have been next?

"So what now?" I ask. "Are you going to arrest him?"

Jake snorts. "Based on a water bottle that you handed me? I don't think so. But we're going to try to bring him in for questioning. Hopefully, he will cooperate. Once we actually fingerprint him and match that up, then we're in business. Although it still might be tricky to get an arrest warrant. We'll see."

Of course, I was hoping Jake would tell me that he was going to bring Tom in and throw him in jail immediately, but that obviously isn't how things work. The thought of Tom being set free after they've questioned him is terrifying. I have to believe that if there's enough evidence, they're not going to let him leave.

But if there isn't enough evidence, if he does get released, then what? Will he know I was the one who turned him in? Will he want to get revenge?

"Is the police car outside my building?" I ask.

"It is," he confirms. "And if the department doesn't want to allow it anymore, I'll get in my car and sit out there myself. Don't worry. I'm not going to let him hurt you."

"Yeah."

"Syd? You okay?"

"I just…" I squeeze my eyes shut. "I can't believe I was so stupid. I thought he was a great guy. I mean, yes, he wasn't perfect. But I had no idea…"

"Please don't beat yourself up," Jake says. "I told

you—I met Brewer myself. And honestly, I'm shocked. I liked the guy. It just shows you never know. These guys who are really charming and smart and good looking can fool everyone."

"I still feel stupid."

"Would it make you feel better to know that it's because of you that we might be putting Bonnie's killer behind bars?"

He's right. If I hadn't dated him, he would have just gotten away with it all. And now, because of me, Bonnie will finally have justice.

"Call me if you have any updates," I tell him.

"I will if I can."

And now all that's left to do is wait.

CHAPTER 56

I am driving myself completely out of my mind in the apartment waiting to hear from Jake, so I decide to walk over to the yoga studio. There's a six-o'clock class, and I figure that will keep me occupied until dinner time. Not that I expect to have any sort of appetite. I attempted to choke down a sandwich for lunch, and I ate about a quarter of it.

I called Gretchen to see if she wanted to join me, but she was busy with Randy. So it's just me walking by myself to the yoga studio. At least Tom is at the police station, probably behind bars, so I feel safe. Well, safe-*ish*.

There are only about half a dozen women in the class today. I roll out my mat in the corner of the room and grab a few yoga blocks as well. Arlene comes into the classroom, her ponytail swinging behind her head. She smiles and gives me a big hello.

"Just you today?" she asks.

"Just me."

"By the way," Arlene says, "I wanted to tell you that I saw you with a young man on the street last week. He had black hair and he was very handsome."

"Um, thanks."

She frowns. "I hope it's not out of turn to say this, but he had a very dark aura around him. It was extremely unsettling for me."

Well, that may have been because he killed a bunch of women. "Huh."

"I tend to be very intuitive about this sort of thing," she says. "I just think you should be very careful around this man."

Where were you a few days ago, Arlene? "Don't worry. He and I aren't seeing each other anymore."

"Oh, thank heavens!" She clutches her narrow chest. "I have to tell you the truth, Sydney. When I saw that man, I wanted to run over to you, grab you by the shoulders, and tell you to run away."

Great. Even Arlene knew my boyfriend was a creep.

The yoga class lasts a little over an hour. Usually, I find the stretches very relaxing, but today my body doesn't want to cooperate. Every inch of me feels tight, and when we do the meditation at the end, my mind won't stop racing.

What's going to happen to Tom now that the police are onto him? Will they end up arresting him today? Is he in jail right this moment? Will they search his apartment and find more evidence of those girls that he killed? Maybe a stash of the hair that he sliced off their scalps?

When the class ends, I grab my purse and dig out my phone. My stomach fills with butterflies when I see a missed call from Jake. No, *two* missed calls.

That's not a good sign.

I click on his name to return the call, and almost instantly, he picks up the phone. "Sydney," he says.

"Did you bring him in for questioning?"

"Yes, but—"

"Is he in jail?"

There's a long silence on the other line. "No. We had to let him go."

"What?" I cry. "But you confirmed it, right? You fingerprinted him and it was a match, right?"

"It was a match," he confirms, "but that's not evidence of wrongdoing. All it proves is that he was in their apartments at some point in the past."

"But that's really suspicious! Couldn't you have—"

"He has an alibi, Syd."

I frown. "An alibi?"

"For the night Bonnie was murdered. He has an airtight alibi for the entire night."

What? "Are you sure? Maybe whoever gave him his alibi was lying."

"He was working at the hospital the whole night," Jake says. "Multiple people saw him there. There are cameras too. It's rock solid. There's no way he could've killed her."

I am stunned. I was *certain* it had to be Tom. His fingerprints were in those girls' apartments. Even *Arlene* thought he had an evil aura!

I guess it's good to know that I wasn't dating a murderer, but at the same time, I have even more questions. If Tom didn't kill those girls, who did? And why was he hiding his relationship with Bonnie? Why was he calling me from a burner phone?

Somehow, even though he has an alibi, I'm not certain that Tom is innocent.

"You okay, Syd?"

"Uh-huh." I swallow a lump in my throat. "I'm just...
I don't know what to think anymore. You really don't
think Tom killed those girls?"

"Like I said, he could not have done it. What he told
us is that he's been dating a lot of women, and just by
chance, he happened to have gone out with both of them."

"And you believe that?"

"I do, Syd."

"So..." I tug at a lock of my hair. "If I told you I was
going to go out with him again, you would be fine with
that?"

Jake is silent for several beats on the other line. "No,"
he finally says. "But not because I think he killed anybody."

I let that statement just sit there for a moment, because
I don't know what to say.

"Listen." Jake is the first to break the silence. "Brewer isn't
going to hurt you. Like I said before, he is a solid guy. I trust
him. But I'll keep an eye on your building anyway, okay?"

"You don't have to do that."

"Yes, I do."

I consider asking Jake if he'll come over to escort me
back to my building from the yoga studio. But that would
be ridiculous. Yes, it's now dark, but it isn't even that late.
There are still people out on the street. I am perfectly safe
walking home. Especially now that I know my boyfriend
is definitely not a serial killer.

Although there is still a killer out there. Somewhere.

I grab my coat, say goodbye to Arlene, and head out
into the cold, dark night. The temperature has dropped
abruptly in the last couple of weeks, and winter is setting
into the city. We might end up having snow for Christmas.

When I get closer to my building, I see somebody sitting on the front steps. It's a man, and he looks familiar, even with a beanie stuffed on his head and wearing a coat. As I approach, the man stands up to look at me, and in the glow of the streetlights, I can clearly make out his face.

It's Tom.

CHAPTER 57

BEFORE

TOM

As the clock ticks closer to one in the morning, I lie awake in bed, staring at the ceiling, wondering if I'm making a terrible mistake.

I love Daisy, and I want to see her more than anything. I want to explain to her that I would never do anything to hurt her and that I want to be with her, no matter what her father thinks of me. I want to try to convince her I'm a good guy, even though that might not be the truth.

But the more I think about it, the more uneasy I feel.

Because the truth is I'm not a good guy. I killed somebody. And every time I look at Daisy, I have terrible thoughts. Yes, I want to kiss her, but I also want to do a lot of other things to her. Bad things.

This won't end well for either of us.

But there's another thought that keeps nagging at me.

Slug heard my conversation with Daisy. Which means he heard when and where we are meeting, and if he doesn't trust me to take care of the situation with Daisy, he might take matters into his own hands.

What if Daisy is in danger?

I sit up straight in bed. I'm getting more worried with each passing minute. Slug has already done some terrible things, and the last task he needs to complete to ensure our freedom is to take care of the "Daisy situation."

I wish I could text her, but it doesn't look like any of my text messages to her have been read. I'm willing to bet her parents confiscated her phone. Or blocked me. I can't risk texting her about our meeting.

I look down at my watch. It's half past midnight. It will take me twenty minutes to walk to the Dairy Queen—fifteen if I sprint there. I could try taking the Chevy, but I'm worried the sound of the garage door opening would wake my mother, and then she'd keep me from leaving. Or worse, involve the police. And my bike has had a flat tire since the fall that I never got around to replacing.

No, it's better to go on foot. If I leave now, I should make it before Daisy arrives. And if Slug is there, I can get rid of him. Or at least make sure he doesn't do anything stupid.

I throw my hoodie sweatshirt back on and stuff my feet into a pair of sneakers. I am moving fast, but I've wasted another several minutes, and I'm definitely going to have to hurry to get there before Daisy does.

I better check Daisy's house first. If she hasn't left yet, I can head her off at the pass. A lot depends on this.

Maybe her life.

I sprint over to Daisy's house as quickly as I can, cutting through a neighbor's yard to save a couple of extra minutes. I'm out of breath by the time I make it back to

Daisy's, and I waste no time rounding the side of the house to get to the back door.

The Driscoll house is silent. Daisy's parents are either asleep or her father is in the field. And more importantly, Daisy's window is dark.

Damn. I missed her. This is bad.

Worse, I sacrificed at least five minutes to make the detour to Daisy's house. Five minutes I didn't have to spend. Five minutes when something terrible could be happening.

I better run.

I run as fast as I can all the way to the Dairy Queen. By the halfway point, I am deeply regretting not taking my mother's Chevy. I'm so hot, I rip off the hoodie and wear it around my waist. And the worst part is, I don't think I'm even going to make it by one.

Daisy, please hang in there.

Okay, I shouldn't panic. Maybe I'm overreacting. Maybe Slug isn't planning anything. Maybe Daisy is going to be fine.

When I arrive at the Dairy Queen, Daisy's mother's Lincoln Continental is parked in the lot. Apparently, she was smarter than me and grabbed the car. And then my heart sinks when I see the car parked next to hers.

It's Slug's Oldsmobile.

Daisy is here, and so is Slug. And I can't see them anywhere.

My T-shirt is soaked with sweat. I'm breathing hard from my run, but I can't afford to stop, even for a second. I have to make sure Daisy is okay.

I walk around the side of the Dairy Queen to the back parking lot. My heart is pounding, and it's not entirely from my fifteen-minute run. I'm late, but only by about two minutes. Nothing could possibly have happened in two minutes.

Could it?

As I get closer to the back, I start to get even more nervous. Why is it so quiet back there? If both Daisy and Slug are together, shouldn't I hear some noise? Talking? Shouting? *Something?*

No, something is wrong. I'm sure of it.

"Daisy?" I call out.

Dead silence.

My panic is mounting. It occurs to me that I should have brought some kind of weapon, although I don't know what. I could have grabbed a knife from the kitchen. Because if Slug is here, he sure as hell brought a weapon. And I might need a weapon of my own to defend her. And if he did anything to hurt her, I'll need it to kill him.

When I finally round the corner of the Dairy Queen, I freeze in my tracks. Way at the other end of the small lot, I see a lump. As I get slightly closer, I realize it's a body. Lying on the ground, not moving. And there's another person standing over the lifeless lump.

I am far too late.

Oh Christ, Daisy...

CHAPTER 58

PRESENT DAY

SYDNEY

For a moment, I consider making a run for it. I don't want to talk to Tom, that's for sure.

But where am I supposed to go? He's in front of the entrance to my building. Also, according to Jake, he's not a killer. So really, I should have nothing to be scared of.

Except for the fact that I turned him in to the police, and he probably knows it.

"Sydney," Tom says as he rises to his feet, "we need to talk."

My body goes rigid. "Do we?"

"You told the police that I killed a bunch of people, so yes, I think we do."

I suck in a breath. "I...I didn't..."

"Detective Jake Sousa is your ex, right?" He arches an eyebrow. "A cop named Jake? I figured that one out."

I flinch. "Fine. I told him."

His shoulders sag now that he has confirmation. "My God, Sydney. How could you think I did that?"

"I don't know." I hug my arms to my chest, and not just because it's close to freezing out here. "Maybe because you dated a girl who lived in my building who was murdered and you never bothered to tell me. How about that?"

"It…it wasn't that serious."

"You're lying. She told me it was getting serious. You told me yourself that you were at the tail end of a relationship."

"It wasn't serious," he insists. "Bonnie and I were casual. Maybe we considered taking it to the next level, but not really. It's not like you and me."

"You and me?" I burst out. "Yeah, why don't we talk about that? What's going on between you and me anyway?"

"How can you ask me that? You're my *girlfriend*."

"Am I? Then how come you only contact me on a *burner phone*?"

Tom opens his mouth, but no sound comes out. He doesn't have an answer for that one.

"Exactly," I say.

"Okay, fine." He shakes his head. "I'm an idiot, and I have commitment issues. Okay? But I'm working on it. Because I really, really like you, Syd. And"—his brow creases—"I don't want this to be over."

I stare at Tom, standing in the street in front of the stairs to my building. Despite everything, I'm still desperately attracted to him. And Jake has reassured me that he is not a serial killer.

But it doesn't matter. I can't continue dating Tom. I don't trust him. Maybe he didn't kill anyone, but there's something about him that's not right. He's been lying to me about too many things. I'd be an idiot to give him another chance.

"I'm sorry," I say. "I don't think—"

Before I can find the right way to tell him that we are officially breaking up, a voice squeals from behind me: "Sydney! Oh my God, Syd, is that *him*? Is that *Tom*?"

Oh great—it's Gretchen and Randy.

I turn around and find the two of them coming toward us, Gretchen's hand clutching Randy's arm. She's got on a white puffball hat, and Randy is wearing a black trench coat. I can't believe that after all the time I've been trying to introduce Tom to Gretchen and Randy, it's finally about to happen when we are seconds away from breaking up.

"Hi!" Gretchen chirps. "You must be Tom! I'm Gretchen, and this is my boyfriend, Randy."

I look over at Tom, wondering if he'll try to ingratiate himself with my friends in order to suck up to me. But instead, he's just standing there, frozen. He's staring at Randy, his face deathly pale.

"Hey there." Randy raises a hand. "Good to finally meet you, Tom."

Tom reaches out to hold on to the banister. He looks like he's about to be sick. "Hi," he finally manages.

"Oh my gosh," Gretchen gushes. "He's just as handsome as you said he is, Syd."

Tom is still staring at Randy. It is the strangest thing. Does he think he recognizes him from somewhere?

"Sydney." Tom tries to grab my arm, but I shake him off. "Can I talk to you for a moment? *Privately?*"

I glance over at Gretchen and Randy, who are giving me curious looks. I don't want to talk to Tom privately. I'm done with him, and there's no point in drawing this out. "Actually," I say, "I'm going to go inside. It's cold out."

"Can I come in and talk to you?" Tom asks.

"I'd rather you didn't." I give him my coolest look, just in case he doesn't know where he stands. "I don't think we have anything else to say to each other."

"Sydney." He's speaking through his teeth now as he grabs my arm. "I *really* need to talk to you. *Now.*"

Despite everything else, Tom has always been a gentleman to me. But now that I'm ending things, I'm discovering a different side of him. He's never grabbed me this way. He's never refused to leave when I asked him.

But to my surprise, it's Randy who steps between us, puffing up his chest. He is much scrawnier than Tom but several inches taller. "Sydney says she doesn't want to speak to you right now. So I think you need to leave."

Tom glares up at Randy, venom in his eyes. "This really isn't any of your concern."

"I'm *making* it my concern."

The two of them are staring each other down. Finally, Randy takes a menacing step forward, and Tom releases my arm. "Fine." His gaze darts between me and Randy. "*Fine.*"

Gretchen puts her arm around my shoulders, pulling me close for comfort as we walk up the steps to the front door. Randy lingers behind for a few moments, still in that standoff with Tom. Finally, he follows behind us. And when he closes the door to the building, Tom is still standing there, at the foot of the stairs.

"Oh, sweetie!" Gretchen cries. "What happened out there? Are you okay?"

My eyes well up with tears, but I don't want to cry in front of her and Randy. "I'm okay. I promise."

"You need to come inside with us," she says. "I insist."

She looks at Randy for confirmation, and he nods.

"You shouldn't be alone in your apartment with that guy hanging around outside. Come to our place for a bit."

"I'll make dinner!" Gretchen says excitedly.

They are right. I definitely don't want to be alone right now. "Well," I say, "okay."

As Randy is unlocking the door to their first-floor apartment, my phone buzzes in my purse. A text message. I pull it out, and a message is waiting for me on the screen. It's from Tom.

You need to get out of there right now.

And then the next message comes in all caps:

YOU ARE IN DANGER!!!

I am genuinely sick of this overly dramatic bullshit. Bubbles appear on the screen to indicate that Tom is still typing, but I don't want to hear it. So before any more messages pop up on the screen, I block his number.

There. Now I have nothing to worry about.

CHAPTER 59

Gretchen starts cooking dinner when I get into their apartment. She's making some sort of casserole, which seems to involve putting basically everything from the fridge into a nine-by-eleven-inch pan and then sticking it in the oven at 400°.

"Trust me," she says, "it's delicious."

"I don't know how it could not be delicious given how much cheese you just put in that pan," I tease her.

She winks at me. "The secret to everything that tastes good is cheese."

I laugh. I'm definitely feeling better since leaving Tom in front of the steps of the building. There's still a heavy feeling in the pit of my stomach, but I did the right thing. Even if Tom isn't a serial killer, he was not a good boyfriend. Like he said, he was terrified of commitment. I mean, when he met my friends, he looked like he was practically going to have a heart attack.

Good riddance.

While we're waiting for the casserole concoction to bake in the oven, Randy decides to take a shower, and Gretchen shows me some of the photos from her exhibit at the museum. I feel terrible that I didn't manage to make it there one more time before it closed, but she is really understanding about it.

"My God, Syd," she says, "you've been through so much lately. And you already saw it once."

"It was amazing. Truly."

I flip through the photographs, which shows how much work Gretchen put into it. The exhibit was about flower species dating back to the Middle Ages. It's both spectacular and incredibly colorful.

That's why she was at the museum the night Bonnie was killed. When she claimed she had been with Randy, but instead, he was in our apartment building, all alone.

I can't help but feel uneasy about that. Okay, Randy just defended me, and I'm grateful for that. But now that Tom has a rock-solid alibi for the night of the murder, we still don't know who killed Bonnie.

It wasn't Randy, though. I'm sure of it.

To my amazement, the ant farm has been mounted next to the bookcase. I genuinely thought Gretchen was going to toss it out the window, the way she was talking. "I can't believe you let him keep the ant farm," I say.

"I know." She rolls her eyes, but she's smiling. "I must really love that lunkhead, huh?"

I can't help but feel a jab of sadness. Will I ever feel that way about anyone? It's possible someday I will, but it definitely won't be Tom.

The timer goes off, which means the mystery casserole

is done. Gretchen pulls it out of the oven just as Randy emerges from the shower. With his hair plastered to his skull, he looks almost painfully skinny. He flashes us a big smile. "You ladies need help?"

Randy grabs some dishes and utensils, I carry the casserole, and Gretchen fishes out a bottle of wine from the cabinet over the refrigerator. A few minutes later, I am scooping casserole onto my plate, and when I taste it…it's not that bad! Actually, it's pretty good. Before I know it, I have demolished half a plate of casserole.

"This is delicious, Gretchen," Randy says happily. "You're the best cook ever."

She giggles. "No, I'm not. I mean, it's a *casserole*."

"Yeah, but"—he grins at her—"somehow, you make everything taste so good."

She beams. "Well, I love to cook for you."

Randy stares at her for a moment. He plays with his fork, pushing some of the casserole noodles around his plate. After what appears to be several seconds of internal debate, he gets out of his chair. While I watch in astonishment, he drops down onto one knee.

Oh no. Not right now—not right in front of me. *Please* no.

"Gretchen," he says, "I love you so much."

Her mouth is hanging open. "Randy…"

Okay, this is happening.

"I really do. In fact, I don't know what I would do without you." He digs around in the pocket of his jeans until he pulls out that blue velvet box. How long has he been carrying that ring around with him, waiting for the right moment? "And that's why I never want to be without you. Gretchen, will you marry me?"

Her eyes are shining, brimming with tears. "Oh my God, yes! Of course! Of course I'll marry you!"

Randy slides the white-gold ring with the tiny diamond onto Gretchen's slender finger. And I was right—she doesn't care what size the diamond is. She's just so thrilled that he asked her to marry him. And then he helps her to her feet and kisses her.

It's absolutely the sweetest thing I have ever seen.

And I think I'm about to start crying.

They are happy tears. Well, mostly. I'm not going to say it isn't depressing that my best friend is getting engaged on the same day that I've had to end the most promising relationship I've had in the last several years. But I'm happy for her. I truly am.

"Excuse me," I say. "I'll give the two of you some privacy."

They barely even hear me. They're too busy making out.

I hurry off to the bathroom, my eyes heavy with moisture. No, I'm not going to cry right now. I just need a minute to pull myself together, then I can go back out there and be super happy for my two friends.

The first thing I do in the bathroom is splash some cold water on my face. Naturally, I look extremely splotchy. When I look at my reflection right now, I can't even understand why a guy like Tom would have *wanted* to date me. He is gorgeous, and I am maybe a step up above plain. What on earth did he ever see in me? No wonder he didn't want a commitment. If I were a supermodel, it would be a different story.

I use the toilet, and when I'm done, naturally, it doesn't want to flush. There's some sort of irony in the fact that

I'm in the super's apartment and the toilet doesn't work. I'm sort of reluctant to interrupt Gretchen and Randy's romantic moment to ask him to help me get the toilet to flush down my pee.

Well, I don't need him. As I said to Bonnie, I know how to fix the toilet.

I pull the cover off the tank. My experience is that there is a lever in there that sometimes gets stuck—the toilets in these apartments are pretty poorly made. Sure enough, the lever is stuck, and after I get it free, the toilet flushes no problem. I may not be successful in love, but at least I'm successful in fixing toilets.

But then, when the water in the tank goes down, I see something else.

It's a plastic bag.

It's a freezer bag—the same kind of airtight bag I used to store the water bottle with Tom's fingerprints on it. Why is there a freezer bag inside their toilet tank? That's super strange.

The bag seems to be taped in place. Curious, I pull it out to see why it's there. I imagine bringing it out and showing it to them. You guys are never going to believe what I found in your toilet!

And then I see what's inside. And I realize that I will not be showing it to them. Not now—not ever.

Because the bag is filled with locks of long hair. At least half a dozen of them.

And each one is tied together with a different-color ribbon.

Oh my God.

Randy is the killer.

CHAPTER 60

I stand there in the bathroom for at least two minutes, hyperventilating with panic.

I can't believe this. And yet…it makes too much sense not to be true. Randy had the key to Bonnie's apartment. Randy has no alibi. Randy is decidedly creepy.

If only I had told Jake the truth. Why did I let Gretchen talk me into keeping my mouth shut?

I wish I had my phone. I could call Jake, and he'd drive over here with sirens blasting. He might already be outside. But I left my purse out in the living room. I can't contact him without going back out there. And the idea of going back into the living room with that man fills me with terror.

But what can I do? I've already been in the bathroom way too long. At some point, Randy is going to get suspicious. And since he knows what he's got hiding in here, he'll likely do anything to protect his secret.

I drop the bag of hair back in the toilet tank and replace the cover. I try not to think about the fact that one of those locks of hair belongs to Bonnie. Randy murdered her, and he stored her hair in the toilet. It's just too awful for words.

And now Gretchen has agreed to be his wife. That's even *more* awful.

I compose myself as best I can. I can't let on what I've found. As I put my hand on the doorknob, a wave of dizziness comes over me. I push it away and open the door. I am going to have to put on the performance of a lifetime. At least until I can text Jake and get out of here. I just have to act natural to make sure Gretchen isn't in any danger until the cops arrive.

"Hey, what happened in there?" Randy asks when I come back into the living room. They have finally stopped kissing and are cuddled together on the couch, Randy still drinking from his wineglass. "We were worried!"

Does he suspect what I might have found? I attempt to laugh, although it doesn't sound like a normal human laugh. Oh well. "I should probably get going. I'm sure the two of you want to celebrate together."

Randy looks like he's about to agree, but then Gretchen jumps off the couch and grabs my arm. "Don't be silly! I bought this cake at that amazing bakery down on Twenty-Seventh Street this afternoon, and I thought we could share it now. I just put it out on the table."

I rub my stomach. "Actually, I am *so* full from your delicious casserole."

Is that a good enough excuse? Do I have to tell them that I have my period?

"Oh come on, Syd!" Her eyes are shining. This has probably been the best day of her life, and it's about to become the worst. "Please stay for cake. Come on. It's my engagement night!"

I look over at Randy. His eyelids seem to be sagging a bit. I guess the excitement of getting engaged has been too much for him.

Before I can come up with another excuse, someone bangs on the door. There's a doorbell, but this person doesn't seem at all interested in using it. They slam their fist into the door four times in a row.

"Sydney! Are you in there? Sydney!"

It's Tom's voice. Crap, someone must have let him into the building.

"Oh no!" Gretchen frowns. "Why is he still bothering you? God, some men are so awful!"

You have no idea, Gretchen.

Gretchen walks over to the door. She presses her index finger against her lips to tell me to be quiet. I glance over at Randy, who doesn't seem to be paying much attention to me, thank God. He looks like he's almost dozing off. I grab my purse off the coffee table and rifle through it to find my phone.

Damn it, where's my phone?

"I'm sorry, Tom," Gretchen says through the door. "Sydney isn't here at the moment."

"Bullshit!" He slams his fist against the door again. "I know she's in there! Let me in! Let me in or I'll call the police!"

"And tell them what?" Gretchen says shortly. "That you're banging on my door and demanding that we let you in? *We're* the ones who should call the police!"

I had my phone in my purse—I'm sure of it. Tom texted me before I walked into this apartment, and I had it then. And after I blocked his number, I put it back in my purse. So where is it?

I bend forward, trying to get a better look inside, and a wave of dizziness comes over me again. What is going on here? I only had one glass of wine.

I look over at Randy on the sofa. His eyes have drifted shut completely. I can't believe he's sleeping through Tom banging on the door this way.

"You know what I'll tell the police!" Tom hisses through the door. "Let me in right now! I swear to God, Daisy, you better not hurt her."

Daisy? Who is Daisy? What is he talking about?

"Daisy!" He is shouting now. "Daisy, let me in right now!"

"Why is he calling you Daisy?" I ask Gretchen.

She turns away from the door, her expression thoughtful. "The thing is, Sydney," she says, "there are a few things about me that you don't know."

And then she turns back to the door and twists the lock.

CHAPTER 61

BEFORE

TOM

D aisy?" I gasp.

Daisy turns away from the body on the ground, and I can see her tear-streaked face. I also see the gun in her hand. She lets it drop, then she runs in my direction, the tears flowing freely. She doesn't stop until she has propelled herself into my arms.

"Tom!" she sobs. "Oh, Tom! I was waiting here for you, and he…he came at me. He had a *knife*."

That bastard. He did exactly what I thought he would do.

She buries her damp face in my shoulder as I cling to her. "I almost didn't bring my father's extra gun, but I thought I might need protection out here. If I hadn't…"

If I hadn't… I can't even contemplate the end of that sentence. If she hadn't brought that gun, Daisy would be lying dead in the parking lot of the Dairy Queen right now. And I would be murdering Slug with my bare hands.

"What happened?" I ask.

She pulls her face away from my T-shirt. She's so beautiful, even when she's crying. *Especially* when she's crying. "He was waiting for me here. He told me all this terrible stuff. He said that he…he killed Brandi and Alison. And that now he was going to kill *me*."

"Jesus," I breathe.

Even though I know it's true, there's a part of me that doesn't want to believe Slug could do all that stuff. I could believe he was a Peeping Tom, but until recently, I never would have believed that he was capable of killing someone, much less mutilating a bunch of girls. He *loved* girls. He just couldn't get them to like him back. People thought he was weird, yeah, but that's because they didn't understand him. He just thought insects were the coolest thing. He talked about wanting to be an entomologist—a bug scientist.

That's never going to happen now.

Slug, why did you do it? I would have gotten you a girlfriend somehow if you wanted one so badly.

"I better call my father," Daisy says through her tears. "He's going to be furious with me for sneaking out, but he needs to know what happened."

"Your father?" I take a step back, ready to bolt. "Daisy, if you call your dad, he's going to snap handcuffs on me and take me to jail."

"No, he won't!" She looks affronted. "Slug told me he killed Brandi and Alison all on his own. You didn't have anything to do with it! Don't you understand? This *clears* you."

"Right, but…" I rub the back of my neck. "If it's all the same to you, I'd rather get out of here. If your dad sees me here, I don't know if he's going to believe anything I say."

"I need you, Tom." She frowns. "You have to back up my story that Slug was trying to attack me."

"But I didn't see him try to attack you."

She throws up her hands. "So what? I mean, look at him! He was waiting for me here. He was obviously going to attack me. And he came with a knife, for God's sake!"

I step over to where my best friend is lying dead in the parking lot of the Dairy Queen, bypassing the kitchen knife lying next to him. There's a puddle of crimson spreading below his body and across his chest. His lips are slightly parted, and there's a trickle of blood running out the side of his mouth. His brown eyes are open, staring at the stars. In the moonlight, you can't see his acne, and he looks a lot younger. He reminds me of the way he looked when I first sat next to him in the cafeteria and he was so happy just to have a friend.

"He's a monster," Daisy sniffles. "He killed my best friend."

I put my arm around her again as she dissolves into fresh tears. It looks like I'm going to have to stay. But she's right. Her story absolves me of any guilt. Maybe the chief will even let me date her again.

I realize I've got to tell my mother what's going on. She's also going to be furious that I left the house in the middle of the night, but it would be worse if she woke up and found my bed empty. And I have a feeling I'm going to be here for a while.

I pull my phone out of my pocket. I had it on silent during the night, and I got a text message about twenty minutes ago, while I was walking over here. Weirdly, it's from Slug. I read the message, my heart speeding up again:

Hey, Daisy asked me to come meet her at the Dairy Queen. Maybe together we can convince her not to say anything.

Okay. That's strange.

And then something else strange hits me. Something that had been percolating in the back of my head finally rises to the surface. When we were talking about the problem with Daisy, Slug said I should handle her "the same way you handled Alison."

At the time, I thought he was being sarcastic, but he didn't *sound* sarcastic. A terrible thought suddenly occurs to me:

Slug thought *I* was the one who killed Alison.

Now that I think about it, how could he have killed her? We were driving around most of the night. And it's not like Alison would have left her house in the middle of the night to meet *Slug*. There's only one person who Alison trusted, who could have lured her out of her house without a fight. It's definitely not Slug. It's not me either.

"Daisy," I say, "you said that Slug surprised you by showing up here?"

She bobs her head. "He was hiding in the shadows when I arrived."

"But his car was in the parking lot. Didn't you see it?"

She wrinkles her pert little nose. "I didn't know that was his car."

"Well, you knew it wasn't *my* car. So whose car did you think it was at one in the morning?"

"I don't know. A random parked car then."

"Uh-huh." I look at my best friend's body, still splayed out on the ground. "And while he was getting ready to attack you, that was when he told you about all the other girls he killed?"

Daisy stares at me, her lips turned down. "I don't know what you're implying." She looks over at my phone, which is still in my right hand. "What's on your phone? What's got you so worked up?"

"Nothing—" I start to say, but before I can even finish the word, Daisy reaches out and snatches the phone right out of my hand. "Hey! Give that back!"

But she isn't listening. She's staring down at the screen, and even if I got my phone back, it's too late at this point. She reads the message from Slug.

"Oh, I see." She nods slowly. "You think that I set him up. That I lured him out here just so I could kill him. Is that what you think?"

"Well…" No, of course I don't think that. Daisy would never do something like that. Not my Daisy.

She swipes at the screen on my phone, and I realize she has just deleted the text message. When the message is gone, she hands my phone back to me. "And what if I did?"

I suck in a breath. "*What?*"

"Jesus, Tom." She bends down to pick something up off the ground, and I realize the gun is back in her hand. "The two of you were pathetic. Slug gets himself caught peeping in windows—that's bad enough—but then you just let Alison walk away after she sees you putting a dead body in the trunk of your car. I snuck over to see you that night, but then I ended up seeing everything you did through the side window of your house. All your stupid decisions. I mean, do you *want* to spend the rest of your life in prison?"

My head is spinning. I can't believe the words coming out of Daisy's mouth. "You killed Alison," I manage.

"You say it like it's a *bad* thing." Her clear blue eyes widen. "Tom, she was going to call the police about you. Do you know that? And believe me, she hated you. Every chance she got, she would try to convince me to dump you." She smiles at me. "She didn't see the potential in you that I do."

It suddenly feels very hard to breathe. "What about Brandi?"

"You were *kissing* her, Tom." Her pale eyelashes flutter. "You and I were supposed to be together. I couldn't have that! She was all wrong for you. Trust me—I did you a *massive* favor."

"You tortured them," I gasp. "That's what the news said."

"I mean, a little." She shrugs. "I had to have some fun with it, didn't I?"

I suddenly realize my knees can't support me anymore. I crouch down in the middle of the parking lot, spots floating before my eyes. This can't be happening. The girl I love didn't just admit to killing three people. This has got to be another one of those wild dreams of mine. Any second now, I'm going to wake up covered in sweat.

Any second now.

"Stop being such a drama queen, Tom." Daisy kicks me with her sneaker. "It's not like you didn't enjoy slashing your father's throat. You think I don't know you? I do."

"It's not the same. Slug didn't deserve this."

"Didn't he?" She sneers. "I hate to break it to you, but your friend was a pervert. He went all over town peeping in girls' windows. Guys like that don't grow up to be

332

wonderful people. We probably just saved a couple of girls in college from getting raped."

"You don't know that. You didn't know Slug." Although she does have a point. What kind of guy goes around town peeking in girls' windows? No matter how desperate you are, you don't do that. If I had known...

Slowly, I manage to get back on my feet, although I'm still lightheaded. Daisy is holding the gun, and she's pointing it at me. There's an expression on her face that is unfamiliar but at the same time very familiar.

I see it sometimes when I look in the mirror.

I always thought that I was drawn to Daisy because she's so pretty and sweet and *good* and that she brought out the better parts of me. But now I know the truth. The reason I feel connected to Daisy is because she's exactly like me.

"Are you going to shoot me?" I ask.

"I wasn't planning to," she says. "I'd say it's your call. What are you going to tell the police?"

"Daisy..."

"Listen to me, Tom." She shakes the gun at me. "I'll make this really simple for you. I'm not going to jail. So either you go along with my story, and Slug takes the fall for everything, or else I kill you, and you and Slug share the blame."

"Makes no difference to you, huh?"

My voice cracks on the words, and Daisy's face falls. It hits me that despite all the terrible things she's done, she never faked her feelings for me. "Don't say that. I like you, Tom. I *love* you. And if all the murders get pinned on Slug, we can be together again. Won't that be wonderful?"

Despite everything, there's a part of me that agrees

with her. It would be wonderful to be with Daisy again. I had been so scared I would never get to hold her or touch her again—it felt like my life was over. Now she's giving me a second chance. Giving *us* a second chance.

She notices the expression on my face and reaches for my hand. "We could lose our virginity to each other, Tom. That would be so amazing. I've been saving myself for you, you know."

My mouth goes dry at her confession. "Oh."

"My point is we could have everything. We could spend the *rest of our lives* together." Her voice lowers to a sultry tone. "That's what you want, isn't it?"

It used to be *everything* I wanted. "What about my father?"

"What about him? He's a drunk. Nobody cares what happened to him." She offers me a smile. "I will make sure my father doesn't dig too deep. Being the daughter of the chief of police has its advantages."

I don't doubt that. Even if I pretend to go along with her story for now and then turn on her when the police arrive, nobody will believe me. Chief Driscoll would never believe that the apple of his eye is a homicidal maniac.

She winks at me, which makes a chill go down my spine. "What do you say, Tom? Do we live happily ever after?"

I make a decision at that moment.

I will keep Daisy's secret.

I won't tell a soul that she murdered two of our class-mates and my best friend. I won't tell anyone that she's a psychopath. I will take her secret to my grave.

I will do this to save myself. But that's not the only reason. I will keep Daisy's secret because I love her. I have *always* loved her—more than anyone I've ever known. And even now that I know how dangerous she is, I don't have it in me to hurt her. And she knows it.

But she and I are over. She won't be my girlfriend anymore. I won't kiss her. We won't lose our virginities to each other. We won't get married or have kids or grow old together. I'll still think about her, but I'll try not to. I love Daisy, but all I want right now is to be as far away from her as possible.

I won't let her ruin me.

I'm better than that.

CHAPTER 62

PRESENT DAY

SYDNEY

My head is spinning.

I'm not sure if it's everything that's happened recently or something else, but it feels like I can barely stand up straight. Still, I'm thinking straight enough to feel horrified when Gretchen lets Tom into the apartment.

Tom's eyes widen when he gets a look at me. He glances over at Gretchen, then back to me. "Sydney," he says, "are you okay?"

Before I can say a word, the dizziness overwhelms me, and I sink to my knees. Even if I wanted to leave this apartment, I couldn't do it. Maybe I could crawl out.

"Jesus Christ!" Tom says. "Daisy, what the hell did you do to her?"

Why is he asking Gretchen what she did? *Randy* is the killer. Except when I look back at Randy, he is still out cold.

"I just thought everyone needed to chill out a bit," Gretchen says. "Especially *her*."

The wine. Oh my God, was there something in the wine I was drinking? Thank God I only had one glass. Randy must have had three. Gretchen barely touched it.

Tom asks the question that's in my head: "What did you give them?"

"Oleander," she answers instantly. "I keep a few leaves handy for emergencies." When she sees the shocked look on Tom's face, she adds, "I didn't give them enough to kill them, but I find that when mixed with alcohol, it makes people extremely drowsy. And as I'm sure you know, Tom, it doesn't show up on a routine autopsy."

A flush enters his cheeks as he stares at her. "I can't believe you. You promised me—no more. You told me you would leave me alone after the last one, Daisy."

Why does he keep calling her Daisy? It's so strange. I look up at the two of them, standing over me while I lie on the floor wondering what the hell oleander is and what it will do to me. At least she supposedly didn't give me enough to kill me.

"Who's Daisy?" I manage to ask, even though my tongue feels like a big lump in my mouth.

"That's what everyone used to call me when I was a girl," she explains. "You know I love flowers—you saw my exhibit—and daisies are my favorite. But I have outgrown the nickname. Nobody calls me that anymore. Well, except Tom here."

"You have a serious problem," Tom croaks. "I had no idea that you...that you were *living* here. Christ. Was that because of Bonnie?"

Gretchen's eyelashes flutter. "I had to keep an eye on

things. So I joined Bonnie's little yoga class. I just wanted to meet this girl that you thought was so wonderful and worthy of your time."

Even with my foggy brain, I register what she's saying. I still remember the day Gretchen rolled out her yoga mat next to Bonnie's. She flashed a big smile. *Hi, I'm Gretchen! This is my first yoga class.* And with her sweet, open face, we both immediately liked her.

Then she met Randy while coming over to visit us. And now she's living with him. Randy was her ticket in.

"You need to leave me alone," he growls. "I can't have a life because of you. I'm lonely as hell, but I'm too afraid to have anything more than a one-night stand, because every time I start to get serious with a girl, her life is in *danger.* Do you know what that's like? I can't even give out my real phone number, because I don't want the cops to track me down! Do you want me to go to *prison*, Daisy?"

"You won't go to prison." She waves a hand. "I always make sure it happens on a night when you have an alibi. Anyway…" She glances in my direction. "It doesn't seem like you're doing so bad for yourself."

Tom's face turns pink. "What do you want from me? Do I have to take a vow of celibacy? Is that what you need me to do so you'll stop killing people?"

"I did you a favor!" she retorts. "You would have been miserable with Bonnie. Or any of those other utterly boring women."

I feel a surge of nausea. Somehow, I got everything wrong. I thought Randy needed Gretchen to be his fake alibi. But it turns out that *Gretchen* was the one who actually needed the alibi.

"You know what I want, Tom?" Gretchen tilts her

head to look up at him, her sweet expression contrasting with the sharp tone of her voice. "I want *you*. That's what I've always wanted. And I know you love me too. Sydney told me that you said you never got over me. Of course, you told her I was *dead*, but I can forgive you for that."

Wait, that girl Tom dated when he was in high school, the one he said was the only girl he'd ever loved…

That was *Gretchen*?

I saw that flash of recognition in his face when Gretchen and Randy appeared. I had assumed he was staring at Randy, but now I realize the truth. *Gretchen* was the one he was shocked to recognize.

"You want me so bad?" He nods at her left hand. "Is that really true? Because it seems like you just got engaged to another man."

"Oh, *him*?" Her lips curl in disgust. "Don't be silly, Tom. I don't even *like* him."

"Yeah, I'm sure."

"It's true. I *loathe* him, Tom."

"You loathe him? I find that very hard to believe."

"Well, believe it." She glances back at Randy. "And I can prove it to you."

The next thing that happens occurs so fast that neither Tom nor I could possibly stop it. Gretchen picks up the knife she had placed down by the cake box. She crosses the room, and I watch in horror as she plunges the blade of the knife into Randy's belly. He was out cold, but for a split second, his eyes fly open. Then she stabs him a second time, and then a third, and this time, blood spurts out of his mouth and his eyes drift shut again. Tom seems to be frozen in horror, watching what she's doing.

"Daisy!" Tom finally yells, snapping out of his trance,

but it's far too late. "What the hell do you think you're doing? Jesus Christ."

She shrugs and finally lowers her hand holding the bloody knife. "I told you I don't love him. Now you don't have to be jealous."

Tom takes a shaky breath, raking both his hands through his hair. "This is nuts. You just killed an innocent man."

"Innocent?" Gretchen sneers. "You know what he used to do? He used to use his keys to go into female tenants' apartments while they were at work and go through their underwear drawers and rub his face all over their panties. Believe me, this wasn't a big loss to society."

Is that true? Did Randy really do that? Despite everything, I believe her. Bonnie always thought Randy was creepy, and she wasn't wrong.

But he didn't deserve to die.

Tom has started pacing the room, looking thoroughly freaked out. Daisy watches him, her eyes twinkling. "Oh relax," she says. "I didn't kill him because of you. I was always going to do it. I taped a bunch of locks of hair in the tank of the toilet, and Randy here is going to take the fall for all those girls who were killed, including dear Bonnie." She flashes me a pointed look. "Poor Sydney here will be his last victim before I come in and stab him in self-defense."

Last victim? Does that mean...

Oh my God, she's really going to kill me. This woman is a total psychopath, and she isn't about to leave behind any witnesses.

I had no idea Gretchen had it in her.

Tom stops pacing and turns to face her. "You need

help, Daisy. I mean it. Let me… Let's go to the police together. I'll explain everything to them. Please."

Gretchen shoots him a dirty look. "Don't act so holier than thou, Tom. You pretend like you're in love with Sydney, but does she know why you really like her?"

He shakes his head, his mouth hanging open. "Daisy…"

"Does she know how you love to watch her bleed?" A smile creeps across her lips. "When she told me that story about how you asked her out after an epic nosebleed, I was like, yes, Tom hasn't changed a bit."

The color drains from Tom's face. "Daisy, don't say that."

"Why not? Don't lie about who you are."

Oh my God, is that *true*?

Maybe it is. He always seemed fascinated by how easily I bleed. Our first date was after a nosebleed. The first time we made passionate love was when I sliced my finger cutting up a lime.

Gretchen claims Tom is just like she is. And I'm beginning to worry she's right.

My fatigue is almost overwhelming, but at the same time, adrenaline is keeping me awake. These two are both out of their minds. I've got to figure out a way out of this apartment before I end up like Randy.

But how?

"I know how much it turns you on when she bleeds," Gretchen says. "You're too much of a wuss to cut into her yourself, but I can do it." She reaches out to touch his arm, and to my dismay, he doesn't pull away. "I can help you with that. We can watch her bleed together. We'll have so much fun together."

Tom doesn't tell her no. In fact, he can't seem to tear

his gaze away from her. I remember how he talked about that girl he loved back in high school. *This* is the girl. This is the only girl he ever loved—the one he can never get over.

"I love you, Tom," she murmurs. "And I know you love me too. You're the only man I have ever loved or will ever love. We are so much alike."

He shakes his head, almost imperceptibly.

"Don't say no." She takes his hand in hers. "You love me. You'll never be happy without me."

"That's not true."

"You and I are meant to be together," she insists, "and you know it."

CHAPTER 63

BEFORE

TOM

I've got my arm around Cindy's shoulders as we walk out of the theater where we just watched *Blood Lake 2*, and I'm holding her close to me to stave off the February chill. The night is frigid but clear enough to see the moon above us, and it's so peaceful. I'd love to just enjoy a quiet walk home with my girlfriend, but Cindy's mind is only on one thing.

"That was hands down the most disgusting movie I've ever seen!" Cindy rants. She can't seem to shut up about it. "Seriously, Tom! I thought I was going to lose my lunch."

"Uh-huh."

"That scene where the killer slices open Kay's stomach and her intestines fly out everywhere…" Her whole body shudders. "That might've been one of the most disgusting things I've ever seen. I'm going to have nightmares over that for weeks. *Weeks*, Tom!"

"Yeah," I mumble.

She tilts her heart-shaped face up to look at me

accusingly, the edge of her white puffball hat nearly concealing her eyes. "How could you take me to that awful movie? I thought you saw the first one! Didn't you realize how awful it was?"

"Sorry. The first one was different."

I don't tell her that the only thing that disappointed me about *Blood Lake 2* is that it wasn't nearly as gory as the first *Blood Lake* movie. But it made up for it with *phenomenal* special effects. It looked as real as any of the patients I cut into during my surgery rotations in medical school.

She smacks me in the arm, but it's playful. We've been dating eight months, and it's starting to get serious. I just turned twenty-six; so far there's only been one girl I've ever been in love with, and it's not Cindy. But that girl was a freaking *psychopath*, and Cindy is nice. There's potential here. I could imagine settling down with a girl like Cindy. Getting married. Having kids. Maybe a dog.

"I suppose I can forgive you," Cindy finally says thoughtfully. "After all, you're going to be a surgeon, so that sort of thing doesn't bother you as much."

"Actually," I say, "I decided not to apply for a surgery residency."

She stops walking so abruptly that she nearly stumbles. "Seriously? But it's all you ever talk about!"

She's right. Becoming a surgeon has been my dream ever since I can remember. But when I got into the operating room and was staring down into the chest cavity of a fellow human being as it filled with warm, pulsating blood, it became painfully clear that it wasn't the right career path for me. I finalized my residency applications last night, and even though it nearly killed me, I applied to only pathology programs, where my only patients will already be dead.

It was for the best. And anyway, it's done.

"I changed my mind," is all I can come up with by way of explanation.

She cocks her head to the side. "You are quite the mystery, Tom Brewer."

I walk Cindy the rest of the way to her apartment building as she continues to rant about *Blood Lake 2*. More and more often, I've been spending the night at her place, but tonight I don't really feel like it. So I don't ask to come up, and she doesn't offer.

I walk home by myself. It's a thirty-minute walk, and it's below freezing, but I've got a warm coat and a beanie, and somehow I barely feel the cold. I'm the only one on the street, and my mother would probably be furious with me if she knew how often I walk around Philadelphia alone at night. But I like to be alone. There's no one I've really managed to connect with out here. Making friends has always been hard for me, and that hasn't changed. I buried the only close friend I ever had back in high school.

Anyway, I'm fine on my own. I worry about my mother much more than she worries about me. She hasn't remarried or even dated—as far as I know—since my father "disappeared." The investigation into his disappearance was shockingly minimal. As it turned out, my dad had been racking up debts all over town, and he'd gotten on the bad side of a few dangerous people, so everyone figured he took off to escape having his kneecaps broken. It didn't hurt matters that the daughter of our town's police chief was on my side, telling her daddy how I helped save her life.

But my mother knows who was responsible for what happened to him. We've never discussed it, but I see it in her eyes every time I visit her. When I told her I'd decided against becoming a surgeon, she said, *Thank God.*

When I get back to my apartment—a small one-bedroom that's a short drive from the med school campus—I yank off my hat and coat, then make a beeline for my laptop on the futon in the living room. I couldn't enjoy the movie while Cindy was sitting next to me shooting me disgusted looks the whole time, but I bet I can find some of the better scenes online. I'd rather watch them alone. What was I thinking when I brought Cindy to that movie? Maybe I'd hoped she'd…

Well, never mind. That was stupid.

I place my laptop on my thighs, but when I get my hands on the keyboard, I don't search for *Blood Lake 2* videos. Instead, I do something that I find myself doing just a bit too often lately. I load up Facebook and search for Daisy Driscoll's page.

Of course, she calls herself Gretchen now, but I'll never be able to think of her that way. We're not Facebook friends, but I know from previous experience that her profile is public. I scroll through her feed, pausing at a selfie she took of herself a few days ago. I used to know that face so well. I used to smile every time I saw it.

And then I catch a glimpse of a movie marquee captured in the background of the selfie: *Blood Lake 2*. I wonder if she went to see it. And if so, did she go alone? After all, no one knows she enjoys movies in which characters get their faces ripped off by disembodied hands emerging from the lake. Nobody knows the real Daisy Driscoll.

Only me.

I close my eyes. For a second, I allow myself to imagine an alternate universe where Daisy and I can see *Blood Lake 2* together, and then, after it's over, we can go back to her place and make passionate love. For hours.

I whip out my phone and bring up my address book. This is the third phone I've had since high school, and it's got Daisy's number programmed into it, even though I've been careful to avoid her since graduation. I don't know why I keep transferring her number into my new phones. I should delete it. Block her.

But I never do.

Impulsively, I click on Daisy's name and start a new text message. After a moment of thought, I tap out a message:

Hey, how are you doing?

I stare at the words. Wow, that sounds *so* lame. Daisy and I haven't spoken in eight years—well, except for that one time in college when I was dating that girl who drowned over the summer and she came to the funeral. Daisy probably barely remembers me, and I'd seem like such a loser if I sent her a random text like that on a Saturday night. It's not even what I really want to say.

I delete the text before I can do something dumb like hitting Send. I chew on my lower lip, and then, before I can stop myself, I type a second message to Daisy:

I miss you.

Christ, that's even worse. If I send that, she's going to

think I'm drunk and looking for a booty call. I delete it and nearly toss my phone aside, but I can't stop staring at Daisy's name at the top of the screen. You know you've got it bad when even looking at a girl's name makes your heart skip a beat. And now I find myself typing the words that have been running through my head all night and for the last eight years:

I don't think I can live without you, Daisy.

No. *No.* I can't say *that*, for God's sake. I can't say *anything* to Daisy Driscoll. It'd just be asking for trouble. No, it's better to focus on Cindy, who is sweet and pretty and doesn't like horror movies, just like any *normal* girl. And I like Cindy. I really do.

Okay, I'm not *in love* with her, but I could be. I will be.

I delete the message to Daisy, then I bring up Cindy's name in my contacts. I'll call her, and if I take my car, I can be over at her place in five minutes. She'll help me forget all about Daisy, I bet.

I click on Cindy's name, and I feel only a slight twinge of regret when it rings on the other end of the line. I brace myself for Cindy's high voice, but to my surprise, she doesn't pick up. The phone rings and rings, then finally goes to voicemail.

Huh. That's weird. I only dropped her off less than an hour ago, and it's not close to bedtime yet. Why isn't she picking up her phone? Cindy *always* answers her phone. Where could she have gone?

But I'm sure she's fine. After all, what could have happened?

CHAPTER 64

PRESENT DAY

SYDNEY

I've got to get out of here.

Gretchen intends to kill me. That much is clear. And Tom has mixed feelings at best, and even if he wants to save me, I'm not sure he can. Gretchen means business, and he doesn't seem to have it in him to stop her.

But what can I do? I have no idea what the combination of oleander and alcohol does to a person, but I can barely move. I make an attempt to sit up, but a wave of nausea comes over me, and it's all I can do to keep from vomiting all over the floor.

"You're not going to get away with this," Tom says to Gretchen. "The police are going to figure out what you did. They're not going to believe Randy was attacking you when he's lying dead on the sofa."

"So I'll *move* him," she says impatiently.

"You know," he grunts, "we can tell on the autopsy if a body has been moved after death."

"Can you?" Her eyes light up. "How?"

"It has to do with lividity," he explains. "That's the bluish-purple discoloration that occurs on the skin after death. And gravity is what causes it to pool in different locations."

She nods, fascinated. "And how long does that take to set in?"

"Well…" Tom begins.

Oh my God, are the two of them really standing there geeking out about the decomposition of dead bodies while Randy is lying dead a few feet away and I'm clinging to consciousness on the floor? Is this really happening?

But no, this is good. They're so intent on each other that they're hardly paying attention to me anymore. This is my chance to get out of here.

I take a deep breath, pushing away another wave of nausea. I don't have to do much. All I have to do is get to my feet and make a run for the door that is less than ten feet away. Thank God Manhattan apartments are so tiny.

I summon all my strength, trying to get to my feet. But right away, my arms and legs start to tremble. I can't do it. The oleander Daisy drugged me with has hit me too hard.

Could I crawl? It isn't that far. Except if I do that, how will I reach the lock on the door?

Oh God, this is impossible. I'm going to die here. As soon as Tom finishes teaching Gretchen about livor mortis, she's going to use that knife to stab me to death. Then she'll store my hair in the toilet tank.

I don't want it to end this way. I loved Bonnie, but I don't want to end up like her. I want to *live*. And Jake will never, ever forgive himself if I die here tonight.

But what can I do?

Just when I'm weighing my limited options, I hear a

noise from outside. The noise is growing increasingly loud, and it takes my drugged brain several seconds to identify it.

Police sirens.

Gretchen's eyes fly wide open. "What the hell? Sydney, you called the cops? But...how? I took your phone!"

Oh, that's why my phone wasn't in my purse.

"Sydney didn't call the police," Tom says. "I did."

Gretchen yanks her hand away from him like she's been stung. "*What?*"

His expression is grim. "I did it before I knocked on the door. I told them everything. I...I'm sorry, Daisy."

"Tom, how could you?" she bursts out, her face pink. I've known Gretchen for a year, but I have never seen her this emotional before. "After everything we've been through, how could you do that to me?"

He just shakes his head.

Gretchen steps over to the window, careful to stay out of clean sight. "Shit," she mutters under her breath.

"I'm so sorry, Daisy." His voice breaks on the words. "I had to do it. I couldn't let you...you know..."

She stands there for a moment, holding the knife in one hand, the other balled into a fist. "There's another way out of here. Randy showed it to me. It's like a secret back exit through the laundry room. I can get out through there." She looks up at him. "*We* can get out."

"Daisy..."

"Tom, come with me." She steps closer to him, her eyes shining with excitement and determination. "Come on. You know we've both been miserable alone for the last twenty years. This is our chance to actually be happy." She takes his hand again. "I want to spend the rest of my life with you. I want to have a family with you."

"A family? Daisy…"

"It won't happen with anyone else but me," she says, "and you know it. There is nobody else who could possibly understand you the way I do. With anyone else, your life would be a lie."

He shakes his head again, but with less conviction than I would have hoped. "Daisy."

"Please." Her eyes spill over with tears. "We've been apart for twenty years, and it's sucked. I'm sick of living that way. Aren't you?"

"What are you asking me?" He frowns at her. "You really want me to give up my entire life to be with you?"

She's quiet for a few beats. "Well," she says, "yes."

"Daisy."

She stares up at him with shining eyes. "I…I can't live without you, Tom."

At first, I'm certain he's going to tell her to go to hell. He's got a life here. A career as a medical examiner. He wouldn't give that all up to go on the run with some psychopath who has already murdered God knows how many people.

But then I see the way he's looking at her. And I realize what his answer is going to be.

"I can't live without you either," he says softly.

In the distance, the sirens are growing louder. Tom swears under his breath.

"We have to go," he says. "Quickly."

Gretchen's face lights up. I thought she'd looked happy when Randy asked her to marry him, but I now realize that was fake happiness. I have never truly seen Gretchen happy until this moment. "Great. Let me just get rid of our little witness here."

She means me. Gretchen's knife is glinting in the overhead light, and it's very clear what she means to do. She's going to get rid of me the same way she got rid of Randy. And when the police arrive, they're going to find two dead bodies in this apartment.

I am too weak to get out of here. I've been trying, but I can't even crawl, much less make a run for the door. I'm completely at her mercy.

This is it. The end. I'm going to end up like Bonnie after all. In a casket, buried in the ground for all eternity. Jake will probably be the one to find my body, and it will wreck him.

Don't blame yourself, Jake. Nobody could have seen this coming.

But just as I'm bracing myself for the inevitable, Tom reaches out to grab Gretchen's wrist. "If you touch Sydney, I'm not going with you. Do you understand me?"

"But she knows everything!" she pouts.

His voice is stern. "You don't hurt Sydney, okay? If I go with you, this needs to stop. The killing needs to stop."

Gretchen looks down at me with unadulterated disgust on her face. I can't believe I thought this woman was my best friend. She really had me fooled. She is truly diabolical.

Good luck, Tom.

"You don't really mean that," she sneers.

"I do." His gaze is unblinking. "No more. That's my condition if I go with you. Nobody else dies, Daisy."

She tilts her head to the side, considering this. "Even if they deserve it?"

"Well," he says after a pause, "that's different of course."

His answer sends a shiver down my spine. But his

ultimatum works. Gretchen tosses the knife on the coffee table, and then the two of them run out the front door together. It slams shut, the sound echoing through the small apartment, and it's only when the police start banging on the door a few minutes later that I finally allow myself to pass out.

EPILOGUE

SYDNEY

I'm juggling two bags of groceries as I unlock the door to my building, and that's when my phone rings.

It's been a month since Gretchen Driscoll and Tom Brewer vanished off the face of the planet. Or at least that's how it seems. I woke up in the hospital a few hours after the police showed up at my building, still groggy but incredibly grateful to be alive. When my nurse saw that I was awake, she said to me, "There's a detective who asked me to call him immediately when you woke up."

That was Jake, of course. Even though there was a manhunt in progress, he dropped everything to race over to the hospital to see me. After all this time, several years too late, he had truly figured out how to make time for me.

And it's his name flashing on the screen of my phone right now.

I manage to get inside the door, where a blast of heat greets me. I dump my groceries on the floor of the mail room before taking Jake's call.

"Hey, Syd," he says.

"Hey."

"You have plans tonight?"

He knows I don't have plans. After Tom and Gretchen escaped through the back entrance, the entire police force launched a full-scale manhunt. After all, the strands of hair in Gretchen's toilet linked her to multiple murders, not to mention that of Randall Muncy. The police were desperate to find them. But both of them abandoned their entire lives and vanished into nothingness together.

Jake was only a small part of this manhunt, which eventually included the FBI. But he took on a much more reasonable task. He appointed himself my official bodyguard, "in case they come back."

When he told me that, I challenged him. Not that I didn't want him around, but I reminded him about his busy schedule. He brushed off my concerns. *I'm going to make time for what's important.*

And he has. He really has.

"I don't have plans," I say as I settle down onto the bench in the mail room. My frozen TV dinners are all melting, but that's okay. Jake has been bringing in dinner most nights anyway.

"Excellent," Jake says. "I was thinking that while I'm keeping watch over you tonight, I could bring over some burgers and fries. What do you think?"

Although nothing has happened between us over the last month, we've spent every evening together. I'd forgotten how much I enjoyed his company.

A smile twitches at my lips. "You know," I say, "it's been an entire month. Gretchen and Tom are almost certainly long gone. I don't know if you need to protect me quite so intently anymore. I do have my dead bolt."

"Well, you know, better safe than sorry."

"I'm just not sure it's necessary."

"Oh." Jake is quiet for a moment. "I don't have to do it anymore if you don't want me to. I don't want to bother you, Syd. If you don't want me keeping an eye on you anymore, I don't have to do it."

"I don't," I say.

"Right." He can't mask the disappointment in his voice. "Okay. No problem. I…uh… I'll leave you alone then."

"But…" I shift my phone to my other ear. "If you would like to come over tonight with burgers and fries and *spend time with me*, that would be okay. In fact, I would like that very much."

I can almost hear him smiling on the other end of the line. "I'd like that too."

I'm giving Jake another chance. He desperately wants it, and I want it too. If there's one good thing to come out of all this, it's our realizing what we lost when our relationship ended. But it's not too late to give it another try.

After all, if Tom and Gretchen can be happy together, why not me and Jake?

Plus, my mother will be thrilled. Hopefully, I'll be able to give her a grandchild a little before I'm ninety.

Jake promises to be over at seven, and I hang up the phone with a smile on my face. I can't wait to see him. Tom never had any chance of being the One, but I'm pretty sure Jake might be it.

I grab my keys again and open my mailbox. There is the usual mix of bills, letters from my college alumni association asking for money, two catalogs advertising a variety of chocolates and one offering lingerie. And there's one other piece of mail that is a little more unexpected. A white envelope with my name on it but no return address.

That's strange.

My name and address are handwritten. The black ink is big and loopy, with all the letters in capitals. I stare at it for a moment, my heart fluttering. I wonder if I should call Jake back and ask him if it's safe to open this mystery letter. But if I do call him, I'm sure he'll make too much of it. He'd probably have a SWAT team here within the hour.

So I rip open the envelope.

And I let out a gasp.

Inside the envelope is a lock of scraggly, dirty-blond hair. Even though I should probably be careful touching anything from this envelope, I can't help but pull it out. From the length of the hair, it looks like it would have fallen just below the shoulders of the owner, and it is tied together with a red ribbon.

What *is* this? And why was this sent to me?

Maybe I still do need Jake looking out for me.

As I'm trying not to panic, a small, ripped piece of paper flutters out of the envelope. It falls to the ground, face-down. Before I can stop myself, I grab the piece of paper. The writing on it is identical to that on the envelope. I sink back down onto the bench as I read the words that the sender has written:

Sydney,
   Kevin won't be bothering you ever again.

—Tom

I stare down at the note that Tom wrote to me about

the man who had attacked and stalked me for months. I had assumed that he and Gretchen were halfway across the globe by now. But maybe not. I can't help but remember the last words the two of them exchanged before they took off.

Nobody else dies, Daisy.

Even if they deserve it?

Well, that's different of course.

Apparently, Tom thought Kevin deserved it.

I frown down at the note. I should save this to show Jake. I should definitely save this. Even after everything Kevin did to me, did he really deserve to die? There should be justice for his murder, just like anyone else's.

Right?

I sit on the bench, staring at the note for much too long. Finally, I slip it and the hair back in the envelope, doing my best to seal it closed once again. And then I toss it in the trash before heading upstairs to my apartment to get ready for dinner.

THE END

READING GROUP GUIDE

1. Compare Sydney and Bonnie's approach to dating. What are the pros and cons of using dating apps? Have you ever used one?

2. Is Slug a good person? Why do you think he and Tom stick together?

3. After Bonnie's murder, it becomes apparent to Jake that a serial killer is on the loose. What is the killer's MO? Who do they seem to target, and why?

4. Why does Alison hate Tom so much? Are her feelings justified?

5. Count the ways Tom seems like a perfect boyfriend. In what ways does he seem…not so perfect?

6. Sydney can't help but feel unsettled around Randy. Why is that?

7. Consider Tom's mother's choice to protect her son, though she suspects he's guilty of something terrible. Do you think she made the right decision? What would you have done in her position?

8. This story is told between two perspectives and timelines. Did this make the read more suspenseful? Were you able to predict any of the twists?

9. What do you think happened to Kevin? Do you think he deserved it?

10. Discuss Sydney's future. Then, discuss Tom's future. Do you think each are happy?

ACKNOWLEDGMENTS

The battery in my car died yesterday.

My husband helped me jump the car, and we assumed it was because I hadn't driven it in over a week and it's the middle of a New England winter. But then this morning, the car was dead again, and with my husband still asleep and only twenty minutes to make it in time for the late bell at the middle school, I knew I had to put on my big girl pants and jump the car myself. Weirdly enough, the hardest part was figuring out how to open the door to my husband's Prius, which had the jumper cables inside. The key looked like something from a modern art exhibit about the future.

But I did it. And amazingly, I didn't even electrocute myself.

I had been hoping maybe I just hadn't let the car run for long enough yesterday and that when I tried starting it again this afternoon, it would come to life without a problem. But nope, that was not the case—my car is dead yet again, and I just called AAA to come replace the battery.

What on earth does this have to do with the acknowledgments? Okay, okay, I'm getting to that.

I always struggle to write the acknowledgments, because they're such an important part of the book, and I

ABOUT THE AUTHOR

#1 *New York Times*, *USA Today*, *Publishers Weekly*, and *Sunday Times* internationally bestselling author Freida McFadden is a practicing physician specializing in brain injury. Freida is the winner of both the International Thriller Writer Award for Best Paperback Original and the Goodreads Choice Award for Best Thriller. Her novels have been translated into more than thirty languages. Freida lives with her family and black cat in a centuries-old three-story home overlooking the ocean.

worry so much about leaving someone out or not thanking them properly. So I always postpone it for as long as I possibly can. But now AAA is on their way—allegedly coming in twenty minutes—and I told myself, "Freida, you've got twenty minutes to make these acknowledgments happen. Stop procrastinating and just *do it.*"

And here I am, having already blown fifteen of them writing a story about my car not starting.

First, I want to thank my mother for her multiple readings of this book. I think she even understood the ending on the first try this time—maybe. Thank you so much to my awesome woman power writing group friends, Maura, Rebecca, and Beth, who provided some amazing feedback. Thank you to Val for the help with proofreading. I also want to express my eternal gratitude to my Facebook moderators—Emily, Daniel, Carrie, Nancy, and Nikki—who have been so incredibly supportive.

My immense appreciation goes to my agent, Christina Hogrebe, and the entire JRA team—you have no idea how much it means to have a supportive agency behind you. Thank you to Jenna Jankowski for your insightful comments and feedback, as well as to everyone else behind the scenes at Sourcebooks for an incredible job. (I'm going to pre-thank Mandy Chabal for all the marketing she will do after I write this.)

And as always, a massive thank-you to all my readers! I am so grateful to all the readers out there who have come along with me on this wild ride. The readers are why I'm doing this in the first place, so I can't tell you how much all this support has meant to me.

Oh my God, AAA still isn't here! Sixteen more minutes??? Come on!